THE D'ALBIAC INHERITANCE

AN ELA OF SALISBURY MEDIEVAL MYSTERY

J. G. LEWIS

For my niece Corrina Sephora Mensoff, an extraordinary artist and all-around inspiring human.

ACKNOWLEDGMENTS

Many thanks to Rebecca Hazell, Betsy van der Hoek, and Judith Tilden for their thoughtful readings of the story and their helpful insights and suggestions.

CHAPTER 1

ilton, Wiltshire, May 1231
Ela climbed the wooden stairs to the viewing gallery with her heart in her mouth.

"Is this young Richard's first time jousting at a tournament?"

Ela turned to see her old friend Anne de Quercy. "It is." She smiled bravely.

"Are you dying inside?" Anne, an older woman, her silver hair hidden beneath a crisp white veil, peered at her with a warm, pale blue gaze.

Ela sighed. Her son would be mortified if she told people she was anxious for him. "Sir William Talbot insists that he's ready, but as a mother I can't help but have some trepidation." She glanced down at the lists, where jesters still tumbled around to entertain the crowds

"Of course you do, it's only natural," said Anne, ushering her toward the front of the gallery filled with mothers, grandmothers, aunts and other matrons and widows. The blushing and giggling young girls watched from another gallery on the far side of the men's gallery.

"He's a skilled rider," said Ela, trying to convince herself. "And handy with the lance." His brother Stephen was actually better at both, and often bested him in their practices. But as the older of the two Richard was compelled to compete first or become a laughingstock.

"And the instruments are blunted, don't forget that," said Anne. "The worst part of losing is having to part with a beloved horse. And the expense of lost armor is no joy, either."

Ela prayed that Richard wouldn't have to forfeit the kind chestnut mare who'd faithfully given him so many hours of practice over the last two years. That was indeed the worst loss, though sometimes the winner would allow the horse to be purchased back for a price.

"Look, they're at the lists! Richard looks so dashing in the Longespée colors." Anne smiled down to where Richard stood at one end of the jousting field. His face hidden beneath his helmet and every inch of his body covered in mail and embroidered cloth, he was unrecognizable except for the six rampant lions on his tabard.

"Do you know his opponent?" asked Ela. She didn't recognize the red and white cloth with a pair of blackbirds embroidered onto it. "I admit I don't attend a tournament unless I'm compelled to, so I'm not familiar with the current slate of combatants."

"I'm afraid I don't know the lad personally and he wasn't at Hertford last month. The herald said that his name is Charibert d'Albiac. I daresay his mother is here among us." Anne looked around the crowd of women, all in white veils, who gazed down at the lists below.

"There's no need to find her." Ela didn't really want to meet the woman whose son was about to attempt to knock hers from his horse. She didn't like tournaments any better than Pope Gregory, who had issued a papal bull against them only three years earlier. Or old Henry II who had banned them entirely during his reign to stop his knights from injuring or killing each other. Unfortunately, the young king Henry III had no such compunction. Perhaps he was keen to find the best fighters in his kingdom who might help him regain the family lands in France lost by his father King John.

"There they go!" The two riders now stood at each end of the lists, surrounded by their attendants, horses shifting impatiently as their riders held the reins tight and readied their lances. On a trumpet blast, the horses shot forward and the riders galloped toward each other, separated only by a waist-high wooden fence erected to keep the horses apart.

The trumpet flourish continued and Ela held her breath as they raised their lances. Both thrust hard and she heard the thump of wood against shield. She stifled a tiny cry as Richard rocked in his seat.

"He's steady!" cried Anne, as Richard galloped past his opponent, still safely in his saddle. "And he got a good blow in, from the looks of it. They'll examine the lances to see which is more cracked." Both men had dropped their lances. Once contact was made, a combatant could be unseated by the thrust of their own lance. Sometimes an unsuccessful jouster would drop his anyway, to make his failure less obvious.

Two men in colorful garb retrieved the fallen lances and took them to the Earl of Surrey, who was judging the tournament. Ela could scarcely conceal her relief that her son was unharmed, but she still said a silent prayer that he wouldn't be declared the loser already based on the blows inflicted.

The earl declared the lances equally damaged. The attendants handed each man a spear for the next contest in the tournament. Ela wasn't so worried about this part. Knights didn't often get badly injured during this contest since the spears broke easily. Dishonorable maneuvers, including a blow to the horse or to the opponent's head, were strictly forbidden and grounds for a combatant to be disqualified or declared the loser.

Still, Ela found herself perspiring and wished she could ask Elsie for a handkerchief to discreetly dab her face. Elsie was down below, arranging refreshments for Richard, Stephen, Bill Talbot and little Nicky, who'd also insisted on coming to watch his big brother.

The spear contest passed uneventfully, with each party sustaining two broken spears in a series of four contests.

"Your Richard is putting on a marvelous performance," cheered Anne. Other women Ela knew had also offered her congratulations on her son's brave comportment. She hoped their kind words weren't premature. After the spears, the young men fought with swords on horseback. She could see that Richard was growing tired. His heavy armor and the heat and discomfort of his helmet must be weighing on him. Still, he stayed on his horse, and so did his fellow combatant.

But the worst was yet to come.

"Hand to hand combat!" announced the herald. "With axes!"

Even though the axes were blunted, and there was no further danger of a fall from the horse, the heavy steel rained hard blows and even a big man could find himself knocked unconscious by a blow to his helmet. The illustrious William Marshall, veteran of countless tournaments, had told bracing tales of putting his head on an anvil to have his dented helmet pried off his throbbing head by a blacksmith.

Their attendants helped the boys down from their horses, and each was handed his own gleaming, polished—but blunted—axe. Sir William Talbot, as her sons' instructor in the martial arts, had worked with the blacksmith to refine the size and weight of the blade and fussed over the exact shape of the carved handle to make the axe as nimble and easy to wield as possible. Ela wished for Bill's reassuring presence at her side right now, but men were not allowed in the women's galleries.

The two young men rushed at each other, axes raised. Ela quietly closed her eyes, and whispered a quick prayer, as the first blows fell. A gasp from the crowd tugged her eyes open. Richard lay on the ground, unmoving. "What happened?" she asked Anne.

"The other young man struck him with such force!" Anne peered down.

Ela gathered her skirts and ran for the stairs. Perhaps Richard would be mortified to have his mother rush to his aid, but she could hardly gaze down on her wounded son, applauding his opponent's victory.

By the time she was on the ground at the edge of the lists, she could see Bill Talbot bent over him, along with his attendants. She gasped with relief as they helped Richard to his feet and removed his helmet. The other young man raised his fist—axe still in it—in triumph.

Ela knew that Richard having to be helped back to his feet was a concession of defeat, so her relief at him showing signs of life was tempered by her knowledge of how mortified he'd be by the defeat, not to mention the loss of his horse and armor.

She stood silently, at the edge of the lists, as Bill helped Richard off the field of combat. The crowd roared as the victor removed his helmet and bowed toward the gallery of young ladies. Their murmurs of approval brought a smile to other men's faces.

"He caught you hard in the arm," said Stephen, with unusual gallantry toward his older brother. "I doubt I could have stood up against that myself."

"He certainly did," said Bill. "The mail is broken and bent.

If I didn't know better, I'd say these marks were made by a sharpened axe."

"Did anyone test the axe blades before the contest began?" asked Ela.

Bill glanced at Stephen. "Did you see it? I saw them test the sword blades, and the spears were provided from a great store of them that didn't belong to either combatant. But I never saw anyone test the axes."

"I'd like to see his opponent's axe," said Ela with sudden determination.

"Mother, no!" cried Richard, in desperation. "I lost and that's all there is to it." He winced as an attempt to move his injured arm pained him.

"Not if he cheated," said Ela. "And if we're to determine that, I must see it at once before it's spirited away. Don't you agree, Bill?"

Bill, always loath to disagree with her, hesitated. "Questioning the results of a bout can be seen as unsporting."

"Fighting in a friendly tournament with a sharpened axe is unsporting."

"That is true."

"You must ask to see the axe," said Ela to Bill. "My sons will never forgive me if I insist on it myself."

"I can hardly refuse the command of my countess," said Bill, as much to the boys as to her. "I shall speak to the herald at arms and ask if he examined the axe blades."

ELA HOVERED NEARBY while the attendants dressed Richard's wound inside a small tent, one of several set up for the purpose of tending wounds or changing clothes. He had some nasty cuts on his upper right arm where the mail—

possibly driven by a sharpened axe—had cut through his padded undercoat and into the skin beneath.

"It's fine, Mother," Richard insisted. "Don't make a fuss. I tried my hardest and he bested me. I just want to go home." She could tell he was fighting back tears, either from the pain of injury or defeat, or both.

"We will, my dear, but first we must determine if the contest was fair. Are you going to forfeit your best horse to someone who cheated?"

Richard groaned and now tears did spring to his eyes. "Poor Maisie! She deserves so much better than me. I can't believe I lost her and to some upstart no one's ever heard of."

Ela had every intention of trying to buy the horse back, but she didn't want to get Richard's hopes up when the effort might prove futile.

"I'll let you ride my horse," said Stephen. "You're a good enough rider for her now."

"I don't want to ride her!" shouted Richard. The black mare was their father's last destrier and a spirited mount who was particular about who she allowed on her back. "I don't want to ride anything ever again. I want to be a bishop, not a knight."

Ela's heart sank. She felt deep sympathy for her peaceful son. "You can be a knight and a bishop. It's your duty to be ready to defend the kingdom, even if you intend to devote your life to God one day."

"So you keep telling me. And now I've lost my horse." He buried his head in his hands.

Bill entered the tent through the curtained doorway. "You were right. The axe was sharp."

"I knew it! What now?"

"I reported it to the Marshall at Arms. The opponent's victory has been declared null and void and he'll be booted from the tournament." He looked at Richard. "If you want, you can claim his horse and armor as yours."

"Yes!" cried Stephen. "You're the winner!"

"No, I'm not. But I thank God I can keep Maisie. I don't ever want to enter a tournament again." He held his sore arm.

"You're the winner, lad. You need to get out there and take a bow for the ladies." Bill grinned at him.

"Really?" Richard blinked in confusion.

"Let's get your cloak on, shall we?"

ELA WAS in two minds about whether to pursue taking the opponent's horse and armor to teach him a lesson. Richard didn't much like the idea—he was a kind boy and inclined to follow the biblical wisdom to treat others as you'd like to be treated. She, however, wanted the other young man to feel the sharp blade against his own skin, as it were, so he'd learn from his mistake.

She decided to insist on a meeting with him—and Richard and Bill—so she could at least give him a piece of her mind.

The other young man was tall and well-built, running slightly to fat. He'd removed his helmet to reveal a mop of reddish-gold hair over a florid but handsome face, streaked with rust from the inside of his helmet.

Bill introduced her to the combatant—Charibert d'Albiac —as mother of his opponent and also high sheriff of all Wiltshire. Instead of the apology she'd expected, he greeted her with a scowl. "It was a fair fight and your son is the cheater."

"I'm reliably informed that your axe was sharpened," said Ela coldly. "And now you add insult to injury."

"What's the point of wearing armor if every blade has to

be filed smooth as a baby's teething rattle?" Charibert tilted his head.

"This tournament is a place for young men to test their skills and prove their prowess, not for the king's best men to maim or kill each other. Your insolence and lack of contrition tells me that we must insist on taking your horse and your armor in recompense for your misdeeds."

"No!" Charibert's round face displayed a look of sheer panic. "My mother will make me wait an age before she buys me more."

"Where is your mother?" Ela looked around. "Is she still in the gallery upstairs?"

"No." Charibert scowled at her. "She wouldn't come. She hates jousting."

"And your father?" She asked more gently, given that it was far from unusual for a young man's father to have died in some battle or other.

"Dead. And my two oldest brothers. All dead. I should be master of my estate, but my mother clings to the reins with a death grip and won't let me take it over."

Can't say I blame her, thought Ela. "No doubt she does not think you ready to assume the responsibilities, and based on what I've seen today I'm inclined to agree with her."

"It's none of your damn business, anyway!" he shouted, baring his teeth like a young animal.

"Don't you dare speak to your countess like that!" barked Bill Talbot, stepping forward. He raised his hand as if to clap the insolent young man across his flushed cheek.

Ela held up her hand to stop Bill. "It is indeed my business, as it appears you have committed a crime in my jurisdiction. Sharpened blades are strictly forbidden in this tournament."

"If you're the sheriff of Wiltshire, then I appeal to you for the right to command my family's estate!" continued the boy, raising his voice. "It's within the boundaries of this shire and is mine by right as the oldest living son. She can't keep it from me."

"Perhaps you've forgotten that your mother is entitled to a share of the family estate, according to the precepts of the Magna Carta." Ela had helped a dear friend secure her own widow's share when her husband died suddenly.

"I don't care what the Magna Carta says," hissed the boy. "Everyone knows that the oldest son inherits the estate."

"If you are still in your minority, then your mother is fully entitled to manage all your affairs."

"I'm not! I'm a full-grown man, not a child. I should be able to buy myself a new horse and armor if I need them, but I can't! I must be able to compete in the upcoming tournament at Brackley. How else am I supposed to demonstrate my prowess enough to be made a knight and make my way in the world?"

"A knight lives and dies on his honor. A man who fights in a friendly tournament with a sharpened axe has no business becoming one."

"If I had access to my estate I wouldn't care if I were a knight or not. My father's been dead for six years and it should be mine by now to manage as I please."

Ela could quite see why this young man's mother didn't feel him ready to take on the great responsibility of an estate, especially if her happiness would then depend on his generosity. "Did your mother inherit the estate from her parents in her own right?" That made a difference. Ela had inherited Salisbury Castle and most of her manors from her father, the second Earl of Salisbury. This gave her the right to claim them for herself after her husband's death.

"No! The estate was in my father's line. His forbear fought alongside William the Conqueror and he was granted the manor for his bravery. The estate has been passed along the male line ever since. She's holding onto it in defiance of the law."

"Mind your tone," snapped Bill. "You're speaking to your Countess."

"You've convinced me that my son Richard should benefit from gaining your horse and your armor." Ela glared at him. "You clearly need to be taught a lesson about arrogance as well as honor."

"No!" He let fly a curse. "You can't do that. I won fair and square."

"Would you like to spend a night in the dungeon at Salisbury Castle?" asked Bill pleasantly.

"You can't do that."

Ela summoned two guards to come closer. "I think you'll find that I can."

CHAPTER 2

*T*he next morning, Ela had just finished her breakfast of apricots and soft cheese, and risen to attend to the day's business, when Bill entered the hall. He approached and spoke in hushed tones. "How long do you intend to keep the young ruffian locked up?"

"I've sent for his mother. I wish to warn her that her son is unruly and likely to get himself into trouble far worse than being ejected from a tournament for sharpening his blade. I'd appreciate the same information if he were my son."

"When do you expect her?"

"She's coming from a fair few miles away, but I'm sure she'll arrive today. In the meantime, young Charibert has time to consider the error of his ways. This brief punishment will hopefully save him from a more damaging mistake in the future."

"That's a nice horse that Richard won off him yesterday. Well trained and pliable. I put him through his paces early this morning."

"I already told Richard that I don't intend to keep the horse, or the armor. I want to teach the young man a lesson, not blight his chances in life. Richard was in agreement. He's shown great nobility of spirit from start to finish."

"And he fought bravely yesterday. Young Charibert would be a fearsome opponent even with a blunted blade."

"I noticed that, and I suspect he'd make a fine knight for the king's army if he can learn to govern himself appropriately. However, I've seen too many brave and foolish young men set their lives on the wrong course and end up with their head in a noose."

"I can't say I've ever seen a sheriff imprison someone in order to stiffen his moral fiber."

"Perhaps more mothers should also be sheriffs and the kingdom would suffer less from men who abuse the power they wield." She'd had to wrest her sheriffdom from the clutches of Simon de Hal, a man who used cruelty and violence to rain terror upon his subjects. "And I'm pleased that Richard is able to learn some lessons in life from this experience. As you know, I'm no fonder of tournaments than the late Henry II, but I don't seek to deprive my sons of the ability to serve their king in combat. The training you provide and their readiness for war were very important to their father, whose legacy it falls to me to uphold."

"Which you do with courage and honor, my lady."

"Even though sometimes I want to shriek and hide my face in my veil when they engage in combat," she whispered. "But don't tell anyone that."

"Your secrets are safe with me, my lady."

MATHILDE D'ALBIAC ARRIVED at the castle shortly before the bells for Sext.

"She arrived on horseback with a boy leading her on foot,

Mother!" marveled Stephen. "I saw them enter the courtyard."

"No wonder it took so long," said Ela. "But not everyone is comfortable in command of a horse. Please send word to the dungeon for them to send Charibert up here at once."

Ela was curious to meet the woman who'd raised young Charibert. She half expected a fiery woman—with her son's fiery hair color—to storm into her castle and insist on liberating her precious boy at once. She was surprised, then, to observe that Mathilde d'Albiac was a soft-spoken woman with dark eyes and modest manner, her hair entirely hidden beneath a heavy veil.

"I'm terribly sorry for any trouble my son has caused," she began. "He's a headstrong boy and has unfortunately been deprived of a father's guidance for much of his childhood."

Two guards brought Charibert into the hall. Ela was relieved to see that he'd been offered a comb and a bowl of water to refresh himself, as people often looked much the worse for wear after a night in the bowels of the castle. She didn't want to frighten his mother any more than she already had.

Before he'd even crossed the hall to reach them, Charibert started barking orders. "They've taken my horse and my armor, Mother. You'll have to buy me more at once. I command it."

"Silence!" cried Bill, raising a hand as if to strike him. Charibert, to his credit or otherwise, didn't even flinch.

Mathilde looked horrified. "Charibert, mind your tongue in front of your countess."

"This is all her fault! I'm imprisoned for no crime."

"Your son cheated in the tournament at Wilton," said Ela calmly. "By fighting my son with a sharpened axe. Up until then he'd fought bravely and with honor, and the contest was evenly matched, so he ruined his chance at an honest victory."

"For shame, Charibert!" said Mathilde in hushed tones. "What would your father say?"

"My father is dead, and will never say anything," said Charibert sullenly.

"Don't say such things. Your father lives and will return to us any day now."

Ela's ears pricked up. "Your husband is missing?"

"Indeed he is, my lady. Left to fight overseas and has been missing for some time."

"He's been missing for six years without so much as a letter or a whisper of news," snarled Charibert. "If that isn't dead, I don't know what is."

Ela looked at Mathilde, waiting for her to scold her son for such cold words. Mathilde just shifted awkwardly from one foot to the other, and looked at Ela. "It is a long time, to be sure. But I feel sure in my heart that he still lives."

Even Ela felt that her hope was likely misplaced after six years. Still…. "My own husband went missing for over a year. The entire kingdom and even the king became convinced he was dead. I, like you, felt sure he lived—and indeed he did! He'd been shipwrecked on the Ile de Ré and suffered so badly from his injuries that the monks had to nurse him back to health for a full year before he was well enough to return home."

"He came back?" Mathilde looked intrigued.

"He did. So if you are sure that your husband lives, I can give you hope. I never doubted that my dear William was alive."

"Perhaps my husband languishes in a Saracen jail," said Mathilde quietly.

"Like your son is languishing in an English one!" cried Charibert.

"Don't speak to your mother so curtly," admonished Ela. She now suspected that Charibert's rude manners sprang from his mother's quiet demeanor. It seemed she did not rule her son with a firm enough hand, and in the absence of his father... "Does Charibert have a tutor, or a sword master? Someone to school him in the art of being a gentleman?" Bill Talbot would gnaw off his own arm before letting one of her children cheat in a tournament.

"He did, my lady. Since he has gained his majority I'm afraid he refuses to be ruled or schooled by anyone but himself." She glanced at Charibert. "He's furious that the king has not yet deigned to make him a knight, and is convinced that he can only win the honor by displays of...chivalry on the tournament ground."

"There's certainly nothing chivalrous about competing with a sharpened axe," said Ela. "And being ejected from the tournament at Wilton will surely work against your aims."

"If I'm the best fighter, I shall be recognized."

"You are a good fighter," said Bill Talbot. "Or you wouldn't be able to hold your own against the lad I've trained from the cradle. You might even have won if it weren't for your illegal ruse."

"His horse was nimbler than mine. And his armor lighter, and his helm of finer construction. He had every advantage over me." Charibert's sullen expression made him look like a spoiled toddler. "My mother refuses to invest in my future, even while she holds my inheritance out of reach."

"That's not true, Charibert." Mathilde looked mortified. "I bought the finest horse Sir Roger could find and he put years of training into him."

"None of that would matter if I could just command the estate that my father left me." Charibert jutted out his chin. "Father isn't coming back. At what point will the law consider him dead?"

"A person who's been missing for seven years may be presumed to have died," said Ela. "Before that time you'd have to instigate a court proceedings to have him declared dead." Mathilde turned pale. "There may come a time, I'm afraid, when such events must come to pass. But let me reassure you that, as your husband's widow, you have protections under the law and are entitled to the use of one third of the estate for your life."

"I have two young daughters, only fourteen and sixteen. Charibert has declared that their future prospects are none of his concern." Mathilde didn't look at her son as she said this. Clearly she expected that he'd try to throw them all out on the street if he could get his hands on the family estate.

"This is the very reason why the Magna Carta enshrines property rights for widows," said Ela. "I had a say in its creation myself and witnessed its signing." She looked coldly at Charibert. "So sons no longer determine the fate of all in the family when their father dies."

"I wish to instigate legal proceedings to claim my estate," said Charibert.

"You're a prisoner right now," said Bill. "And have no right to instigate anything." He turned to Ela. "Should I put him back in the dungeon?"

Mathilde gasped. Obviously, her son's cold and crude behavior had not extinguished her maternal feeling.

Ela hesitated. She wanted Charibert to sweat. Still, she didn't want to torture his mother. "Charibert has paid for his misdeeds by being expelled from the tournament and locked up overnight. He's had a taste of what will befall him if he lives by his own rules instead of those of the kingdom. I intend for him to return home with you—with his horse and armor—that he may one day prove himself to have learned his lesson and to be able to fight with honor and decorum."

Charibert brightened. The smirk creeping across his face

almost made Ela change her mind. She said a silent prayer that her own dear sons never displayed such willful arrogance.

"As high sheriff of Wiltshire, I forbid you to enter any more tournaments this calendar year."

"No! I've already put in my entry for Brackley. They say the king himself will be there."

"King Henry III has no personal interest in tournaments that I'm aware of. I've certainly never seen him at one and he is my children's cousin. As it stands you've proven yourself to lack the honor and dignity of a true knight this season. A year will allow you time to reflect on your life and prepare yourself for the hard choices of manhood."

Charibert looked like he wanted to protest, but, happily, he thought better of it. Or perhaps he realized that her authority did not extend beyond the boundaries of Wiltshire and he intended to go ahead with his entries as planned.

A WEEK LATER, Charibert was back in Ela's hall. He stood in the line of petitioners who approached her dais one at a time to press their case. In front of him was a woman who claimed she'd been given clipped pennies as payment for a bale of fleeces. She wished to press charges against the man who'd paid her with them. Ela promised to summon him before the jury and sent her on her way.

Then Charibert approached. He wore a smart dark blue tunic with black and red trim that would have looked fine on someone with darker coloring. He, by contrast, looked alternately pale and florid. He didn't bow, or offer any conventional pleasantries. "I wish to pursue my claim against the estate. You said that my mother has a claim to a third, but it's too small and unprofitable to divide. She can find a new husband and take my sisters to live under his roof. Then she can marry them off as well."

Ela's heart ached for poor Mathilde having to go to war against her own son to keep a decent roof over the heads of her daughters. Mathilde's marriage prospects were almost non-existent without significant property to her name, especially since she was past child-bearing age. The same might well prove true for her daughters if they didn't come with a promising dowry. Even a great beauty could have trouble finding a suitable match if she didn't come with property or a purse of coins in these materialistic times.

And Ela had learned quite a lot about Montaigu d'Albiac. "I asked my garrison commander for information about your father and his military service." Charibert looked shocked. "You're surprised? Perhaps you didn't realize that the king's garrison lives inside the walls of my castle. I was sad to learn that your father distinguished himself—" She hesitated, and held Charibert's gaze. "For profligacy and dissolution. I hear he lost a great deal of money and property at dice and thus your estate has already shrunk considerably because of his actions."

"I didn't say I was sad that he was dead," said Charibert, stiffening. "Just that he is dead."

Ela felt a sudden surge of sympathy for Charibert. "And I learned that both of your brothers died in the siege of Bedford Castle. My commander remembers that they were caught up in the melée and unhorsed and trampled to death."

To his credit, Charibert did flinch at this information.

"Were you close to your brothers?"

"Of course I was. We were brothers, though I was a few years younger. My father insisted on training them himself and wouldn't let anyone else near them with advice on horsemanship or swordsmanship. Since I've had the benefit of instruction from another, I know he didn't teach them all they needed to know. I'm sure I could have bested either of them before the end of a trumpet blast."

Ela felt sad for the young men who'd been sacrificed for their father's misplaced pride. "Your father himself was a proficient fighter, I'm told."

Charibert held himself straighter. "Perhaps I inherited from him what my brothers didn't."

"Vicious was the word used." Ela peered at him. "So I do hope not." She let that sit in the air. "My garrison commander could not offer definitive information on whether your father is alive or dead. It's quite common for soldiers to decide they prefer life in the holy lands—where it's warm all year long and a little gold can keep a man in great comfort. He thought it possible that your father lives there still, perhaps with a harem of concubines to occupy his time."

Ela chastised herself for poking Charibert's hide, which was likely bruised and battered enough by his father's poor choices. Still, this scenario was exactly what her garrison commander had suggested, before apologizing for sharing such crude sentiments with a lady.

"In such circumstances a man is hardly going to write home to his family to excuse his absence but is more likely to stay quiet and keep his whereabouts mysterious. I was given to understand that your father had spent every penny to his name and lost most of the estate. I suppose he chose to fight overseas for a chance to rebuild his family fortunes through pillage and plunder."

"Such a quest is hardly unusual."

"No, indeed it is not." Ela sighed. Her own husband was not immune to enriching himself with the spoils of war. "I do wonder how your mother has managed to support you all with the remains of the estate. I hear there are but a hundred acres of land left to it."

"She took an interest in breeding a particular kind of sheep whose wool has sold well. And she had the men dig fishponds and set snares and otherwise wring food from the woods and fields. She's not as foolish as she seems."

Ela wanted to laugh at this combination of compliment and insult. "So she's managed to keep you all alive and provide you with a horse and armor and the training to—almost—beat one of King Henry III's cousins on the tournament ground and you show such little gratitude? Perhaps she deserves the manor more than you do."

Charibert's lip twitched. "I'm the oldest living son and it's my right to inherit."

"Only if your father is dead."

"It's been six years. I'm petitioning you, as sheriff of Wiltshire, to have him declared dead."

"I suspect such a declaration would have to come from the king himself, given that your father is a noble and there's an estate involved. It's entirely possible that the king may take a dim view of you inheriting since you disgraced yourself in a tournament last week."

Charibert hesitated. "I don't believe that."

"And I don't believe the king will declare him dead without significant proof. Perhaps you should journey to the holy land to search for him yourself."

"He's not in the holy land. He's dead!" Charibert almost shouted the last part. "Since you persist in ignoring my pleas, I'm forced to share information that I'd far rather have kept to myself."

"What's that?"

"I believe that my mother killed my father."

CHAPTER 3

*E*la stared at Charibert d'Albiac in stunned silence for a moment. This was certainly a new twist in his ruse. And it was a clever one, since—as sheriff—she could hardly ignore a charge of murder. "What evidence do you have to back up this accusation?"

"I don't know where she hid the body, but I believe that he came back from the siege of Bedford Castle without my older brothers and started to…misuse her."

"You witnessed this?"

"I saw it with my own eyes. She was distraught about losing my brothers. He would lash her with his tongue when she cried. He was home for about six months. At first, he had money that he'd been paid for them to fight in the siege, and was happy drinking and gambling. Then the money ran out and he stayed at home drinking and barking insults at her. Then one day he was gone."

"Where did she say he'd gone to?" Ela could easily believe the scenario thus far. It matched everything else she'd heard about Montaigu d'Albiac.

"Mother said he'd headed back to Egypt to fight the

Saracen and win more gold. I was furious with him for leaving without saying goodbye to me, his only surviving son. I intended to chastise him for it when he returned. For more than a year I nursed my grudge against him. Then I noticed that my mother no longer seemed to expect his return."

"What do you mean?" The line of petitioners behind him grew longer as he stood there. One woman held a chicken in her arms, which was flapping and squawking. Ela's desire to dismiss Charibert and never see his arrogant face again warred with sudden curiosity about his story.

"She never received any letter from him, and didn't complain about it. She didn't admonish me with promises that I'd be punished when my father got home. She just stopped talking about him altogether. One day I asked her if she thought he was dead." He paused and looked reflective for a moment.

Ela grew impatient. "And what did she reply?"

"She said he's alive and that I must pray daily for his safe return. This sat oddly with me, because why would she want his return? He was nothing but a thorn in her side and the estate is more prosperous with him gone."

"Did you ever accuse her of killing him?"

"No. I could hardly accuse her of murder then ask her to buy me a fine horse and armor, could I?"

Ela thought that she wouldn't put that past him at all, but she supposed that he did have a point. "So you kept quiet, knowing that you needed her to provide for you until you were in your majority."

"Yes. I knew better than to bite the hand that quite literally feeds me. But now that I'm a man, I'm tired of living at her whims. My father is dead, whether in Saracen lands or buried under the vegetable patch at Neversend. I have no wish to see my mother hanged, so don't think that, but if she must hang for me to finally gain my estate, then so be it."

The clamor of the hall, busy as it was with soldiers, servants, petitioners and her own family, seemed to hush almost to silence. Ela watched Charibert's face to see how his words would sit with him now that he'd said them aloud.

He did look uncomfortable enough to shift his rather substantial weight. "As I said, I don't want to see it, but…." His face reddened.

Ela inhaled slowly. "I understand that such an accusation is not brought lightly. If you were to falsely accuse her, and she were to hang, do you realize that even if you escaped a charge of murder, you would suffer all eternity in the fires of hell?"

His florid face twitched. "I'd hardly say it if I didn't think it true. I did say I've no proof."

Ela wondered how far he'd really be prepared to go with this accusation. "So, shall I send men to dig up the gardens and grounds around your family's estate, in search of a body?"

"Yes."

Poor Mathilde. Ela didn't think for one moment that such a mild-mannered woman would kill her husband. She didn't look capable of killing a mouse, let alone a man. But such an accusation could not be ignored, especially if Charibert intended to use it to press his claim to the estate. If he wrote to the king insisting that his mother had murdered his father, King Henry's first question would be to ask if the sheriff had investigated the crime.

~

"I HARDLY KNOW WHERE TO BEGIN," admitted Ela to Bill Talbot that evening, as they sat in the hall after dinner. A fire burned in the great hearth and the children sat near it, Richard and Stephen recounting old tales of battles and chivalry that would probably give the younger children nightmares. "If Mathilde is suspected of murder then she should appear before a jury to answer questions that might go some way to reveal her guilt or innocence. But I have no reason to suspect her of murder beyond her son's accusations."

"And he's a callow youth who's already proved himself to be untrustworthy and capable of cheating to get what he wants. I could have trained that gelding into a fine mount for young Nicky." Ela knew Bill would have preferred her to deprive Charibert of his horse and armor.

"He is, so I'm disinclined to believe him. However, I can't just ignore his petition to gain control of his estate. If his father truly is dead, and the estate is not his mother's in her own right, then he may well be entitled to the lion's share of it."

"More's the pity."

A peal of laughter drew their attention to Stephen and Richard. The laughter came from Elsie, who hovered nearby. "I'm glad the boys are so kind to Elsie. Some girls would never recover from what she's been through." The poor girl had lost her parents in a horrific manner and been sold to a child-slaver by her aunt and uncle. "It's wonderful to see her coming out of her shell."

Bill peered at the little group. "It was kind of you to give her a place as your personal maid. She could barely carry a platter when she first arrived."

"She grew up on a remote farm in the country. I doubt that her family owned a single plate. Sometimes I have to remind myself that other people's lives are so different from ours that it's like we're living in different worlds."

"Young Charibert d'Albiac certainly needed to be brought back to the harsh realities of this world. Imagine thinking that you can get away with cheating—against the king's cousin, no less—in front of a great crowd of people?"

"He's young, Bill. And from what I've learned his father was almost a monster. His entire childhood took place under less than ideal circumstances. He may yet mature into a decent young man. And his family lives here in Wiltshire. I don't wish to antagonize local nobles if I can avoid it, especially ones with considerable fighting prowess such as he displayed against Richard. He may yet prove valuable as a knight for King Henry."

"A young man willing to accuse his own mother of murder to gain his estate shows no honor, in my estimation." He leaned in and spoke softly. "Imagine if young William accused you of poisoning his father so that you could take control of Salisbury Castle?"

Ela blinked. "William knows I loved his father dearly. He'd never think such a thing, let alone say it aloud."

"Indeed he would not, my lady. But I hope to underscore what a shocking accusation this is."

"I admit that my main concern is making sure that poor Mathilde doesn't hang for a crime she didn't commit. Hence my hesitation to call a jury and even plant the idea in anyone's mind. But should I then send men with shovels to tear up her demesne? Such an act implies a suspicion of guilt. And does a failure to find her husband's body there prove her innocence? Or does it suggest that she was cunning enough to hide it well?"

"The best way to protect Mathilde is to find her husband alive."

"I very much doubt that he is alive, either in the Holy Land or elsewhere. Given that we live at the heart of the king's military operations, the whereabouts of most knights can be discovered quite easily. And no one seems to know what happened to Montaigu d'Albiac. If he was as reckless a gambler and fighter as has been suggested, any number of people may have wanted to kill him."

Bill hesitated and peered into his cup of wine. Then he looked back at her. "Far be it from me to suggest anything... untoward. But if a body were to be found somewhere—somewhere very far from the d'Albiac estate or even from England—and declared to be the corpse of Montaigu d'Albiac, would not that protect Mathilde's interests?"

Ela wasn't sure whether to laugh or protest in horror. "Bill, I can't believe you'd suggest such a thing. And no, it wouldn't protect her interests. She insists her husband is alive and thus she must hold his estate in his stead. If his death was confirmed, she'd lose her estate—or the bulk of it —to her son overnight."

"Better than swinging from a gibbet." Bill took a sip of his wine.

"I don't intend to resort to any ruse. I wish to discover what actually happened to Montaigu d'Albiac."

"Charibert implies that Montaigu d'Albiac came home from fighting and never left again because his wife killed and buried him. The garrison records should at least show if Montaigu left England again after his six months at home."

"Excellent suggestion. If he left again, we can hunt him—dead or alive—overseas rather than digging up her herb garden. I shall consult the garrison records tomorrow morning."

THE NEXT DAY Ela summoned the garrison commander and requested to consult the record books. He took her to the rooms, up against the castle's outer wall, where military records were held. Great leather-bound log books, written in the crabbed hand of a former clerk, held information about the movements of various knights and important soldiers—their departures, their returns, and a red line drawn through their name if their life was known to be lost.

Records from 1225 showed Sir Montaigu d'Albiac on a list of those engaged on a voyage to Gascony. The king's brother Richard raised the expedition. Ela's late husband had traveled with them, so she knew something of their exploits. They had taken Poitou without bloodshed, then gone on to besiege Rieux and Bergerac. On the list of men presented by the clerk, several names were now lined through in red, with a red date scratched next to their name, and others had return dates written next to their names in black.

Montaigu d'Albiac's name, conversely, was lined through in black.

"What does that mean?" asked Ela of the clerk.

This clerk was a middle-aged man with close-cropped dark hair. "It means that he didn't fight with Richard's men after all."

"So he was supposed to go but he didn't turn up?" Her heart beat faster. Was there even the tiniest chance that Charibert was right to think his mother killed his father?

"That's one possibility. It could be that he made other arrangements and went elsewhere instead. If he was a man who liked to fight then that more-or-less diplomatic mission may not have been to his taste."

"He would have had no chance to enrich himself, I imagine."

"Indeed not, my lady." The clerk looked relieved that she'd understood him without him having to say it.

"Knights can pick and choose the missions they go on?"

"Rather they can buy their way out of forays that they don't wish to go on. If they have enough money to do so, of course."

"Would there be a record of such monies being paid?"

"In an ideal world, yes, my lady."

"Since we are not in an ideal world, what exactly is your meaning?"

"I don't know if he paid money to avoid service or if he simply didn't go. The former clerk who crossed out his name might have known, but he died of a fever two winters ago."

Ela sighed with exasperation. What was the point of keeping incomplete records?

"And there are no records of him being called to serve on a later expedition?"

"Not in these books, my lady."

THE NEXT MORNING, Ela and Bill set out early to visit Mathilde at her manor.

"It's a long ride," observed Bill, as they trotted down from the castle mound, guards clattering behind them. "I'm surprised you didn't send John Dacus instead."

She did frequently employ her co-sheriff on the longer and more tiresome journeys their work entailed. But today Ela had left her co-sheriff to deal with the line of supplicants needing help with one matter or another. "It's a beautiful day for a ride. Why should Sir John enjoy the wildflowers in the hedgerows while I listen to people squabbling over who a loose piglet belongs to?"

That wasn't the only reason, though. "And I wish to see Mathilde in her home and get the measure of her character. Her husband not arriving for military service, then disappearing altogether around the same time, is troubling."

"You're starting to think that she did kill him?" asked Bill. They trotted through a field where the spring grass glistened with dew.

"No. Well, my mind is not entirely closed to the possibility, but I think it unlikely. And I feel sympathy for her predicament. Not everyone is happy to see a woman in command of her own manor and money."

"So you wish to form your own opinions more carefully before you bring her before a jury to question her about her husband's disappearance."

"Exactly. If she's brought before a jury and accused of murder, I'm afraid that things might quickly turn against her. Her own son accusing her of such is very damning."

They cantered up a short hill, which led to a magnificent view across Salisbury Plain. They slowed to a walk and she patted Freya's neck.

"Charibert cheated in a tournament in full view of half the nobles in the south of England," said Bill. "Surely this calls his character and his accusation into question?"

"It certainly does in my mind. But I've seen how quickly a persuasive speaker can get the jury on their side. Young Charibert is very insistent—a bully, even—but that, combined with his youth and golden-haired, pink-cheeked charm, might persuade the jury to think him a hero. I've seen it happen before. And Mathilde is so soft-spoken. I worry about whether she'll find the gumption to protest her innocence when her son is the accuser."

"Does she even know her son has accused her of murder?" asked Bill.

"I have no idea."

CHAPTER 4

*T*he house at Neversend was a low, sprawling manor that appeared to have grown and changed under several different owners. An arched stone gatehouse was the most impressive part of the manor demesne. It led them into a courtyard where buildings of different sizes hunkered against each other. The white render of the manor house had washed away to reveal the stonework below, and Ela could see old, filled-in archways and openings where doors and windows had been moved at some point in the past.

"I don't know why I was expecting a castle," said Ela, as they rode up the track toward the sprawling manor.

"Charibert's warlike demeanor, perhaps," said Bill cheerfully. "And perhaps there was one at some point."

"If their ancestors were as difficult as the current generation, it may well have been slighted." A family whose castle was deliberately destroyed after a defeat often rebuilt it as a stone manor, but without permission from the king in the form of a license to crenelate they could not rebuild it as a castle.

They spoke softly, so as not to be overheard. The clatter of their horses' hooves drew a woman to the door, wiping her hands on her apron.

"Ela, Countess of Salisbury, is here to meet with the mistress of the house," said Bill.

Charibert appeared behind the woman at the door. "I see you've come to investigate my claim." Triumph shone on his face.

"Your claim?" Ela stared down at him from her horse. "I'm here to investigate the charge of murder that you've laid at the feet of your mother."

The woman in the apron gasped. "Whatever can she mean?" she asked of Charibert.

"Fetch Mother at once," he commanded. Then he turned to Ela and Bill. "Do come in."

Ela bristled. This hall was still his mother's to command, not his. He should be ashamed of himself for making such a bold and—she assumed—unfounded accusation to gain control of the property.

Two girls appeared in the hallway. "What's amiss? Why is Dottie shaking and crying?" asked the taller of the two. She looked out the door toward Ela and Bill. "Who are you?"

"I am Ela, Countess of Salisbury." The girls, apparently less truculent than their brother, politely paid their respects and didn't ask further questions.

A guard held Ela's horse while she dismounted. Mathilde had appeared in the crowded doorway. "Is there a private room where we could talk?" asked Ela. She didn't wish to ask Mathilde if she'd killed her husband in front of his children.

Mathilde nodded, clearly agitated, and ushered Ela and Bill into the house. The guards stayed outside with the horses, where a stable boy was summoned to bring them water.

Charibert hovered nearby, and Ela made a point of asking

him to leave her to conduct her inquiries in peace. She watched Bill put his hand on the hilt of his sword, and she felt sure he'd be happy to knock Charibert off his feet with it if the occasion presented itself.

Mathilde closed the door behind them, sealing them into a smallish sitting room with several mismatched wood chairs arranged near an empty fireplace. Ela noticed the swept fireplace and the clean fire tongs. The stone walls bore signs of earlier decoration that had faded or chipped off, much like the facade of the building. A small carved wood cross hung above the mantel, with the shadow of a much larger one—since removed—hovering around it. The faded wall decorations—painted red lines to suggest stone blocks—were brighter in a large rectangular patch on another wall, suggesting that perhaps a tapestry had once hung there. The overall impression was one of genteel poverty in reduced circumstances. This matched everything Ela had learned about the family's fortunes under Montaigu d'Albiac.

"Has Charibert done something?" asked Mathilde anxiously.

"In a way, yes," said Ela. Clearly, the servant had not repeated news of the murder accusation to Mathilde. "I'm afraid that your son came to my castle to pursue a claim to your family estate. He also suggested that you might be guilty of the murder of your husband."

Mathilde stared as if uncomprehending. "Me?"

"He said that he thinks you tired of your husband's profligacy and verbal abuse and decided you'd be better off without him. To maintain control of the estate in his absence, you insist that he's still alive and might return at any moment."

"But that last part is the truth!"

"When did you last hear from him?"

33

Mathilde's face crumpled. "Not since he left. But I know he's alive. I'm sure of it."

"You don't even know where he is."

"He's in the Holy Land."

"There's no record in the garrison commander's books of him going there under the auspices of King Henry or anyone else."

"He wasn't under the auspices of anyone. His only interest was in the opportunity to gain riches. For all I know he intended to fight for the French, or even the Saracens themselves."

Ela sighed. Such a suggestion did seem plausible given Montaigu's urgent need for money and his taste for battle and excitement. Such mercenary activities weren't even uncommon. "Did he travel with anyone?"

"He may have, but he mentioned no names to me."

"Did he say where he was going?"

"To the continent, he said. I asked where, but he told me...he told me to shut my mouth. He said it rather more rudely than that. I didn't press him. I'd learned not to."

"His treating you cruelly does give you a motive to kill him," said Ela softly.

"How would I have killed my husband?" Mathilde's voice broke. "He was a man over six feet tall and quick as a fox."

"As sheriff, I'm afraid I've learned there are many ways a woman can kill her husband. Poison is the most popular since no strength is needed, only subterfuge." She watched Mathilde's face carefully to see her reaction. Mathilde did look horrified—but was that a sign of guilt? "I know a case where a wife smothered her husband with a pillow while he slept. She claimed he died peacefully in his sleep, and she might have got away with it, but their young son saw it happen from the doorway and told a neighbor."

"Perhaps the son wanted his mother out of the way so he

could seize his inheritance," rasped Mathilde. "How could you prove if a man is smothered or if he died in his sleep?"

Ela looked at her in surprise. Has she pondered the best way to kill a man without detection? "The coroner has ways of determining when and how a person died that don't seem obvious to a layperson."

"Does my son think I buried the body?" Her red-rimmed eyes stared. "I don't know how I could even move his body across a room, let alone dig a hole and..." she burst into sobs.

Her emotion seemed genuine, though perhaps her panic and sorrow were for herself and her rapidly shrinking prospects for a promising future.

"Your son didn't speculate on such things. Of course, in the absence of a body, murder can be hard to prove. The coroner himself has told me that when the body can't be found, it's difficult to secure a conviction."

"So they would only hang me if they found his body?" She seemed to brighten.

"I can't promise that." The jury and the judge at the assizes were human and thus unpredictable. "But would you allow my men to dig on your manor to see if they can find the body? If you withhold permission they may well see that as proof of guilt."

She hesitated. "Where will they dig?"

Was she guilty? "Wherever they see fit. Your willingness to let them dig anywhere would go a long way toward proving your innocence."

"Then I suppose I have no choice. They must dig wherever they will."

Mathilde shook all over as if chilled by a cold wind. Her hands trembled. "My son Charibert has accused me of such a terrible thing?"

"I'm afraid so." Ela wanted to reassure her that she didn't

believe Charibert, but that would undermine her impartiality as sheriff, so she held her tongue.

"He would have me hang so he can take possession of this house and the remaining land on which it stands." She looked past Ela as if talking to herself. Then she looked at Ela. "I've done everything I could to raise him to be a gentleman in his father's absence, but it seems I've failed. And now I must be condemned to die as well."

Ela's heart clenched. "Don't speak too soon. You've not yet been tried, let alone convicted."

"My husband lives, I tell you!"

"What makes you so sure?"

Marguerite looked down. "I'm not sure I should tell you."

"Why not?"

"Because it may make me look more guilty." She looked behind Ela again. "The truth is that from the day I met my husband—we were betrothed when I was fourteen and married when I was sixteen—I felt a sense of chill dread. His very presence stirred feelings of unease inside me."

"What did he do to inspire such aversion?"

"He never hit me, if that's what you're thinking. Rather he ignored me. He went about his business—drinking, gambling, out all hours with God only knows who. He acted as if I didn't exist. Except in the bedroom. There he just used me as if I was a garderobe to relieve himself in."

Shocked, Ela struggled to keep her composure. She fought the urge to cross herself at such crude talk.

"After our sons were killed in battle my grief drove him to anger which only deepened my misery."

Sympathy stirred in Ela's chest. "I suppose you must have been relieved when he went away."

Mathilde, who'd been looking past her this whole time, now met her gaze. "But that's just it. I don't feel any sense of ease or peace. I feel like he could blast through that door at any hour of the day or night, face red with drink and eyes blazing, shouting that he needs to raise a hundred pounds by sunup."

Mathilde's eyes filled with tears. "If he were dead, surely I'd no longer dread his imminent arrival?" She looked past Ela again. "I feel in my bones that he's still alive out there somewhere. His spirit persists in this world. I'm sure of it."

Ela found Mathilde's terror of her husband rather damning. Could Mathilde have killed him and then somehow convinced herself that she didn't? Such delusion was not unheard of. And her guilt might rattle her nerves enough for her to feel the same dread as when he lived.

"We shall certainly go to all possible pains to discover him —if he lives. I've sent word to contacts in a few different places abroad. We shall see if we can rouse some news of him."

"If they find him, will they bring him back?" Her worried gaze filled Ela with sorrow.

"I suppose his return—or not—would be his decision. He's not accused of a crime. But evidence that he lives would surely exonerate you of his murder."

"Then I suppose I must pray for it," said Mathilde doubtfully. "If he lives, he may return to torment me. If he doesn't, then my son Charibert will try to exile us from our home. How shall I look at Charibert across the dinner table when he's accused me of such a terrible thing?" This thought seemed to occur to Mathilde for the first time. Her face crumpled. "Do you think he really believes me to be a murderess?"

Ela swallowed. She had no good answer. Was it worse if her son thought her a killer, or if he had simply lied to sacrifice her life out of greed? "You must bear it bravely and pray that your husband will be found alive."

And that we don't find his body buried beneath your herb

37

garden.

~

TWO OF ELA'S men started digging, using shovels they'd brought from Salisbury. Ela stayed to watch the digging—or rather to observe if either Mathilde or Charibert had any unexpected reactions.

Mathilde stayed inside the house—probably weeping or praying or both—but Charibert came out and hovered over the men as they dug. After some time, he strode over to Ela, who stood watching with Bill.

"This makes looking for a needle in a haystack seem like child's play," said Charibert. "Even if they turn up the entire estate they might miss him. He could be buried just one foot deeper than they dig."

"Do you think your petite and slender mother dug a hole six feet deep?" asked Ela.

"I don't know. Maybe she had someone else dig it?"

"Who?" Ela was curious if Mathilde had any confidants. "Do you have male servants who might have been employed to either commit or conceal such a crime?"

Charibert appeared to consider this quite seriously. "None still here, but it's a possibility. There was old Alf. He's dead now but was a strapping man who worked here his whole life."

"I suppose we must dig deeper, then," said Ela coolly. "We wouldn't want to miss evidence of a crime."

As the digging went on, Charibert grew more agitated. He paced back and forth in the gardens, where herbs and root vegetables and even small trees were being uprooted, then hastily replanted. Perhaps he didn't like to see such wanton destruction of their useful foodstuffs and despoiling of the estate he hoped to soon command.

Especially if he knew that there was no chance they'd find a body.

"How long are you going to go on digging? Charibert's red face loomed over Ela, tall and broad, and intimidating.

"Would you like us to stop?" she said pleasantly. "If you'd like to retract the accusations of murder that you made against your mother, we can all go away at once." She silently prayed he'd take that course.

"I never said that I'm certain he's buried here," said Charibert sullenly. "I didn't see her kill him and dig a hole. I just think that's what happened."

"We'd certainly have a much easier time finding the body if you did see her bury it, wouldn't we?" said Bill cheerfully. He enjoyed watching Charibert squirm. "What do your sisters think of you accusing your mother of murder?"

"How would I know? You should ask them."

ELA SHRANK from interviewing Mathilde's daughters, but by now they must have found out why the sheriff's men were tearing their garden apart. Ela went back to the door of the manor house, and Bill knocked and asked the servant to fetch them.

After much bustling and consternation from within—they could hear it through the closed door—two red-eyed girls came to the door. Mathilde, from behind them, introduced them as Helene and Joan. Helene was the oldest and dried her eyes vigorously on a handkerchief while her mother spoke. "It's all lies," Mathilde protested. "Charibert is willful and selfish but I can't believe he'd make such a baseless and dangerous accusation."

"Are you aware that he wants to take control of the estate and force the rest of you to leave?"

The girls nodded. Joan, the younger, spoke up. "He's been saying that ever since he reached his majority. He wants to be master of the estate."

"He'll probably gamble it away," said Helene.

A fierce shriek drew Ela's attention to another girl, physically restraining a boy of about six. "Let me go!" he shouted.

"I tried to keep him upstairs," said the girl apologetically.

"Who is this?" Ela asked Mathilde.

"He's my grandson, Charley. The son of my boy Alain who was killed.

"I see. And this young lady is your son's widow?" The girl's familiarity with the boy—she wrapped her arms around him—suggested that she was his mother rather than a servant. There was an odd silence.

Mathilde drew in a shaky breath. "Agnes was my personal maid."

"Oh." The current fashion for pious and modest clothing made it hard to tell nobles from servants when there was no fur-trimmed cloak or crisp white veil to distinguish them.

Mathilde rubbed her palms on the front of her gown. "I'm afraid Alain took advantage of her. Charley was born after my son was killed. Alain never learned of the boy's existence."

"Oh." Were there any men in this family who weren't reprehensible? Even Charley, struggling and writhing in his mother's grasp, seemed like rather a handful. "So your household of dependents is even larger than I previously thought?"

Mathilde nodded silently. "What will happen to them all if I hang?"

It was a very good question, and not one Ela could answer.

"My lady!" one of the guards had rushed up behind her. "We've found a body."

CHAPTER 5

*E*la's heart sank, no doubt along with the heart of everyone else there. Except Charibert. He leaped into action and sprinted to where the guards were digging.

"We must send for the coroner at once," said Ela. "Don't disturb the bones further until he's arrived."

One of the guards was dispatched to Salisbury to fetch Giles Haughton.

"How can there be a body?" whimpered Mathilde. "When I didn't kill my husband."

"Perhaps they've unwittingly dug up an old grave," said Ela hopefully. "I recall one instance where human bones were found that turned out to be from the time of the Roman occupation of our lands—complete with Roman coins and pots."

"This one's fairly recent," said the guard who'd come to get them. "There's no doubt about that."

The younger daughter, Joan, burst out in racking sobs. The older one, Helene, bravely kept her composure. "I wish to see this body," she said. "There must be some misunderstanding."

41

The guard led them to a spot beneath a spreading apple tree. They'd dug among the roots and revealed the bones of a human hand. Helene gasped when she saw it. Ela crossed herself.

"The bones aren't buried deeply enough for it to be a proper grave," said Bill Talbot quietly.

"No. Likely whoever put them here counted on no one digging around the roots of a mature apple tree," said Ela. "Which does suggest a murder."

"And while the flesh is gone, the sleeve is still intact." A green linen cuff lay crumpled around the bones. "So this body is not ancient."

Mathilde peered at the hand, her own hands pressed to her mouth. "Whoever can it be?"

"Why can't they keep digging?" pressed Charibert. He paced around the tree. "It must be Father."

"Charibert, how can you think such a terrible thing?" asked Mathilde.

"It didn't have to come to this," said Charibert coldly. "If you'd just given me my rightful inheritance on my majority, I'd never have said anything."

"She didn't kill him, you wretch!" cried Joan, through tears.

"Then who is this?"

Ela glared at him for a moment, wondering if a more callous youth had ever lived. "We will learn more in good time when the coroner arrives."

THE BELLS for Nones had faded away before the guard returned with Giles Haughton. He jumped down from his bay palfrey and greeted Ela, who introduced him to the group of white-faced, red-eyed women, and pointed out young Charibert, who stalked nearby.

"Are you the coroner?" asked Charibert crudely, marching over.

"You've accused your own mother of murder?" asked Haughton, as if he'd never heard of such a terrible thing. Which, quite possibly, he hadn't.

"I only wish to see justice done," said Charibert, looking slightly chastened. His red-gold hair shone in the afternoon sun and excitement flushed his boyish features. "Can they dig the rest of the body up yet?"

Haughton tut-tutted disapprovingly and ignored his question. He walked around the apple tree, surveying the site, then quietly instructed the workers to keep digging.

As they shoveled the earth away, it became clear that they had only part of a body—a headless torso to be precise. The flesh was gone but the top half of a green tunic, with no ornamentation around the cuffs or neckline, remained. Ela tried not to recoil as the remains were pulled from the soil and placed on a linen cloth that Giles Haughton had brought with him.

"Girls, I don't think you should see this," said Ela, ushering the young ladies away.

"I think we should," protested Helene. "This is not our father."

"How can you tell?"

"He never wore green."

"That's true," chimed in Joan. "He had some green woolen hose that he wore when it was very cold, but he didn't own a green tunic that I remember."

"This is valuable information," said Ela. "Though I worry about you seeing horrors that you'll never be able to unsee. As sheriff, I can tell you that some sights will haunt your nights for many years to come."

"No horror chills me more than the prospect of our dear mother hanging from a gibbet," said Helene. Her lips pressed together in her white face. "Anyone who knows her will vouch for her good and kind character. Some mothers would have blamed Agnes for her condition and even sent her and the baby away, but our mother has welcomed her into our family as if she were our sister and little Charley our youngest brother."

Ela noted with relief that Agnes and Charley were nowhere to be seen. An impressionable young boy should certainly not see the grisly remains emerging from the soil.

Further digging around the apple tree produced the remains of the legs, bare of clothing and shoes, and the head —fleshless but with remaining wisps of light brown hair.

Helene and Joan peered anxiously through their fingers— and amid fervent prayers—at the bones emerging from the soil. Giles Haughton placed the bones on his cloth and arranged them into the shape of a man.

Charibert kept popping up and peering, then heaving a sign and pacing around the garden. Ela had an eerie feeling that he was almost as surprised as everyone else that bones had turned up, and so quickly. He wasn't saying anything, though. He hadn't exclaimed that the bones were definitely his father. And the girls hadn't cried with relief that they weren't.

"That is our father's hair color," admitted Helene, when pressed. "Though it looks rather long."

"Hair keeps growing after death," bleated Charibert.

"It does not," said Haughton. "That's an old wives' tale. Was your father a man of diminutive stature?" he asked Charibert, who looked at him blankly. "Was he a small man?"

"No! Of course not." Charibert seemed offended by the suggestion. "He was as tall as me. Taller even—" He broke off, likely looking at the bones and coming to the same conclusion that Ela did.

"These are a woman's bones, aren't they?" asked Ela.

"I will need to examine them more closely to be sure, but the shape of the pelvis suggests that they are the bones of a woman, rather than a small man."

"How can that be?" protested Charibert. "When it's my father that's dead?"

"How long ago was this person buried here?" asked Ela of Haughton. "Can you tell from the state of decomposition?"

"It's quite a few years," said Haughton. "Enough for all the flesh to have decayed away. At that point, it's hard to tell if it's five years, or fifty. I may learn more if I examine the fragments of clothing. Their construction may reveal more about the date. This apple tree is not ancient, though. I'd say it's no more than twenty years old, and she was buried among the existing roots—even divided into pieces to fit there—which to me suggests that the burial is within the last ten years or so."

Ela shuddered at the thought of someone cutting up this woman's body to conceal it.

"How do you think they cut her up?"

"The bones are cut clean, rather than severed with saw marks. I'd venture to say it was done with a hatchet or sword or a similarly sharp instrument designed to slash through bone and flesh in one cut."

Ela looked at Mathilde, who gazed intently at the bones, hands still pressed to her face. "Mathilde, do you have any idea who this might be?"

She looked up at Ela, pulled her hands away from her face and swallowed visibly. Her eyes looked as if she's seen a ghost—as well they might. "I do. I think it's—" her voice seemed to catch in her throat.

"Cathy Cross," said Charibert suddenly, staring at the bones. "She had a green dress like that."

"Who was she?" asked Ela.

"She was a kitchen girl here for several years. She was a good worker and the cook liked her, then one year her whole temperament seemed to change. She became distracted and difficult and given to fits of crying. Then one day she disappeared…" Mathilde trailed off, staring down at the assortment of bones in their partial green shroud. "But who could have killed her?"

Not Charibert, thought Ela. He'd never have encouraged them to dig in the garden if he'd buried a body there. Besides, he'd have been a boy when this woman was killed. "How long ago did she disappear?"

Mathilde appeared to do some calculations in her head. "I'd say it was ten years ago. In the summer."

"Did you report her disappearance to the sheriff?"

Mathilde frowned. "I don't suppose we did. We thought she'd left of her own accord. She'd seemed so disgruntled and unhappy in her employment. She had relatives in Somerset so I suppose we thought she went home to them. I intended to follow up with them but Montaigu told me not to bother, as she'd grown so lazy and idle."

Montaigu. In addition to being a gambler and a wastrel, was he also a murderer?

Mathilde paused, perhaps wondering the same thing.

"Where is Montaigu?" asked Haughton.

"That is indeed the question of the hour," said Ela. "I came here in the first place to investigate Montaigu's disappearance. His son Charibert," she pointed to the boy, "had accused his mother of possibly killing him, so the guards were searching the grounds for his body—and came upon this one."

"You can't stop searching for him, he might still be here," said Charibert brusquely.

"One murder at a time, young man," said Haughton giving the boy a severe look. "My mortuary table doesn't fit two corpses at once. I do hope that you're not going to suggest that your mother killed this poor girl. She doesn't look like she has the arm strength to make such a clean cut." He stared at Charibert.

The boy's arrogant demeanor melted into the pouty expression of a toddler being sent early to bed. "No. I wasn't going to suggest that. Mother always liked Cathy and was upset about her leaving."

"Yet you think her capable of murdering her husband in cold blood?"

Charibert hesitated, perhaps not realizing he'd be called upon to defend his outrageous accusations in front of so many people, including his mother and sisters. "My father was a very difficult man."

"Most men are, I'm afraid," said Haughton. "And most women are long-suffering to the point of sainthood." Ela resisted the urge to nod in agreement. Her own husband, charming as he was, could be high-handed and insensitive to the point of cruelty without even noticing. She couldn't imagine being married to a man who squandered their daily bread and their children's futures. "Luckily that is rarely cause for murder. I'm not saying women don't murder their husbands—they do—but it's not common. And I've certainly never seen a body butchered by a woman with such deft and skilled violence."

Ela crossed herself yet again, beset by a sudden vision of the poor girl's terrible end. "She must be given a Christian burial."

"I shall arrange it with the parish priest," said Mathilde

grimly. "And I shall endeavor to inform her family, if they can be found."

"In the meantime, I must remove the bones and her dress to my mortuary to see if I can find more hints of exactly how she died and who may have dispatched her. I'd bet my life that it's a man, and a strong one who's skilled in the use of a sword."

Montaigu d'Albiac. Ela turned to Mathilde. "Do you know of any reason why your husband might want to kill this girl?"

Mathilde, lips pressed together, shook her head. "I doubt he even noticed her existence."

"You shall be summoned before the jury in Salisbury, not to face charges of murder, but to provide all the information you can about this girl so that her killer can be found."

ELA CALLED for the jurors to meet in the castle mortuary the next morning. Giles Haughton had laid out the skeleton of Cathy Cross on the scarred wood table, assembling the severed sections of the body into a whole.

"Someone wanted to make sure she'd never be found," said Stephen Hale, the cordwainer.

"And in any other circumstance they'd have been successful," said Ela. "The guards only dug under the tree because we were already searching for the body of a murder victim and wanted to dig in places that might be considered safe from disturbance."

"But this isn't the body you expected?" asked Stephen Hale, the cordwainer. "I confess to being confused."

"Indeed, it isn't," said Ela. "We sought the body of Montaigu d'Albiac, the lord of the manor who disappeared some six years ago. His son has tried to convince us that

Montaigu was murdered by his wife, but I suspect it's a ruse to seize his inheritance against his mother's will. I have, however, instructed the guards to keep digging. Who knows what we might find at this point?"

Giles Haughton showed the bones, including the places where they'd been severed with a sharp blade. "A swift strike," he observed. "By someone with a very sharp blade and considerable strength."

"That's the truth, indeed," said Peter Hardwick, the butcher. "My apprentice couldn't do this, even with the finest tool in my shop."

"I believe that a sword made these cuts," said Haughton. "I tested a few different weapons on the femur of a recently butchered heifer and the cuts most resemble those made with Sir William Talbot's broadsword, which he was kind enough to wield for me." He turned to where Bill stood behind the jurors.

"Was the cut difficult to make?" asked Ela.

"For me, no." Bill spoke calmly. "I spend my days training your sons in the art of knighthood, and wielding a sword with speed and force is an essential part of our training. Any trained knight could do this."

"Could my sons?" asked Ela, genuinely curious.

"I suspect they could, my lady."

Ela fought the urge to cross herself. She should be pleased that Richard and Stephen were able to defend their own bodies, the castle, and the king's realm with such vigor.

"So is it likely that Sir Montaigu d'Albiac killed this girl?" asked Stephen Hale. "She could easily have been dead six years or more. There's precious little flesh left on the bones."

"It's certainly a possibility," said Ela. "But if a trained youth could make these cuts, there are three more suspects—his sons."

"How old are they?"

"Only one lives, and he's eighteen—that's Charibert, the one who's accused his mother. The others are some years older and were killed fighting in the years before their father disappeared."

"So it could have been one of the older brothers. Charibert would have been too young if he's only eighteen now."

"And he'd hardly have invited the sheriff's men to turn up his home turf if he'd hidden a body there."

"Unless he wanted us to find this body." This idea had occurred to Ela. "Though I can't think of a good reason for that and he seemed both surprised and displeased that our investigation was rerouted by its discovery."

"How are we able to confirm the identity of the dead woman?"

"Everyone in the household agreed that it was a kitchen girl called Cathy Cross. She wore a green dress, her hair was this same color, and her height and build were fitting."

"No one missed her when she disappeared?" asked Stephen Hale, the cordwainer.

"No. She'd turned strange and distant in the months preceding her disappearance, and somehow this convinced everyone that she'd just left of her own accord." Ela swallowed. "And a thought occurs to me about what might have happened."

All the jurors turned to look at her.

"One of the dead sons, Alain, got a different servant girl pregnant. She's still there in the house, with her child who's now a boy of seven. I wonder if perhaps he interfered with Cathy Cross as well, and ultimately killed her."

The jurors shifted as they gazed at the poor girl's bones. "That would explain her change of disposition, I suppose," said Hale. "Did she say something to her mistress?"

"Apparently not. Most girls don't. They fear they'll face

blame for seducing the young man. And sometimes they feel that they are to blame in some way. It's an unfortunately common problem, I'm afraid."

"I suppose that if she got pregnant he'd hardly be expected to marry her, then being from different stations in life," said Howard.

"It's true. She'd likely have been expected to quietly disappear."

"Or, in this case, perhaps she was made to quietly disappear," said Peter Hardwick, the butcher.

"There's no way to tell if she was pregnant or not, at this point," observed Haughton.

"I suppose it hardly matters," said Hugh Clifford, the wine seller. "If all the suspects are either dead or missing, our investigation seems doomed to run aground."

"I'd like to know everything there is to know about her death," said Ela. "Since we have an ongoing investigation on the d'Albiac estate. If Sir Montaigu d'Albiac can be found alive, we may want to charge him with murder."

"Does that seem likely?" asked Clifford.

"I wish I knew. His son Charibert suspects that he's buried in their demesne, but his mother claims that he lives because she can feel it in her bones, or some such. There's a significant possibility that we'll never find hide nor hair of him, dead or alive, but the search continues, both at home and abroad."

CHAPTER 6

That night after dinner in the hall, Ela once again noticed Elsie laughing and smiling at every one of Richard's utterances, no matter how banal. The events of the last few days produced grim ruminations over how a servant girl can find herself in a compromising situation with a young master. While she didn't notice Richard encouraging the girl, she decided to have a quiet word with him.

She drew Richard from his chess game and into the hallway that led from the great hall toward the private chambers.

"What is it, Mother? Stephen may well move a piece on the board and cheat in my absence."

"Do you really think your younger brother capable of cheating?"

"Absolutely. You know what a ruthless competitor he is. He'll do almost anything to win." Ela decided she would have to speak to Stephen as well. She certainly didn't want a young Charibert growing under her roof. "But I took the precaution of memorizing the entire board and I shan't let him get away with it."

Ela cleared her throat. "I notice that Elsie seems to be rather enchanted with you lately."

"Elsie?" He looked like he had no idea who she was talking about. "Your maid?"

"Yes, of course. What other Elsie would I mean?" This feigned ignorance set her nerves on edge. Her suspicions deepened. "Have you been doing anything to encourage the girl?"

"Encourage her to do what?"

"Richard, stop being so obtuse. Have you been…making eyes at her or complimenting her or otherwise giving her reason to believe you favor her?"

He stared at her, as if incredulous. "Elsie? She's as dull as a mounting block and a similar shape as well."

"Don't say such things."

"Well, she is. How could you possibly think I'm interested in her? I doubt any man will be. She's plain as can be with that pale, pudding face. She's not even a competent maid."

"She absolutely is!" Ela's heart now burned with indignation for Elsie, who'd endured far too much cruelty in her life. "She's an excellent and solicitous maid."

"Well, I daresay she's better than Hilda…" He laughed, remembering the incorrigible beauty who'd turned the household upside down. "But I hardly think she'd extinguish your memories of Sibel."

"Sibel was the lady's maid of a lifetime. I'm only too grateful that she has been able to marry and have a child despite me enjoying the benefit of her companionship for so much of her life. I doubt any maid shall be Sibel's equal, but Elsie has matured and grown in leaps and bounds and I'm most satisfied with her."

"Well, you can rest assured that I have no interest in flirting with her, or doing any other inappropriate things with her." Richard's face showed anger rather than amusement at the accusations. "I'm hurt that you'd think so little of me, Mother. You know that I am to be a bishop and I don't say that just to spit words into the air."

"I truly believe you have a calling, my dear. I apologize for accusing you of anything. It's just that the d'Albiac household has turned up two such cases and set my nerves all a-jangle over it. Can I count on you to tell me if you see anything similar in our household?" She'd always worried about her oldest son, William, whose dashing good looks and striking height were paired with considerable fecklessness. She'd been greatly relieved when she managed to get Will safely married off without incident.

"You don't have to worry about Stephen. He still thinks girls are a nuisance to be avoided at all costs. If I have even the tiniest illicit thought about Elsie—perish the thought—" He paused and shook his head as if the idea was unthinkable. "I'd spend a week on my knees in prayer."

"Thank you, Richard. I'm sorry to have troubled you. I just wasn't sure if Bill Talbot deigned to talk to you about such things."

"He doesn't." Richard laughed as if the idea was unthinkable.

"That's what I thought." Ela certainly didn't want to raise it with Bill, either. The subject would be embarrassing for both of them. She'd tried several times to convince him to remarry in the decades since his wife died, but he wouldn't hear a word of it. "But I'm grateful to hear your convictions on the subject. Please, go back to your game."

"ELSIE, fetch us a jug of small ale," barked Richard coldly, without looking up from the last few moves of the game.

Elsie hopped into action, almost running to the kitchen.

"Richard, you should always say please," scolded Ela.

Richard just looked at her.

Elsie returned with the jug, and started to pour out the ale into Richard's cup.

"Not so fast! It'll splash."

"I'll be careful, sir." Elsie looked up at him, flustered, then her hand shook, splashing ale onto the tablecloth.

"Now look what you've done!" The wet stain spread across the linen toward the chess board, and Richard swept up the wooden board with both hands.

"I'm so sorry, sir. I'll go fetch a cloth."

Richard stood, moved a step to the left, then set the board down too hard so the pieces fell over. "Ugh, now the game is ruined! What a clumsy girl."

Elsie, close to tears, now ran for the kitchen.

"Richard, don't be so sharp with her."

"Should I sigh and simper and whisper sweet nothings to her?" asked Richard quietly. Ela drew in a breath. Richard was clearly furious about her accusations—and her lack of faith in him—and not about to let her forget them. She didn't want to make a scene in the hall, especially in front of poor Elsie, who now hurried back in with a cloth and a bowl of water to mop up the mess.

"I can remember where the pieces lay," said Stephen. "Especially since I was about to win."

"The hell you were," retorted Richard, clearly irritated with his brother as well. "Let's go sit over there where it's quiet and there aren't any nuisances hanging around." He picked up the board and headed for a table far away from the fire.

Ela watched as Elsie, red-faced and mortified, scrubbed at the stain on the tablecloth, then gathered up the soiled linen and took it away. Elsie sneaked a hurried glance at Richard, who now sat on the far side of the hall. Ela's heart ached for her. Perhaps the girls in the d'Albiac household had been foolish enough to fall for the charms of their young masters, even knowing in their heart of hearts that nothing but suffering could ever come of such longing.

≈

SEVERAL DAYS LATER, Ela met with her co-sheriff John Dacus to discuss how to proceed with the d'Albiac problem. They sat in the armory. She'd recently had two chairs placed near the fire, as she found it to be an ideal place for private discussions with her staff. The castle's impressive collection of swords, halberds, pikes and lances shone from the wall, where they hung in decorative patterns.

"Well," said Dacus, "We've dug up the entire garden around the house and a good deal of the land near the sheepfold and the byres, including the midden." Dacus was a handsome man in middle age, with silver-streaked dark hair and warm brown eyes. "We found a good deal of rubbish, including some that likely dates back to former centuries, but there's no sign of Montaigu d'Albiac."

"I am relieved to hear that because I never thought Mathilde capable of murder. No other bodies?"

"No, thank goodness. There is a family cemetery near the ruins of an old chapel and they're still sorting through that slowly and in a respectful manner, but so far no suspicious or recent bones have been found."

"The dead girl's family couldn't be located, so I suppose we must arrange a Christian burial here in Salisbury for her."

"Perhaps it's merciful that her parents and siblings will never know what happened to her," said Dacus gently.

"I suppose there's some sense to that, but it galls me that there's no one left to seek justice for her."

"Except the office of the Sheriff of Wiltshire," he said cheerfully.

"Indeed, except that of our three suspects in her murder, two are known to be dead and one is missing without a trace. This makes a trial difficult to arrange. I suppose I should be grateful that Charibert hasn't accused his mother of the killing," said Ela with a sigh.

"He probably would if he thought he could get away with it, but no one would believe a diminutive and soft-spoken lady capable of wielding a sword hard and fast enough to cut clean through bone."

Ela had wondered if she herself would be able to do such a thing. She was as tall as many of the men in the king's garrison, and possibly fitter. However, her swordsmanship potential was something to speculate upon with Bill Talbot over a cup of wine, not to propose to her long-suffering co-sheriff. "I wouldn't put it past Charibert himself if he were older at the time of her death, but he would have been twelve or younger, so—although I find him arrogant and disrespectful to an extraordinary degree—I can hardly accuse him of murdering the girl."

"Most likely Montaigu d'Albiac committed the murder, I suppose," said Dacus. "But there's been no news of him."

"I wish someone had at least seen him. Then Mathilde could come out from under the cloud of suspicion that her son has conjured over her. Still, I suppose it will dissipate over time. I see no need to arrest her for the murder now that we've combed over the property and all but proved that he isn't buried there. Charibert is still pushing to have his father declared dead, however, since his main goal is to claim the estate."

"At what point can his father be legally assumed to be no longer alive?"

"Seven years. That date is almost upon us, so I suppose I must consider his claim. According to the law, his mother is entitled to a one-third share of her husband's estate. It will be hard for her to claim her share though, as there's only the one manor and one manor house. I suppose she could sell her share of the land and buy elsewhere, but most of the land has been sold already. She won't be able to sell enough to buy another suitable property, even a small and remote one, and still have money enough left for an income."

"So in an ideal situation, Mathilde d'Albiac and her daughters would remain as occupants in the house."

"Absolutely, but Charibert has made it clear that he does not intend to let that happen."

Dacus looked appalled. "It's a son's duty to care for his mother, and his sisters."

"Charibert d'Albiac has already proven that he has little regard for social norms, let alone niceties. I suspect he'd throw his mother and sisters out into the street if he could get away with it. And there's another girl with a child—Mathilde's granddaughter—the progeny of one of her dead sons, that lives with them."

"I can see why you're so keen to keep them installed there as long as possible. Still, the law as it's written favors inheritance by the oldest surviving male heir."

"And it is my duty as sheriff to uphold the law."

THE FOLLOWING WEEK, Ela, Stephen and their entourage accompanied Richard to his second tournament. Still smarting from the soft-tissue arm injury he'd acquired at the hand of Charibert d'Albiac, Richard tried to beg off.

Bill, worried that the bad experience would grow in his mind and stunt his future prospects on the tournament ground, was insistent that he get back in the saddle. "You're unlikely to meet another character so underhanded as to use a sharp blade. And your abrasions have healed nicely."

Ela would have preferred that her sons didn't participate in tournaments at all. Still, it was her duty to raise them to be knights and she deferred to Bill's wisdom and expertise on the matter. "We'll all enjoy a grand day out and a fine banquet afterward," she insisted. "You fought so well last time. Your father would be proud."

Now, at the tournament ground, Richard looked resplendent. His polished chainmail glittered in the sun, and the helmet under his arm shone like silver. He stood tall and puffed out his chest, which again bore the Longespée coat of arms—six rampant golden lions in a field of azure. "The pretty girls are looking at you," observed Stephen.

Elsie, there to attend to Ela's needs, immediately turned her head in the direction that Stephen was looking. Ela sighed inwardly. The poor girl was clearly besotted with her son, who still barely noticed she was alive. When he did notice her, he now took the opportunity to scold her for some imagined infraction. Still, his lack of interest was far preferable to a mutual obsession that could lead them astray.

Girls were indeed staring at Richard in his combat finery. Ela recognized the daughters of some of her friends and acquaintances, blushing beauties of sixteen or so, the hair under their fillets braided tightly overnight and released into shiny waves that cascaded about their shoulders, in contrast to the veiled matrons like Ela herself.

The girls had their own gallery, from where they oohed and aahed over the young combatants below. One of these lovelies would be chosen to present the winners with their prizes. In contests fought by the greatest knights of the realm, the prizes might include a gold ring or a fine emerald, or some other expensive trinket. Today's event promised more modest trophies—a silver cup, or a pair of spurs, perhaps. Ela hadn't inquired as to today's prizes, as she didn't want Richard to get excited about winning one. He was there to test his skills and prove his prowess, not bring home booty.

"Charibert d'Albiac is here," said Richard suddenly, shock in his voice.

Ela glanced up. "I suppose there's nothing to stop him attending, as long as he doesn't compete."

"The nerve of the lad," growled Bill. He looked like he'd like to stride over there and give young Charibert a piece of his mind.

"Never mind him. Don't let him be a distraction," said Ela to Richard. "Best of luck to you, though I doubt you'll need it."

Richard, Stephen and Bill headed off toward the lists, with Richard's horse and all his attendants. Ela and Elsie set out for the matron's gallery.

"Would you like a cider, my lady?" asked Elsie, as they passed a stall selling cups of the brew.

"Why yes, I think I would," she said. "And buy one for yourself as well. It's thirsty work standing around outside on a hot day." She gave Elsie some coins and the girl went to stand in a short queue at the stall.

"My lady Ela."

A man's voice made her swing around. *I know that voice.* The familiar low tones sent a cold chill down her spine. Ela turned to find herself face-to-face with Hubert de Burgh. At nearly sixty, he had more gray in his dark hair than the last time she'd seen him, but he still stood tall and straight and his arrogant visage showed little of the softening that could accompany age.

"Sir Hubert." She offered her hand but not a smile. The occasion demanded politesse, not simpering.

He kissed her hand. "It's been some time, much to my dismay. I'm here today at the king's request, to keep an eye out for future warriors to serve our country."

"An ideal place to do so."

"Your son Richard is competing, I see."

"Yes." Her mind started galloping. How did he even remember her son's name? Then she reminded herself that her son was the king's cousin, and it was de Burgh's business to keep himself apprised of King Henry's affairs. "He acquitted himself well at his first tournament two weeks ago."

"I hear there was some upset over his opponent cheating."

"Yes, he used a sharp sword, but Sir William Talbot realized the trickery and brought the miscreant to account."

"And I hear the boy has caused further mischief, in bringing a suit against his own mother."

Ela's hackles rose. Why was de Burgh so interested in Charibert d'Albiac? "Indeed. He wishes to have his father declared dead, but we have no evidence that his father is no longer alive."

"In cases of a long absence, an heir can claim his estate on the presumption of death. As the oldest surviving male heir this young man is entitled to the free and full use of his father's estate. It's the tradition of our land, isn't it?"

Ela tried to keep her face placid. "The Magna Carta has modified tradition to increase the share of widows."

De Burgh's face creased into a slow smile. "I think we all know that the new laws were born out of circumstances necessitating a sort of bargain between the king and his barons. Many of the measures are unlikely to hold up in court."

She stiffened. "I beg to differ. The Magna Carta is the law

of the land." She began to have an inkling of what Hubert de Burgh might be up to. "As a widow, it protects my right to remain unmarried if I so choose." He'd already tried to marry her wealth into his own family by sending his foolish nephew Raymond to court her.

"Did you hear that dear Raymond was killed in France last year?" asked de Burgh.

"Yes. I heard he drowned in the Loire."

"Yes, his horse stumbled on the bank and he fell into the river." De Burgh studied her, perhaps for signs of emotion. He showed none himself. "Do you still rankle with indignation that he proposed to you?"

"Of course. My dear husband was still alive at the time. I found the proposal extraordinary and offensive to a high degree."

"It was my idea, I'm afraid. Naturally I believed your husband to be dead. Are you still angry with me?" His smile didn't reach his eyes.

"It's not in the interests of the crown, the nation or the people of Wiltshire for me to hold a grudge against you or anyone else." She couldn't bring herself to answer his question directly. She hated him with unholy force. No amount of prayer seemed to lift her enmity. She still firmly believed that he'd poisoned her husband, and now he had the nerve to smile down on her here on this sunny tournament ground.

"Your cider, my lady." Elsie returned with the cider in a cheap earthenware cup imprinted with chevrons around the rim. She held her own in her other hand. Then she looked at de Burgh. "Would you like this cup of cider, my lord?"

"Why thank you, how kind." De Burgh took the cup. Elsie looked back at Ela as if hoping she'd done the right thing. Ela wished she could throw her cider at him.

"That's very thoughtful of you Elsie," she said. She

reached into her purse for another penny. "Go fetch yourself another cup." Elsie hurried away.

De Burgh sipped his cider, then stared at Ela intently. "The d'Albiac matter has made me wonder why you have not yet passed the torch—so to speak—to your son William."

CHAPTER 7

"*W*illiam is still young and needs time to mature." Ela spoke quickly, trying to tamp down her rage at de Burgh's insolence. She had answered this question before, though few dared to ask it. "He's barely in his majority. He will be Earl of Salisbury in good time."

"I beg to differ. He's a full-grown man and a knight of the realm now. I wonder if perhaps he rankles at being barred from assuming the mantle left by his dear, departed father."

Ela's hackles rose further. "William is busy with his manors and his new family. I assure you that the situation bears little similarity to the d'Albiac matter. For one thing, I have my choice of manors to retire to, should I choose to leave Salisbury Castle, whereas poor Mathilde d'Albiac has nowhere else to go and a son who wishes to put her and his sisters out of their home."

"Do you not think your time would be better spent nurturing your own children? I find it strange that you wish to trouble yourself with the problems of all Wiltshire."

"Do you find it strange that you wish to trouble yourself with the problems of the entire kingdom?" She lifted a brow.

64

"You've sat at the right hand of one king or another for most of your life. Are you not keen to retire to a peaceful country manor?" She glared at him. They both knew the answer. He'd never willingly leave the corridors of power. Ela continued, "God gave me a head for problem-solving and I'm grateful for his guidance in all that I do. I fully intend to take the veil once my children are grown. Work is already underway on the convent at Lacock where I shall spend my last years, God willing."

"Your devotion to the people of Wiltshire is most inspiring, my lady." A joyless smile tilted the corners of his mouth. "I wish your son Richard all the best in his endeavors on the tournament ground today."

"Your good wishes are much appreciated, Sir Hubert."

He took his leave just as Elsie returned with a new cup of cider. Ela found herself gasping. This encounter felt like a joust or a sword fight. She'd managed to save her skin but wasn't at all sure she'd emerged victorious. In fact, his parting wishes for Richard only served to remind her that with his power and the ear of the king, Hubert de Burgh held the fate of all her sons in his grasping, bloodstained hands.

"Are you ill, my lady?" Elsie peered at her, brow furrowed.

"I'm fine, thank you, dear Elsie." She managed a shaky smile. "The cider is sweet and rich, isn't it?"

"It's delicious, my lady. I've never had better. Thank you so much for buying me some. Did I do the right thing by offering a cup to your guest?"

"You did. Generosity and compassion are two of the finest qualities one can possess and I'm glad to see them shine in you."

Elsie beamed and sipped her cider.

~

ELA HELD her breath as Richard and his horse lined up at the lists. His attendants hovered nearby and even his horse seemed more anxious than usual, prancing and tugging against the bit. At last, the trumpet sounded and Richard shot forward, lance raised.

In moments the tilt was over and both men still sat astride their horses. She couldn't even tell if either one of them had hit the other. What a foolish pastime this was! Why should the flower of England's youth attack each other for sport and risk injury or death? When she'd aired her thoughts to Bill he'd mouthed soothing platitudes about a man's duty.

"He's your son, isn't he?" said a woman in a blue dress that almost matched her eyes. Ela recognized her as Elspet Wimberley, who she met at some of her mother's entertainments. "He just acquitted himself very well. The girls were all atwitter about him before he even rode. If they could vote for the winner he'd be wearing the victor's garland already."

"Goodness, I had no idea." Ela's surprise was genuine. Given Richard's studious nature and demonstrated lack of interest in the opposite sex—confirmed by his fresh disdain for Elsie—she hadn't much thought of their opinions of him. "And mercifully neither does he. He wants to be a bishop and would rather not be here at all. But I'm told he has a duty to defend the castle should the need arise."

The woman laughed. "My son is itching to fight. I keep telling him to wait one more year."

"That's what Richard's younger brother Stephen is like. I suppose I shall enjoy watching him more, knowing that he wants to compete."

"It's not easy being the mother of a young man." The woman smiled. "But at least young men have some agency over their destiny. I worry more about my daughters, whose

66

happiness depends so entirely on us choosing the right husband for them."

The woman then spotted a friend of hers and rushed away, exclaiming something, and leaving Ela rather stunned in her wake. She felt confident that her oldest children were well settled in life, Ida and Isabella married to kind and capable husbands from excellent families, and William married into one of the finest families in the land, with estates galore to manage and a lovely wife to cherish. She wasn't sure why she suddenly felt uneasy. The encounter with de Burgh had rattled her. He had the power to alter the trajectory of her children's lives, and he knew it.

AFTER THE SERIES of fights with the various weapons was over and Richard had battled his way to a narrow victory, Ela hurried down from the stands to congratulate him. His face red and sweaty, Richard looked exhausted. All smiles, Bill Talbot congratulated him on a brave and determined performance.

Ela now noticed that pretty girls, freshly descended from the stands, hovered around whispering and giggling.

"You should be very proud of yourself," she said.

"He won that battle inch by inch!" said Bill. "His opponent was a worthy competitor. Come accept your prize."

An attendant mopped Richard's sweaty brow and helped him out of his decorative surcoat, his chain mail, and then out of the padded garment beneath.

"Praise be to God," said Richard.

"For your victory?" asked Stephen, who stood nearby looking jealous.

"For relief from the oppressive heat of these garments. I don't know how soldiers fight in them for hours."

"It's worse in the midday heat of the Holy Land," said Bill wryly. "The sun there is like a banked fire." He helped Richard into a fine, lightweight cloak of dark blue wool. Elsie handed him a cup of cider, which he took and drank without thanking her. Ela determined to speak to him about that later. It was one thing not to encourage the girl, but quite another to be rude and thoughtless.

Richard was called up to the main stands to accept his prize. On his way there, two lovely girls—one of whom Ela recognized as the daughter of a friend of hers—crowned him with a garland of flowers. Another girl, her long red hair glowing through her gossamer-fine veil, held a square velvet cushion with a ring in the middle. She took the ring in the middle of it—a ruby, thought Ela—and pushed it onto his longest finger.

"Congratulations, my lord," she said with a bow, her pink cheeks flushing darker.

Richard, serious as the bishop he hoped to be, bowed politely to her and the judge and the assembled company, before taking his leave as fast as possible.

"When I win I shall kiss all the girls," said Stephen quietly, once Richard returned. "I've seen a knight do it after he won and took his prize. They seemed to like it."

"You'll do no such thing," said Ela. "You are the king's cousin, not some French adventurer with no care for his reputation. These girls are too polite to act appalled, but they surely would be."

"I'm not so sure. Would you be appalled, Elsie, if a brave knight kissed you?"

"Stephen!" scolded Ela. Now he was just trying to stir up trouble. And it worked. Elsie burst into immediate tears and ran off. "Now look what you've done. Poor Elsie has been through enough in her short life without you taunting her."

"I'm sorry." He had the decency to look chastened. "Should I go after her?"

"No, you've done enough harm," said Bill Talbot. "I shall find her and attempt to mollify her feelings, perhaps with a treat from the pie stall."

"You stay here, Bill," said Ela, "with the conquering hero and his annoying younger brother. I shall find Elsie."

∾

ELA HURRIED off in the direction Elsie had run, heading behind a striped tent selling baked goods. Once behind the tent, out of the fray of the tournament crowd, she couldn't see Elsie. She hurried forward, past the backs of other vendor tents. A large oak tree stood off to one side; perhaps Elsie had headed there to hide?

She crossed the grass, enjoying the brief respite from the chatter and excitement of today's events. The oak had a trunk as wide as a cart, and must have stood sentinel in this grassy field for hundreds of years, perhaps watching real battles between knights of another era. Its spreading branches cast deep shade that promised welcome respite from the warmth of the day.

As she approached the tree, Ela was about to call Elsie's name, when she heard a girlish giggle.

"Elsie?"

Silence. Did she imagine the giggle? There was no sign of Elsie. Ela walked up to the tree, then walked around it. She almost jumped out of her skin when she came upon two people pressed up against the far side of the trunk.

Worse yet, one of them was Charibert d'Albiac. His red-gold hair identified him easily. "What are you doing here?" she asked, in her sharpest sheriff's tone. "You've been banned from tournaments for the year."

69

She took a look at his companion, a young girl hiding her face behind her veil.

"I'm banned from fighting, not attending."

"You'd be wise to stay away from them. Who is this young lady?" Ela had deliberately asked Mathilde d'Albiac if her son was betrothed to anyone. That would give him more motivation to want mastery over his own estate. She swore that he had never been engaged or promised to a girl.

Charibert just stared at her. Ela looked at the girl. "Are you too ashamed to show your face?" she asked her.

The girl dropped her veil and curtseyed, "God go with you, my lady. I wish no offense."

"Gertrude Wimberley?"

The girl looked startled at being recognized. "Yes, my lady."

"I spoke to your dear mother this afternoon while we watched from the stands. I feel confident that she'd be shocked to see you here with young master d'Albiac." Ela resolved to speak to her mother at once and warn her of the danger her daughter had found herself in. Charibert d'Albiac had already proved himself both unscrupulous and determined.

The girl flushed. "I'm sorry, my lady."

"Be away with you!"

The girl executed a fumbled move somewhere between a bow and a curtsey, then lifted the hem of her blue gown and hurried away, veil flapping.

"What are you thinking of?" asked Ela. "This girl is the daughter of a dear friend of mine. Are you trying to compromise her reputation?"

"I didn't drag her under this oak tree." He gazed down at her, insolent. "She came here of her own free will."

"You may not have dragged her but I have no doubt that you coaxed and cajoled her."

"That's no crime."

"Not if you were both peasants, perhaps, but as a noble and—you hope—a future knight, you are quite wrong. It's your duty as a knight to protect and defend the virtue of every maiden in the kingdom. Unless you've made arrangements with her father and her mother and agreed to the terms of your marriage contract, any overtures you make to her could be construed as a gesture of intent to marry, and your refusal or inability to follow through would be seen as breach of promise."

He sneered. "Are you trying to say she could sue me?"

"She could. And so could her parents. Taking a girl behind a tree in private is a very serious breach of etiquette."

"All the more reason to be secretive about it." He shifted his weight and Ela became aware of how he loomed over her. A frisson of unease made her wish she'd brought a guard with her. One had moved to follow her, as usual, but she'd told him to stay put. She'd hoped to have a private moment of womanly reassurance with Elsie, not find herself face to face with a man who was likely to prove one of the worst rascals in the kingdom.

"I know this girl's parents and I intend to warn them about you." She hoped to see a change in his sneering expression.

"They won't say a word. They won't want to tarnish their daughter's reputation by spreading this news abroad."

He was right, of course. "This suggests to me that you've taken advantage of girls before. You seem familiar with the modes and methods of enjoying their affections without the burden of commitment." No doubt it ran in the family. Young Agnes and her baby Charley were living proof. And likely the woman they found buried in the grounds had suffered a similar fate.

"And what if I have? You can hardly prosecute me for a crime I haven't been accused of."

Ela reflected that Charibert was not as stupid as she'd first assumed. His meaty good looks and brash behavior hid a cunning mind that made him dangerous to both men and women. Why did such creatures need to exist, who made life more difficult for everyone? Perhaps it was part of God's plan for humankind to learn to navigate a life around such obstacles.

"I advise you to watch your step, Charibert d'Albiac. I am sheriff of all Wiltshire and I have the king's ear as he is my children's cousin."

He did blink at that last part. "I beg your pardon for any offense I've caused, my lady. Perhaps the early loss of my father has made me coarser than I should be."

"That's no excuse. My own children lost their father at a tender age and I know that your mother obtained instruction for you. Instead of making excuses or finding justification for your bad behavior, why don't you change it?"

"I shall endeavor to do just that, my lady." He offered a small bow. She had no doubt that his intent was mocking, but his demeanor didn't make it overt.

Ela dismissed him, irritated at his rudeness and that he'd delayed her search for Elsie. For all she knew, Elsie had found her way back to Bill and the boys by now.

And she must warn Elspet Wimberley to keep a close eye on her wayward daughter.

ELA FINALLY CAUGHT up with Elsie behind the stands where the audience sat.

"I'm so embarrassed, my lady. Richard and Stephen seem to have the idea that I am making eyes at them and I have no idea how that happened because I swear I would never do such a thing."

"I know you wouldn't, dear Elsie. Your behavior is always impeccable." She sighed and wondered whether to admit it. "I'm afraid I might have put the idea in their heads when I decided to warn them against any flirtations. The difficulties that lusty young men have caused in the d'Albiac family were foremost in my mind."

Elsie stared at her. "You told them I liked them?"

"No, of course not." Ela couldn't remember her exact wording and hoped it wasn't so specific. "I simply warned them not to encourage any of the servants—or any other girl for that matter—with flirtation. They're of the age where it suddenly occurs to young men that they are surrounded by beauty and grace that they've never noticed before."

"I have no beauty or grace," blurted Elsie. "So there's no danger there."

Her round face streaked with tears, poor Elsie was certainly no beauty, and Ela saw no point in applying false compliments. "You have a good heart and tender hands and a sense of loyalty that any man would be lucky to enjoy in his wife. Though I certainly hope that you don't get married for many years. I would miss you terribly as I've become quite dependent on you."

Elsie seemed to consider this. "Sibel was awfully lucky to have a baby after waiting so long to marry, wasn't she?"

"She was indeed. God has plans for all of us. Sometimes they require a great deal of patience. I must beg you to have patience with my sons, who are still children and can display callous foolishness they should be ashamed of."

Elsie considered this also. "Boys do seem slower to mature than girls."

"Indeed they do. They are good, kind boys at heart and I suspect my suggestion that they might be interested in girls has mortified them to the point where they lashed out at you quite without cause. I apologize to you for any offense they've caused."

"I'm embarrassed that I reacted so strongly. I suppose it is because I admire them both so, that it hurt so much."

"You should not be ashamed to have tender feelings. You've been through so much in your short life, many wouldn't have any feelings left at all."

"Sometimes I wish I didn't."

Elsie's tears had dried. Ela pulled a handkerchief from her sleeve and wiped her cheeks. "Have courage. Sometimes life calls for tremendous bravery, as you know. But I must warn you the same as I told the boys—beware of temptations that could distort the course of your life. Some young men are cruel enough to prey on vulnerable and tender young girls for their amusement."

"I know. I shan't let it happen to me, I promise."

"I don't doubt it. I know that you're a sensible girl."

"Unlike Hilda!" Elsie cheered up, remembering her very lovely and equally foolish predecessor. "I shall attend to my duties and keep my mind on my prayers."

"I thank God for bringing you into my life, Elsie. Shall we go rejoin the others?"

"Yes. And I'm sorry for any trouble I caused you."

"Don't apologize. On my way to find you, I saw something that I must urgently address."

ELA FOUND Gertrude's mother and managed to tug her aside to whisper an urgent caution about keeping an eye on her daughter. She whispered the name of Charibert d'Albiac and that he was an incorrigible rascal. Elspet Wimberley looked suitably shocked and appalled and Ela congratulated herself on warning her before some disaster could befall young Gertrude.

She rejoined her entourage—Richard's entourage, really —with considerable relief and they headed for the feast set up in a great striped tent nearby.

Mercifully Charibert seemed to have made himself scarce. The disgust she felt for this young man surprised her. On top of trying to unhouse his mother and sisters, he had shamelessly endangered the reputation of a young girl in broad daylight. And had added insult to injury in the most shocking way when she arrived to reprimand him.

Her deepest well of hatred was reserved for Hubert de Burgh. She remained sure that he'd poisoned her husband and knew full well that he could choose to seek further retribution on her family if he so chose. Living in the same England as de Burgh felt like sharing a cellar with a venomous adder who might strike at any moment.

Still, there was nothing she could do but try to placate the adder—or was there?

CHAPTER 8

Two days later, Ela and Bill Talbot sat in the hall, a plate of breakfast pastries still before them, discussing the merits of entering Richard in one more tournament. Ela was firmly opposed, feeling that Richard had already demonstrated his mettle and should be assured of his knighthood. She saw no reason to risk injury on the tournament ground.

"A letter from the king, my lady." Albert the old porter shuffled toward her, bearing a sealed scroll.

"I wonder if it's an invitation?" she mused. Although King Henry spent considerable time in the area, she didn't often find herself summoned to his side. For one thing, she was a woman, so not likely to be invited to join a hunting party the way her husband would have been. For another, she was twice his age and more of a respected elder than a friend. She sometimes wished that they were closer, since her sons were not that distant from him in age and she would like to cultivate friendship between them, if only to enhance their prospects for being given posts replete with honor and income at some time in the not-too-distant future. "Please read it to me," she requested.

"I'm told it's for your eyes only," said Albert in a guarded tone.

"Really? Who said that?"

"The messenger who delivered it."

"Goodness." Ela took the scroll, still tightly rolled and sealed. "I dare say it's not so secret that I must go read it in my solar. I shall take a look." She cracked the seal and unfurled the scroll. The writing was not King Henry's. He must have dictated to a scribe. The signature, however, was his, and she wondered what missive demanded such a formal and private delivery.

"My dear Ela, I hope this letter finds you well. I hear that my dear cousin Richard has distinguished himself on the tournament ground. You must be very proud of him and I feel sure that this portends a great career for him in our kingdom."

Ela paused and smiled at Bill, grateful once again that he was here to prepare her sons for manhood in their father's painful absence.

"Your younger sons' ascension to manhood brings to mind the question of their oldest brother, William, and when he will assume the role of Earl of Salisbury."

Ela stopped reading. Her heart pounded and her breathing quickened. How dare he? She'd paid him two hundred pounds to regain shrievalty of her own castle—her birthright—and then a further five hundred to retain the titles of Countess of Salisbury and High Sheriff of Wiltshire.

Did he mean to bleed more money out of her?

"Is something amiss?" asked Bill, concern in his voice.

"No," lied Ela. She read on.

"William is now well into his majority, a knight of the realm, and could relieve you of the onerous duties you so bravely took on after your husband's untimely demise. After five years as castellan

of Salisbury I feel sure that you must be ready for a quieter life that will give you more time to enjoy the blessings of your children and grandchildren, or perhaps even the quieter joys of the cloister. My ear is yours. Your affectionate cousin, Henry."

His name was signed with his characteristic flourish.

"The nerve!" she said aloud. Then she looked around to see who had overheard. Albert the porter stood nearby, perhaps awaiting a reply to deliver. The eyes in his wrinkled face had seen almost anything that could happen among men, and even he looked shocked by this outburst. She thrust it at Bill. "Read this."

Bill read the letter, his frown growing deeper.

"Let us speak in private." Ela led Bill out of the hall and into the armory, where he closed the door behind them. "This is Hubert de Burgh's doing."

"I saw him at the tournament," said Bill.

"I spoke with him at the tournament and he said much the same thing aloud. I thought little of it, knowing that I have a very expensive written contract with our king protecting my right to hold the titles and estates of the Earldom of Salisbury for my entire life if I so wish. I dismissed de Burgh like the tiresome buzzing fly that he is to me. And he has turned around and poured poison into the king's ear."

"I suppose you can hardly dismiss the king, despite his youth."

"Indeed not. And the matter of the odious Charibert d'Albiac takes on a greater weight since it sets precedent that I shall perhaps be expected to follow. Charibert d'Albiac is definitely a buzzing nuisance that I'd like to swat away entirely."

"Given his proclivities for disgraceful behavior, I suspect he'll soon go the way of his father and brothers."

"You're right, perhaps, but he can still unsettle or even destroy some innocent lives along his path to ruin.

A knock on the door made them both turn. "I'm in a private meeting," called Ela.

"It's urgent, my lady."

Ela sighed. Bill walked to the door and opened it. Jake, the young porter, stood there. "It's Charibert d'Albiac, my lady."

"Ugh," rasped Ela. "I don't consider any matter concerning that boy to be urgent. He's not nearly as important as he'd like to think. He can wait his turn like all the other petitioners."

The porter looked startled. "But he's not here, my lady. He's dead."

A JURY WAS SUMMONED at once and Ela and Bill set out for Neversend, the d'Albiac estate, with coroner Giles Haughton. The messenger, a young lad from the estate, had arrived breathless and flustered and bearing very little actual information. He didn't seem to know where Charibert lay, how he'd been killed, or where anyone else in the family was at that moment. Ela found herself wondering if he'd been told to plead ignorance so that someone—or someone's—could get their story straight.

When Ela arrived she learned that Charibert had been found dead in his own bed.

"Who discovered him?" she asked. The household was eerily silent, with Mathilde and her daughters hovering at a distance like ghosts. Any of them had motive, since their son and brother had been outspoken about his intent to eject them from the family home if he could.

Haughton bent over the body. He lifted each eyelid in turn and peered at the linings of Charibert's nasal passages.

Then he popped his mouth open with a practiced hand and gazed into it. "He's been poisoned." There were traces of vomitus on the pillow next to the dead man's cheek.

"Can you tell what with?"

"My educated guess would be a high dose of *aconitum napellus*."

"Wolfsbane?" She'd always been told to use great caution preparing herbal remedies from the purple flowers. Mostly she avoided using it in favor of something less dangerous.

"Yes. Also known as Monkshood. It's a very efficacious poison and readily available in the woods hereabouts."

Ela's heart sank. Poisoning was a woman's crime, in general, and held a candle up to the faces of his mother and sisters.

"Would it be administered in food or drink?" Ela looked around for a plate or cup.

"Most likely. It doesn't take much to kill even a big healthy ox like this young man. Vomiting or loose stools are a common side effect." Haughton pulled back the bed cover. "These sheets show evidence of both."

He started to examine his body. "There's a graze on his knuckles. It's fresh and hasn't scabbed over."

"What does that suggest to you?" asked Ela.

"That his hand ran up against something abrasive. Not stone or wood, from the look of it, but something sharper, like chainmail."

"He didn't fight in the tournament. I was there and would have intervened if he'd tried. What other pretext would a man have for wearing chainmail in peacetime?"

"Practice, I suppose. Or an informal fight of some kind." Haughton lifted his nightshirt. Ela fought the annoying but persistent instinct to avert her eyes. Charibert's pale flesh was well-muscled and almost hairless. Haughton eased the nightshirt over his head. "He has an abrasion on his forearm, too." He pointed to a pink area of skin, freshly inflamed. "That'll form a bruise."

"Do you think he was in a recent fight with someone?"

"I'd suspect so."

This cheered Ela. "I welcome the opportunity to seek suspects outside his household," she said softly. "I wonder if Gertrude Wimberley's mother had the opportunity to speak to her husband about Charibert's behavior."

"Who is Gertrude Wimberley?"

Ela explained the impromptu tryst she'd seen at the tournament and how she'd warned the girl's mother. "I suppose I hoped Gertrude's father would warn the boy off. He needed some sense shaken into him."

"Some would even say he'd be justified in killing a man who stole his daughter's innocence," observed Haughton, now turning Charibert over to look at his well-muscled back.

"If the boy had raped her or seduced her into giving him her virginity, perhaps," said Ela, even more quietly. "But I believe I managed to interrupt them before he'd even kissed her. Thus, unless this was not the first encounter between Charibert and Gertrude, he didn't have the opportunity to provide grounds for his own murder."

"I must speak to Gertrude Wimberley's father. If Charibert committed an outrage against his daughter, and he visited the house on the night of Charibert's death, he's an obvious suspect."

"His name is Sir Godfrey. The family hails from Oxfordshire. I've met them at court on numerous occasions, but I don't know them well."

"It was generous of you to warn them that their daughter was in danger."

"I'd have no respect for myself if I hadn't. You don't have to be a sheriff to wish to prevent a crime against a girl's innocence and reputation. I hope I haven't provided cause for a worse crime yet to be committed."

Charibert's body showed no further signs of either injury or foul play. His flesh bore numerous well-healed scars, but they were marks that any young knight-in-training might have gained during his boyhood.

Ela summoned Mathilde and her daughters into their parlor and sat them down near their unlit hearth. White-faced and tearful, they dabbed at their eyes with hand-kerchiefs.

"When did you last see Charibert alive?" she asked of Mathilde.

"I went to bed before him last night. He liked to stay up late into the night talking with whoever was awake."

"And who was awake?" Now Ela looked at the daughters.

"We both went to bed soon after our mother," said Joan. "Leaving him alone in the hall. He was muttering that when it was his hall there would always be good company there to entertain him."

"Two days have passed since I last saw him at the tourna-ment at Brackley. Do you know who he met with during those two days and three nights?"

"Two men came to see him. A Sir Godfrey Wimberley and his son. I offered to have them dine with us, but they wanted to speak with Charibert privately—which they did—and then they left."

Ela looked at Haughton, then back at Mathilde. "Was this yesterday?"

"It was."

"Do you know if they gave him anything to eat or drink?"

Mathilde looked confused. "It was I that offered them food and drink. But, as I said, they didn't accept."

Again Ela looked at Haughton. "Could they have given him poison through a scratch or abrasion?"

"It's certainly possible if the substance is potent enough."

"Did they have an altercation of any kind, my lady?" asked Haughton of Mathilde d'Albiac.

"Not that I saw, though Charibert spoke with them then swept them out of the house before I even had a chance to introduce my daughters. When he returned he said that they were not friends of his and that we had no business knowing them."

As well he might, thought Ela. She looked at Haughton again. "So the Wimberleys had both motive and opportunity."

"Who are they and what have they to do with my son?" asked Mathilde, her voice rising.

Ela hesitated, not wanting to rain blows on a grieving mother. Even if one of her sons had turned out to be a scoundrel, she doubted she'd ever forget the tender moments they'd shared in his infancy and youth. "I'm afraid that I found Charibert attempting to seduce Sir Godfrey's daughter behind a tree at the tournament at Brackley."

Mathilde gasped and clutched a handkerchief to her mouth.

"I believe I interrupted them before he could compromise anything more than her reputation. Naturally, I warned her mother to keep a sharp eye on the girl. A tournament is one of the few places where a girl might find herself in the company of an unknown man and I felt that young Gertrude was in danger."

Mathilde twisted her hands together. "Perhaps they were just innocently speaking?"

"Behind a tree? I prefer to proceed with caution where a young girl's purity is at stake. I'm sure you would feel the same if your daughter found herself in the clutches of a strange young man."

"Indeed I would," said Mathilde apologetically. "But I

can't believe my son is dead. Surely they wouldn't kill him for such a thing?"

Ela had to admit that it didn't seem entirely likely; still, it was a straw that she would certainly be clutching at if she were Mathilde. "Your son was poisoned, my lady. If not by one of the Wimberleys, then likely by someone in your own household."

"Impossible! Who would kill my son?"

You. If she had killed her husband to take control of the estate, then she might have killed her son for the same reason. Ela couldn't entirely rule this out as a possibility. "I'm afraid every member of the household is a potential suspect. Were you all here last night?"

"Yes. Where else would we be?" *Indeed. And where would you go if Charibert were to throw you out?* Mathilde had motivation. Still, Ela found it hard to imagine a mother killing the son she bore and raised. "Sir Godfrey Wimberley must have poisoned him," blurted Mathilde.

"This is indeed a possibility. Though I do find it unlikely that Sir Godfrey, who has a blameless reputation, would lay himself open to a charge of murder."

"I hesitate to say this, but perhaps my son took more liberties with his daughter than we are currently aware of."

"I shall certainly investigate that possibility. In the meantime, my men will search your house for poison. The coroner has a strong suspicion about what type of poison was used."

WHILE THE GUARDS searched the house for traces of wolfsbane—particularly the leaves and stalks, since the flowers didn't bloom until late summer—Ela interviewed Mathilde, both daughters and several other members of the household, including Agnes, their cook and their stable man.

Mathilde looked like a ghost, her face drained of color and her movements wooden. "Are you going to arrest me?" she asked when Ela sat down with her in a small, private chamber.

"Should I?" Ela wanted to give Mathilde the benefit of the doubt, but also enough rope to hang herself should that be more appropriate.

"I didn't kill my son. I loved Charibert even when he tried my patience. He was my last surviving son—I already lost my two older ones. I still can't believe he's gone." Her voice was strangely devoid of passion or emotion. Ela suspected that the shock of his death hadn't fully settled on her yet. "I keep thinking this is a horrible dream and soon I'll wake up."

Ela watched her face closely. "Now you won't have to leave your home."

Mathilde stared at her as if she might be demented. "Do you think that is any consolation to me? Perhaps the very stones and sticks of this house are cursed. How can I lose all three of my sons in just a few short years? With my husband gone, the name of d'Albiac will die as well."

This begged an interesting question. "Will it? Or are there other male cousins who might have a claim on the estate?"

Mathilde looked perplexed. Apparently, this possibility hadn't occurred to her. "None that I know of." It was an unusual name and Ela certainly hadn't encountered any others. "Could they come forward and throw us out, too?"

Would you kill them as well?

Ela had observed that once someone had killed, they were far more likely to kill again. Murder seemed to open the door to a whole new world of problem-solving. If Mathilde had poisoned and buried her husband, perhaps she succumbed to the temptation to secure her future here at Neversend by following the same path.

Except that this time the body didn't disappear. "Who found Charibert in his bed?"

"I did. He didn't come down to break his fast—which wasn't all that unusual. Sometimes he stayed up late and didn't want to rise in the morning. But that's a poor habit for a young man to form, so it was my practice to wake him if he still hadn't come down by the time the bells rang for Tierce."

"Did you realize right away that he was dead?" Ela felt awful asking her. She couldn't imagine the horror of discovering that one of her children had died in their sleep.

"I called his name, and he didn't stir. Usually, he'd roll over and pull the coverlet over his head or something similar. When he didn't move at all by the third time I called him, I approached him and touched him—very gingerly as I didn't want to startle him into striking out or something."

This intrigued Ela. "Has he ever hit you?"

"No." Mathilde looked shocked. "Never."

Ela wasn't entirely sure she believed her.

CHAPTER 9

*E*la interviewed the other members of the household, one by one. Helene, the older daughter, had dark hair tucked into a bun beneath her barbette and fillet. Worry haunted her serious gray eyes. "What will happen now?"

"The coroner will remove your brother's body to the mortuary to do any further examinations he requires."

"Will our mother be arrested?"

Ela anticipated that the question of Mathilde's guilt would arise again. "I can't answer that question for certain. First, we must interview Sir Godfrey Wimberley."

"She didn't kill Charibert. I'm sure of it." Helene's pleading gaze tugged at her heart.

"How old are you?"

"Sixteen," said Helene, looking confused by the question.

"Are you betrothed?"

Helene's gaze dropped. "No."

"May I ask why not?" She wanted to be polite, but a sixteen-year-old noblewoman without a marriage arrangement of some sort was unusual. It also made Helene's future far more dependent on the family fortunes than she might be if she was about to leave for another man's house. This alone might give her the motivation to dispatch her brother before he could throw her out of the family home.

"My mother has not received positive responses to her attempts to find suitors for me. As you can see, I'm no great beauty."

Ela frowned. "You are indeed a beauty." The girl had a bold profile and smooth skin and kind eyes, all atop a willowy figure. Her looks certainly wouldn't deter a suitor. The family's much-diminished fortunes and the precarious state of the inheritance might, though. "I suppose your father's disappearance presents the problem of not being able to carve a suitable dowry out of the inheritance."

"I'm not sure there's much left to carve it from. I'm content to just stay with my mother."

"You must have been concerned that Charibert would cast you out on the street."

"I never thought he would do that. He's selfish...he was selfish and could be foolish, but Charibert wasn't cruel."

Ela begged to differ. He'd deliberately wounded her son in a sporting contest where such malice was explicitly forbidden. He was clearly a young man who'd stop at nothing to achieve his aims.

Joan, the youngest, was shorter than her sister, with a fuller figure and gray-blue eyes. Red-rimmed, her eyes expressed worry as well as sorrow. "Could he have died of natural causes?" she asked Ela, her voice cracking.

"The coroner will examine his body for signs of a natural death, but it seems unlikely given Charibert's age and robust good health. The coroner thinks he was poisoned. Naturally, since you and your mother and sister were in the house with him, I must interview you. Did you see Sir Godfrey Wimberley when he came to call?"

Joan brightened. "I did, and he seemed furiously angry.

He wouldn't take food or drink and wanted to meet with Charibert at once."

"Did you see them together?"

"Not really. Charibert took him into the back parlor and closed the door."

"Could you hear what they were saying?"

"No. Their voices were lowered."

No doubt Charibert didn't want his mother and sisters to overhear the details of his disgraceful flirtation. "Did Sir Godfrey have any bags on his person? A scrip, perhaps?"

"I can't be sure. He wore a cloak."

He could have concealed a tiny phial in the sleeve of his tunic if he came with the intent to poison Charibert. Still, Ela thought poisoning would be an overreaction to Charibert's advances on his daughter. Especially since the whole family saw him arrive. Surely if he intended to murder Charibert, Sir Godfrey would have proceeded with more caution and secrecy.

"Do you have any ideas about who might have killed your brother?"

Joan shook her head, and her eyes filled with tears, suggesting that—difficult as Charibert could be—she still harbored sisterly feelings for him.

Ela also interviewed Agnes, who seemed as stunned as the sisters. Her son Charley hovered around, hiding in the corners, staring at them. "Do you think it's possible that your mistress killed her own son?" Ela asked, in the privacy of the closed room.

Agnes shook her head. "She doesn't have an unkind bone in her body."

"Do you think Charibert would have thrown you all out of the house if he inherited?"

Agnes seemed to consider this. "I can't believe that he would."

And Ela had another question. "Do you think his father is still alive?"

"My mistress certainly always behaves as if he is. She's never for one moment suggested or hinted that he's not coming back. His spare armor and weapons are kept polished."

"Did Charibert use them?"

"No, he had his own made for him. His father was taller and heavier, and Charibert found his sword old-fashioned and unwieldy."

Ela reflected that it must have been expensive to outfit Charibert for his education as a knight, and his mother spending money for new armor and weapons, not to mention trained horses, suggested her commitment to his success in the endeavor. Another reason why it was hard to imagine her killing him. A family's prospects rose and fell with the achievements of the oldest surviving male. If Charibert made a reputation and fortune for himself, it would have lifted the fortunes of the entire family and improved marriage prospects for his sisters. Mathilde had every reason to support and encourage him and hope for the best.

Unless she'd given up all hope.

As Ela and Haughton rode away, Ela found herself hoping that Sir Godfrey Wimberley, who had been a friend of her late husband's, could provide some convincing answers for why Charibert d'Albiac had died in his own bed only a few hours after his visit. She sent messengers to the Wimberley estate to bring Sir Godfrey and his attendants to Salisbury to meet with her in front of a jury the following morning.

They rode through the countryside on a bright, late spring day. The sky was blue as a sapphire and the hedgerows bursting with wildflowers. The glory of the day—such perfection—reminded her that humans had secured their own expulsion from paradise. Even amid such beauty and bounty people still wrought a harvest of evil.

"Should we arrest Sir Godfrey on suspicion of murder?" asked Haughton.

"He's a knight and has never—to my knowledge—been involved in any untoward behavior. He was a friend of the late King John and a regular at court. Right now we only have the word of the d'Albiac household that he even paid a call on Charibert. I can't justify arresting Sir Godfrey on hearsay by a woman accused first of murdering her husband and then of murdering her son."

"I see your point. Will you be bringing Mathilde d'Albiac before a jury?"

"Yes, I summoned her to attend as well. She has not yet appeared before a jury to face Charibert's charges that she killed her husband. Do you think there's even a slight possibility that she killed them both?"

"I've certainly encountered cases where a woman has killed her husband."

"As have I." One such disaster had occurred in Elsie's family.

"But I can't think of a single case where a mother has killed her son."

THE JURY CONVENED SHORTLY after the bells for Tierce. Sir Godfrey Wimberley arrived with a veritable procession of guards and horses and three of his sons, all of them young men not far in age from Charibert. Although he wasn't a particularly tall man, Sir Godfrey exuded an air of calm dignity that gave him an imposing presence.

He swept into the center of the hall, silver hair cropped close, and wearing a green cloak over a dark red tunic trimmed with gold thread. His skin bore the red veins of someone who enjoys the outdoors despite a brisk wind and Ela suspected that he spent a good deal of time hunting.

Three tables were arranged into the customary U-shape for the jurors to sit at, and Ela's guards ushered Sir Godfrey to the empty chair that sat between them.

"I prefer to stand," he said with quiet authority.

Surprised, Ela wasn't sure quite how to respond. Sir Godfrey wasn't an accused criminal in chains so there was no need to secure him to the chair. Still, she saw the tip of his sword pushing at the back of his cloak and resolved that an armed, trained knight, standing poised for fight or flight, should probably be disarmed before cross-examination.

"Sir Godfrey, please hand your sword to my guards during your testimony."

For a moment, she thought he might challenge her. But he unbuckled the sheath from his belt and handed the sword, hilt first, to the nearest guard.

"We are gathered here today to investigate the death of Charibert d'Albiac, known to this court because of his efforts to wrest the family estates from the hands of his mother, in the absence of his father." Ela paused and watched the surprise on their faces. "Sir Godfrey Wimberley was one of the last people to see Charibert alive. Sir Godfrey, could you please explain why you came to be at the relatively remote and obscure place that is the d'Albiac home at Neversend?"

Sir Godfrey met her gaze. "Thank you, my lady. While I in no way wish to implicate you or anyone else in the untimely death of this young man, I think you know that my visit was paid as a consequence of your comments to my wife."

He spoke with easy charm, as if they might be discussing the fine weather for hunting or the merits of a particular horse.

Ela clasped her hands on the table. The next part was awkward as it involved the tender reputation of his young daughter. "Members of the jury, please note that I had quiet words with Sir Godfrey's wife, Elspet, because I saw young Charibert d'Albiac forcing his attentions on their daughter behind a tree at the tournament at Brackley."

A wave of whispers and murmurs arose, not from the jury but from others gathered in the hall.

"Let me assure you that the liberties taken were of the flirtatious kind, and she was not—that I could see—in physical danger, but, as a mother of daughters, I took pains to intervene at once and immediately warned the girl's mother that she was in danger of being seduced by a rogue."

Sir Godfrey's head dipped slightly before he met her gaze. "I thank you kindly for your attention to my daughter's safety. I'm sure it was no small inconvenience to yourself to take action, and at a busy tournament where I hear that your son Richard discharged himself with great honor." He drew in a breath. "My wife did not find occasion to tell me about the incident until we arrived home later that evening. When she did, naturally I wanted to address the matter with this youth. From her description of what occurred, I felt there was reason for concern."

"I agree," said Ela. "Without going into detail about what I saw, I—as a parent—would want to assure that my vulnerable, unmarried daughter did not breathe the same air as Charibert d'Albiac again."

"Again, I thank you."

"Don't be so quick to thank me, Sir Godfrey. My warning and its aftermath appear to have laid a charge of murder at your feet."

She looked at his feet, which—encased in neat brown leather shoes—did not flinch or shuffle.

"I did indeed visit young Charibert and had stern words

with him in his home. I told him in no uncertain terms that if I found him near my daughter he would feel the sharp blade of my sword rather than the sharp edge of my tongue."

"How did he respond?"

"With arrogance," said Sir Godfrey evenly. "But he did ultimately apologize and agree to stay away from her. I left satisfied."

"What was your reaction when you heard he had been poisoned?"

"Naturally I was shocked. A young life lost so suddenly and unexpectedly is a tragedy, especially for his family."

"Did you realize that you might be accused of killing him?"

He hesitated, then jutted his chin toward Ela. "If I set out to kill someone I assure you I would not resort to such a cowardly method as poison."

"Sir Giles Haughton is the coroner. I suspect he has questions for you."

Ela gestured to Haughton, who leaned forward in his chair and tented his hands on the table. "If you were to kill someone, as you suggest that you might, what method would you choose?" He looked genuinely curious.

Now Sir Godfrey did shift his weight, and an expression of confusion crossed his stern features. "I imagine that I would challenge my enemy to a sword fight."

Haughton pursed his lips. "It would be risky to start a swordfight with a man as young, well-muscled, athletic and aggressive as Charibert d'Albiac. If I wanted him dead I doubt I would choose that method myself. Poisoning typically involves far less risk to the life and limb of the would-be murderer." He looked encouragingly at Sir Godfrey. "I'm sure you'll agree."

Ela could see that Sir Godfrey Wimberley's self-assurance had rubbed Haughton the wrong way.

"I am a man of honor above all else. I felt the urgent need to warn the d'Albiac boy to stay away from her, but I felt no such burning impulse to end his life. My daughter has been promised in marriage since she was a child, and her wedding will take place next year. He has no business paying her any attention."

Ela reflected that the girl had hardly been fighting Charibert off. Unfortunately, she seemed to be enjoying his affections. Ela rather thought that Sir Godfrey would be wise to get her safely married off to her betrothed with great haste. She, however, did not intend to further involve herself in the matter.

"Charibert d'Albiac was poisoned with wolfsbane," said Haughton. "A common plant, easily prepared by anyone with a rudimentary knowledge of herbs. It was certainly a very high dose to kill him so quickly. A lower dose might have sickened him, possibly for several days, but the dose he was given likely stopped his heart within an hour of him ingesting it."

"How do you suspect it was administered?" asked Ela.

"Almost certainly it would have been oral. While such a poison can be rubbed into a wound and enter the bloodstream that way, he had no such large wound on his body."

"So he ate or drank the poison?" confirmed Ela.

"Indeed he did."

"Sir Godfrey, did you take food or drink with Charibert during your visit to his house?"

"Not a drop or a crumb. I refused the host's hospitality and certainly did not bring gifts of food or drink with me."

"Did Charibert eat or drink anything in your presence, while you were there?"

"He did not."

Ela summoned Mathilde to rise. "Mathilde d'Albiac, is this true?"

Mathilde nodded. She looked somber and older than her years in a dark gray gown, with her white veil arranged to reveal little of her face. "We offered him spiced cake and wine and he refused them both."

"Did he have access to food or drink in your household at any time during his visit?"

Mathilde thought for a moment. "They went to speak in a closed parlor that has no entrance to the kitchen or the pantries. I don't believe he did have access to any food or drink." She looked sad while she said it, perhaps realizing that in absolving Sir Godfrey of guilt, she was pointing the accusatory finger back in her own direction.

"Does the jury have questions for Sir Godfrey?" asked Ela.

Will Dyer, the cooper, known by all to be direct in his speech, raised his hand. "Sir Godfrey, have you ever killed a man?"

Sir Godfrey looked alarmed for a moment before regaining his composure. "Naturally I have. I fought in service of the crown in France and in the Holy Land. I took more than one life in my role as a knight in the king's army."

"Have you ever killed a man—or a woman—on English soil?" Dyer regarded him sternly, black hair framing his square face.

"I have not," snapped Sir Godfrey, obviously feeling he'd been pushed too far.

"You did suggest that if Charibert were to approach your daughter again, he'd feel the blade of your sword. Is that not a threat against his life?"

"It was intended as a warning, not a statement of intent."

An ill-advised turn of phrase, thought Ela. Still, she didn't think it likely that Sir Godfrey had killed Charibert. Of course, she didn't think it likely that Mathilde had either.

~

ONCE THE JURORS had finished with Sir Godfrey, he was asked to sit to one side and Mathilde d'Albiac was called to sit in between the tables of jurors. She moved slowly and stiffly, as if arthritic, adding to the impression that she was an elderly woman rather than one only a few years older than Ela.

"Are you unwell, Mistress d'Albiac?" asked Ela, with some concern.

"I am grieving the death of my third and last son, my lady," she said, looking directly at Ela. "I have suffered losses in this life that no mother should have to endure and I find their burden heavy to bear."

Chastened, Ela muttered her condolences. "I'm sure you are anxious to find your son's killer."

"Indeed I am."

"Do you suspect Sir Godfrey of killing your son, in a fury over the liberties Charibert took with his daughter?" Ela reflected that she'd only revealed a rather watered-down version of what she'd actually seen. She'd mentioned Charibert touching young Gertrude's hand, when she suspected he'd had his body pressed up against hers.

Mathilde looked down at the table before Ela. "As a mother of girls, I can certainly imagine the rage I would feel if a young man compromised my daughters in any way. However, I struggled to see such a thing as a pretext for murder. If he felt that his daughter's reputation had been gravely endangered, he might have forced my son to marry her."

Ela glanced at Sir Godfrey's face. At this moment he looked as if he'd rather kill his daughter than see her married to such a scoundrel as Charibert d'Albiac. This intrigued Ela. "Sir Godfrey, did you consider insisting that Charibert d'Albiac take your daughter's hand in marriage?"

"Most certainly not. As I previously mentioned, my

daughter Gertrude is already betrothed to a fine young man from a good family. From what you described, she was in some danger, but anything ruinous to her prospects was prevented by your quick action, for which I am eternally grateful."

Ela looked hard at Mathilde. "Mistress d'Albiac, do you have any suspicions about who might have poisoned your son?"

Mathilde's eyelids fluttered and Ela wondered if she was going to cry. Then she looked directly at Ela. "If I knew I would tell you at once. Charibert was my hope for the future. His death leaves me drifting like a rudderless ship."

"Were there any other visitors to your home over the last few days?"

"None other than ordinary tradesmen. A traveling wheelwright came to the door and asked if we had any cartwheels that needed mending. I hired him to replace the rims on the wheels of a old handcart that's used sometimes. We gave him bread and cheese to eat, but he didn't come into the house at any time and, as far as I know, he had no contact with Charibert."

"Did Charibert go abroad at any time during these last few days?"

"Yes, he did. Charibert is... Charibert was not one to sit around the house tapping his toes. He went out on his horse every day, either hunting or riding into a town or village. I used to send him on my errands to buy any sundries that I needed." Her eyes filled with tears.

"Where did he go on the day before he was found dead?"

Mathilde wiped her eyes with a handkerchief. "I wish I knew. I had no errands to send him on and he didn't return with a pheasant or a rabbit or even a wren."

"I'll send men out to the neighboring towns to ask if he

was seen there," said Ela. "In the meantime, do the jurors have any questions for Mathilde d'Albiac?"

Thomas Pryce, the old thatcher, stirred. "Mistress d'Albiac, who inherits the estate you live on now that your husband and son are dead?"

"My husband is not dead."

CHAPTER 10

*M*athilde looked at him steadily. "He is abroad and will return in due time."

"My lady," said Stephen Hale, the cordwainer. "The jury has been informed that your son Charibert had filed documents with the clerk to begin the process of having your husband declared legally dead due to his long absence. Were you aware of this?"

"I was."

"How did you feel about it?"

"Naturally I was opposed to his efforts. Every day I pray for my husband's safe return and I keep alive a flame of hope and faith that he'll be restored to us."

"Would you have continued to live on the estate with your daughters if your son Charibert had inherited?"

Mathilde blinked. "No doubt we would. Where else would we go?"

She's lying. Ela's senses activated. Her sympathy for Mathilde warred with her conviction that the truth should always be revealed in all its dangerous fullness. "Mistress d'Albiac," she said quietly. "Your son had expressed a wish to take control of your manor for himself and to remove you and your daughters."

"I'm sure he would never have done such a cruel thing."

Ela felt satisfied that the prospect of Mathilde's expulsion from the estate had been raised, and she didn't wish to probe further. Let the jurors do their work.

"Begging your pardon, my lady," said Stephen Hale, peering down his long nose at her. "But the jury is fully aware that your son Charibert was not entirely a man of honor. This morning alone we have learned that he took liberties with a young girl who is betrothed to someone else. We have also learned from Sir William Talbot that he attempted to cheat in a tournament by using a sharpened axe in a contest against Countess Ela of Salisbury's son Richard." He paused and a murmur arose in the hall as his words sank in. "And, against your wishes, he's attempting to have your husband declared dead. So it seems that your son is perhaps entirely capable of putting out his mother and sisters to serve his selfish aims."

Mathilde let out a small gasp and pressed her handkerchief to her face. "He's very young."

Mathilde's grief, and her apparent refusal to accept that her son was now irretrievably dead, played on Ela's heartstrings and further convinced her that Mathilde had not killed Charibert.

"Is there anyone else who might benefit from Charibert's death?" she asked, hoping to deflect attention from Mathilde's newfound riches and freedom. "Or had he made any other enemies that you're aware of?"

Again, Mathilde dried her eyes. "Charibert didn't have enemies, as such, but he did rub people the wrong way."

"He certainly rubbed me the wrong way when he injured Countess Ela's son," said Bill Talbot, speaking up for the first time. "But that doesn't mean I wished him dead. Murder by poison requires considerable animosity and forethought. If Charibert was killed in a tavern fight—something that might well have been his fate based on his temperament and proclivities—then such petty squabbles could be the cause. But the person who killed him either acquired or made a toxic potion, put the poison into his food or drink, and waited patiently for it to take effect. Can you think of anyone —male or female—who might have cause to harbor such a strong and stinging resentment against your son?"

Mathilde, now sobbing into her handkerchief, shook her head but didn't manage to utter words.

Ela wondered why Bill had brought this up. He couldn't really think he might be under suspicion. He had a flawless alibi in his constant presence at her side. "You are not under suspicion, Sir William."

"I'm grateful for that," he said cheerfully. "I have hardly had the time or acquaintance to nurse a grudge long enough to plan and execute the poisoning. His killer must have had access to his food and drink. Where did he eat when he was away from home?"

Mathilde looked at him with red-rimmed eyes. "He'd been expelled from the local tavern for punching a customer, so he didn't eat there. He assured me that the customer had insulted a woman but the innkeeper wouldn't believe him. He did sometimes buy a meat pie from the pie shop in Lower Whitcombe, but I can't think of any reason they'd have to poison him."

Ela made a mental note to see if the owner of the pie shop had a young daughter, or might otherwise have suffered at the hands of Charibert. If they could determine that Charibert visited the shop that day, they'd have a new suspect in his death.

Old Thomas Pryce leaned forward. "Who had access to the food served to Charibert the previous night?"

"Well, we all ate together," said Mathilde. "In the hall. Charibert wanted to sit at the head of the table but, as usual, I reminded him that we must keep the seat in readiness for his father, who might return at any time."

"How did he react to that?"

"He grumbled, as he is wont to do. It has become almost a game with him to try to step into his father's shoes."

"What makes you so sure his father is still alive?" asked Stephen Hale.

Mathilde looked at him for a moment. Then she looked past him to where a faded tapestry hung on the stone walls of the great hall. Then she looked back at him. "I can feel it."

"Feel it where?" asked Hale, obviously unconvinced.

"In my bones, in my heart, in my feet and the tips of my fingers." Mathilde spoke as if what she said was completely normal. Ela understood, though. She'd had similar conviction that her own dear husband was alive and trying his hardest, every day, to return to her and his family—and time had proven her right.

"If I may be so bold, my lady," said Will Dyer. "Your husband, Sir Montaigu d'Albiac, gained a reputation as a gambler and a spendthrift."

Mathilde's eyes widened as if she couldn't believe his audacity.

"The court rolls, which show him being sued for repayment of debts and also for non-payment by several local tradesmen, tell the tale. Are you really so anxious for his return? It appears that you have managed his manor well in his absence."

Mathilde looked flustered. "I've certainly done my best to keep the home fires burning. As his wife, I naturally consider it my duty to protect his estate."

"Even from his son?"

"Charibert would have inherited when the time was right."

"Did you consider Charibert ready to manage the estate himself?"

Mathilde hesitated. No doubt she realized that her answer would say as much about her as it would about her son. "Charibert was growing into his responsibilities but still lacked maturity. The incident at the tournament reveals that he was too impatient to win. He broke a rule and found himself eliminated. He displayed the foolish haste of youth. He was a good enough fighter to win without a sharpened axe."

Ela felt her back stiffen. Now Mathilde was implying that Charibert had put up a better fight than her son Richard and that her son had won by default rather than through greater skill. Her blood started to heat, until she realized that her reaction was driven by maternal loyalty rather than common sense. Truth be told, the boys were evenly matched on the tournament ground.

"Your son was indeed a skilled fighter, but a commitment to a fair and just fight is more a sign of a true knight than handiness with a blade—dull or sharp."

"I agree, my lady," said Mathilde. "I was deeply disappointed by my son's behavior. But it illustrates why I didn't wish him to take over the estate. The same youthful haste might have made waste of it."

"If your husband is dead and there are no other heirs, the estate would now be yours. There are no other heirs. Do you still maintain that your husband is alive?"

"I do." Mathilde spoke without hesitation. "I don't know if he will ever return, but I remain sure that he lives and breathes somewhere in this world."

Ela frowned. Did Mathilde truly believe her husband was

alive? Or did she have her own reasons for insisting that he lived?

"If it does turn out that your husband is dead, you cannot be forced to remarry," said Ela. Many women weren't aware of the protections for widows now enshrined in the law. "So you need not fear that."

"I don't fear it," said Mathilde. "My husband would kill any man who tried such a thing."

Ela started. Her husband had felt the same murderous rage toward Hubert de Burgh, after he'd tried to arrange Ela's betrothal to his nephew. William had engaged the king on his side, scolding de Burgh for the outrage. De Burgh had been compelled to make expensive gifts including a valuable warhorse to atone for the grave sin of trying to marry Ela's fortune into his family—while her husband remained alive.

While de Burgh had made lip service of an apology, William had attended a dinner at his house, then returned home only to sicken and die within days. She remained sure that de Burgh had poisoned him out of spite. She'd shared her suspicions only with Bill Talbot and Giles Haughton. She didn't want her sons to know, for they'd surely feel obliged to seek revenge.

Giles Haughton had pledged to sow the seeds of suspicion abroad. From time to time Ela got wind that others suspected de Burgh had a hand in her husband's death, but no one had made a move to charge de Burgh with any crime. He remained the most powerful man in the land after the king so no one, including Ela, dared to so much as raise their voice against him.

Ela struggled to draw her attention back to the proceedings in her hall. "Has your husband written to you during his time away?"

"My husband was not a man of letters, my lady."

"Do you mean that he couldn't write?" Such a thing was

not unheard of, even among nobles. After all, they had others to do it for them if the skill had evaded them in childhood.

"I don't know if he could or couldn't but I never knew him to do it."

"But he never hired someone to pen a letter or otherwise send you word of his whereabouts?"

"No, my lady." Mathilde did look rather embarrassed by this.

"I find this quite extraordinary," said Ela. "After all, you and your children are his responsibility, financial and otherwise." When her husband was injured, and presumed by many to be dead, he hadn't written to her for a full year. But as soon as he was able to communicate he had the monks send a letter to Ela assuring her that he was still alive and would be home as soon as he was able. She was grateful she'd been able to throw it in the face of Hubert de Burgh and his nephew at the time of the outrageous marriage proposal. "Why do you think he wouldn't write?"

"He's always been a man to fully engage in what's happening in front of his face and to forget about the things that are going on behind him."

He's dead, thought Ela. He has to be. "How will you tell him that his only surviving son is now dead?"

Mathilde's face went blank for a moment, then tears filled her eyes. "I will have to wait until he returns."

"What if he never returns?"

"Then I shall die still waiting for him." Mathilde spoke with quiet assurance.

Will Dyer stood up. "It seems an urgent matter to find your husband, my lady. Since you are still accused of killing him, and now of killing your son, only his urgent appearance can secure your liberty and your life."

Mathilde uttered a sob and swayed. For a moment Ela thought she might fall from her chair in a dead faint.

Ela was about to protest that there was not even circumstantial evidence that Mathilde had murdered either of them, but a murmur of assent rose from the jury and spread through the hall.

"She should be tried at the assizes," said Thomas Pryce, without rising. "Two murders under one roof is cause for suspicion."

"Mistress d'Albiac maintains that her husband lives," said Ela, in an effort to stop this barrel picking up speed as it rolled down a hill. "We have no proof that he's dead."

"There was a body found, though, at her house. A young girl. Maybe she killed her, too."

Mathilde let out a wail. Her distress had little effect on the jury and the gathering crowd of soldiers and staff and townspeople in the hall. "Lock her up!" they cried. "Lock her up!"

Ela sighed. She hated to lock people up unless there was incontrovertible evidence against them. For one thing, they might sicken and die in the damp and cold conditions of the underground dungeon. For another, they might fall victim to a miscarriage of justice at the assizes and hang for a crime they didn't commit. Still…

"Mistress d'Albiac," said Ela loudly, to be heard over the din. "It might help your case if you could point the finger of accusation at someone else. Do you suspect anyone else who might have had a hand in the murder of your husband or your son?"

Mathilde shook her head. Ela glanced at Sir Godfrey Wimberley to see how he was taking this. His well-formed features were composed and unreadable. Could he have killed Charibert to prevent him causing further trouble with his daughter? The girl had seemed quite willing to succumb to Charibert's advances. Another incident might have utterly ruined her marriage prospects and even filled her womb with the seed of the seemingly cursed house of d'Albiac. Any father would be skittish at that prospect.

"Are you satisfied that Sir Godfrey Wimberley played no role in Charibert's death?" asked Ela of the jury. "After all, he did travel all the way to Neversend for a face-to-face encounter with the boy."

"But there was no food or drink exchanged," said Stephen Hale. "What other means is there to get poison into a body?"

"Giles Haughton, perhaps you could answer this question?" said Ela.

Haughton leaned forward, frowning. "Ingestion is certainly the most typical means of poisoning. Topical application...to the skin...might well prove ineffective even if there was an open wound, which in this case there wasn't."

"We did notice that Charibert had some small abrasions on his hands, as if he was in a fight," mentioned Ela. "It's possible that he might have had an altercation with someone else."

"A young man, especially one who trains to fight in tournaments, is rarely without a scrape or graze or bruise of some sort," observed one member of the jury.

Ela had to admit that was true. Her sons came home with all manner of minor injuries just from hunting in the forest.

"I had no physical altercation with the boy. We did not touch one another and exchanged words only," said Sir Godfrey quickly.

"Did he seem well when you spoke to him?" asked Ela.

"Well enough, I suppose. I've never met him before, so I'm not familiar with his manner. He did not strike me as ill in any way."

"Did he seem normal to you, as well?" asked Ela of Mathilde.

"I don't remember him being any different than usual. As I think I mentioned, he was often the last in the household to make for his chamber. I left him downstairs in the hall when I went to bed." She looked at Ela. "Could he have already been poisoned?"

Ela looked at Haughton, who shook his head. "Unlikely. It's a fast-acting poison that quickens then stops the heart. The ill effects happen shortly after ingestion. Who else remained downstairs with him?"

Mathilde's forehead creased. Ela could almost see thoughts passing through her mind that she didn't want to utter.

"Who else was in the hall at the time?"

Mathilde's hands fluttered. "I suppose my daughter Helene, was still there, my oldest. She was mending a stocking. But I'm sure she didn't poison him!"

"Did she normally retire early?" asked Haughton.

Mathilde blinked. "Early enough, I suppose. She sometimes goes up early to pray in peace before her sister joins her in the bedroom."

"And when did your younger daughter, Joan, go upstairs?"

"She came up with me. She'd been helping me with some embroidery. We were making a new tabard for Charibert to wear at his next tournament. A tabard with the d'Albiac coat of arms—" She broke into a sob. "And now he'll never wear it, and the d'Albiac name will die with him."

Silence hung in the air for a moment. "Charibert was banned from all tournaments for the rest of the year after he cheated in the tournament at Wilton. Why would you sew a tabard that he couldn't wear until next year?"

Mathilde sniffled. "I know it seems foolish but such a thing soothed and calmed Charibert…gave him something to look forward to."

Ela's ears pricked up. "Why did he need calming?"

Mathilde looked a little nervous. "For the last few years he's talked of little else but competing in tournaments and making a name for himself, so for him to be banned altogether on his first outing…it was quite a blow."

"He was angry?" asked Ela. "How did he express it?"

"Oh, I don't know." Mathilde looked as if she wished she'd kept quiet about the tabard. "Grousing and fuming and stomping about the house. Nothing untoward. Typical behavior for a young man with his ambitions thwarted."

Ela would be mortified if one of her sons behaved like an angry toddler. "Did he take out his fury on you and your girls?" asked Ela. Poisoning was a woman's crime and Charibert lived in a house filled with women. It was entirely possible that one of the girls had tired of their irascible and egotistical brother enough to wish him out of the picture.

"He could be loud and irritable and demanding, but he didn't lay a hand on them, if that's what you mean."

"I shall have to interview your daughters in more detail," said Ela. She hoped this would buy Mathilde some time to exonerate herself in the eyes of the jury.

But it was not to be.

"Matilde d'Albiac should be locked up," said Thomas Pryce again, his watery eyes shining. "She's under suspicion of two murders and must be prevented from killing again."

Nods and murmurs of agreement rose from his fellow jurors.

Mathilde stared at them, too stunned to even cry.

Ela felt a great sigh rise within her. "What of Mathilde's young daughters?" she asked. "Are they to be left to run the manor?"

"How old are they?" asked Whittacre.

"I believe they are fourteen and sixteen," said Ela. "Old enough to care for themselves adequately, but without the experience to keep a household running." Without a firm hand, a manor could quickly fall to rack and ruin, with servants shirking their work or even pilfering from the larders and storage barns. "I shall take on the wardship myself until the assizes. My daughter Petronella will assist in running their household. She has been prepared for such responsibilities since she was small."

No one dared to object. Mathilde was taken away to the dungeon, weeping copiously. Ela drew in a deep breath and went to find Petronella.

CHAPTER 11

"*B*ut Mother, you know I have renounced the world of material cares and wish to devote myself entirely to prayer." Petronella's face looked like a thundercloud. "You can't make me go live in a house of strangers!"

"Soon you shall be safely behind the walls of the cloister at Lacock and shall spend the rest of your life there, as I know you long to do. In the meantime I have need of your wisdom and counsel to manage these girls and their manor."

"I know nothing of running a manor."

"You know everything about running a manor because I have taught you myself."

"You told me that you were preparing me to run an abbey. While I have no wish to take on the responsibilities of abbess, I did not object to learning the tasks required of one. Running a secular manor is entirely different."

"Not in the least. It's almost exactly the same except that no one is required to interrupt their work for regular intervals of worship. There's still a house to be maintained, a pantry and buttery to be stocked, a garden to be tended. There are crops to be sowed and harvested and stored or sold. There are animals to be fed and watered and sheared and milked. While you will not be doing this with your own hands—"

"I do not consider myself to be above humble labor."

"Your humility is to be admired. However, it is often the supervision—or lack of it—that determines the smooth running of a manor or an abbey. Servants need a firm hand to guide them."

"You speak as if they were children."

"I suspect you'll find that many of them are." Ela crossed her arms. "And these two young girls have had their mother taken away from them on the heels of their brother's sudden death—"

"They're saying one of them may have killed him," said Petronella quickly. "How can I feel safe among them?"

"You ask that as if the Lord would not be with you, guiding you at all times," said Ela quietly.

Petronella looked chastened. "May God's will be done."

"It is my will—and God's, I believe—that you help these young women through this difficult time. You can teach them what you know about how to run a manor—or an abbey—and prepare them for a future where they may well find themselves on their own."

"I can speak to them about the solace of the cloister."

"You can." Ela hoped that wouldn't be the sole topic of conversation. "But be understanding if they seek a more conventional life. They are both of marriageable age and could be encouraged to submit to a suitable marriage if I can arrange one for them. In the meantime, let us pray that neither of them is found guilty of murder and that their mother proves to be innocent as well."

"What if they are guilty?"

Ela felt her heart sink at the prospect. "If any of them is found guilty, she will surely hang."

~

THE NEXT MORNING, after Ela had deposited Petronella at Neversend and Petronella had become acquainted with the household, Ela left her there and headed for Lower Whitcombe, the village nearest Neversend. She wished to speak to the owner of the pie shop which Charibert frequented on the day of his death. She also hoped to get a sense of how the local people felt about young Charibert, and whether he had made any particular enemies in the locality.

The pie shop's worn and weather-beaten sign suggested a long time in business, and the delicious smells wafting from the doorway explained its longevity. Inside, a table bore several fragrant pies, some whole and some already in slices. Behind the table stood an older man with white at the temples of his gray hair and sharp brown eyes.

"Good morrow, Mistress. We have lamb and kidney fresh out of the oven and stewed beef in gravy—"

"You are in the presence of Countess Ela of Salisbury," said a guard officiously. Bill was busy at home preparing Richard for his next tournament, and John Dacus had agreed to greet petitioners in the hall in her absence. Thus she was forced to rely on less genial company.

"Begging your pardon, my lady," said the pie shop man, looking entirely unbowed. "I'm sure a countess is as welcome in my shop as any lady or gentleman. I use only the finest ingredients and bake fresh all day long."

"I'm glad to hear that, Master…."

"Dalrymple."

"But I'm afraid I'm not here to buy a pie." Shame, as it was nearly noon and she'd had a long morning. The aroma of his wares—rich beef broth with carrots and mushrooms from the smell of it—tempted her stomach. "Are you aware that Charibert d'Albiac has died?"

"Yes, my lady. The people have talked of little else these last few days."

"Did he ever come into your shop?" She wanted to test his veracity.

"He certainly did, my lady. Almost daily. He had a prodigious appetite, which is typical among men of his age, I suppose, and happily for him he had the means to humor it."

"What kind of pie did he buy on the day of his death?" she asked pleasantly, as if inquiring out of simple curiosity.

"On the day of his death?" The pie man did hesitate and look flustered. "Why, I'm not sure he came in here that day."

"His family tells me that he did. They say he returned home with a slice of pie that he ate in their hall shortly before retiring for the day."

Dalrymple peered at her. "Well, I dare say it was the beef and gravy as that was his favorite. But it wasn't my pie that killed him. He only bought two slices out of a whole pie and I ate one of those slices myself."

"Did you know Charibert well?"

The man swallowed. "I suppose I knew him as well as anyone who comes in here a lot. We didn't make much in the way of conversation, if that's what you mean."

"Did he pay for his pies?"

"Yes. Do I look like I'm running an alms-house?" She watched his neck redden slightly.

"Always? Or did he sometimes chalk up a debt and agree to pay you later?"

"Sometimes he paid later." The man's face darkened. "But I knew he was good for it. The family's noble, you see. Been there at Neversend since the time of the conqueror."

Ela's instincts told her to go further down this path. "Did he owe you any money at the time of his death?"

"A few pennies, perhaps. Nothing to keep a man awake at night." He spoke quickly, clearly agitated. "But I didn't kill him over a few slices of pie if that's what you're getting at."

"I did not mean to imply that you did." The pie seller bringing up the idea of himself as a murderer rather absolved him in Ela's mind. A guilty man would likely steer far clear of introducing that image into a conversation. Still…"Do you have any daughters?"

"Three my lady, all married and with children of their own."

That news extinguished another avenue of motive. "Do you know of anyone in the village who disliked Charibert?"

"You might better ask if I know anyone who didn't dislike him." His mouth tilted up at one corner.

"He was unpopular?"

"I'd say so."

"Could you tell me why?" she tilted her head slightly.

He tilted his head to match hers. Was he mocking her? "Did you ever happen to meet young Charibert d'Albiac?"

Now thoroughly affronted, Ela straightened her back. "I shall ask the questions."

"Begging your pardon, my lady."

She raised her hand, now mollified enough to realize that he wasn't entirely wrong to ask her. "And I have indeed had the dubious pleasure of meeting young Charibert. His blend of imperious arrogance and rude impatience cannot have endeared him to his neighbors."

"No indeed, my lady. He was rude even as a boy at his mother's skirts. Cut from the same cloth as his father and brothers."

"You knew them, too?"

"Yes, my lady. Born and raised here in this pie shop and

I'll die here too, if the Lord wills it. I remember when his father was a boy and would cry bloody murder if the servant didn't buy him two slices of pie instead of one." He chuckled wryly at the memory, then his smile faded. "Hard to believe they're all dead now."

"Can you think of anyone who would have hated Charibert enough to want to poison him?"

He shook his head. "Can't say I do. I'm privy to a lot of the gossip in this village, being behind the counter here all day every day. I haven't heard anyone cursing and muttering about him any more than anyone else. Not lately, anyway."

"If you do hear anything—even the slightest hint or rumor—please send news to me or attend me at my castle. His mother is imprisoned and under suspicion and may well hang for the crime if no further suspects are found."

Master Dalrymple's mouth fell open. "Mistress d'Albiac? Why she's the kindest and most long-suffering woman in England. She'd not murder a mouse if it ate pie off her plate."

"Her son was trying to seize his inheritance from her and throw her out of the house. Hence she has a motive for wishing him removed from the scene."

"I don't believe it for a moment." He still looked aghast. "Surely he must have enraged some mighty lord or even wronged a woman."

No doubt. Ela could think of instances in each case that she'd witnessed with her own eyes. "The fact remains that we need facts and witnesses to prove a case."

"Do you have facts and witnesses against Mistress d'Albiac?"

Ela reflected that if Bill was here he'd have scolded Dalrymple for asking another question. Villagers weren't used to interacting with nobles and had less familiarity with the rules of deference than those who lived in and around a castle. "We do not. However, her fate rests with the justice at the assizes. I have formed a good opinion of her myself, despite a much shorter acquaintance than yours, and I wish to give her every chance at reclaiming life and liberty. I thank you for your time and trouble."

~

ELA REMEMBERED that Mathilde had mentioned a traveling wheelwright coming to the house on the day of Charibert's death. She inquired in the village if any of them had dealings with the man. One of them said that he wasn't a traveling wheelwright at all, but lived right among them.

Directions from the pie man led Ela to the wheelwright's workshop on the outskirts of the village. His barn had a great set of doors, much faded and worn, propped open to reveal a room filled with bits and pieces of wheels—spokes, rims, metal edging—and hammers, awls, wedges and tools of every description. A blacksmith's anvil even stood in one corner. The wheelwright, bent over and shaving away at a curved piece of wood, didn't notice their arrival until one of Ela's guards barked out a greeting.

The man looked up like a startled colt and glanced from Ela to the guards to Ela again. Then he whipped his hat off his head and nodded a mumbled greeting.

"Are you Peter Redditch?" asked Ela, gently, as if she was talking to a flighty horse.

"That I am, ma'am. That I am. What can I help you with? I make wheels of all sizes and mend them too, and my—"

Ela held up her hand. "I'm not here for a wheel, but to ask you about a family who you may have done business with."

"Oh, yes?" He looked nervous, his big blue eyes watery and his pale hair sticking to his forehead.

"The d'Albiac household. I'm told you went to their door to see if they needed work done on any wheels."

His face paled. "I did mend a set of worn wheels for the mistress."

Why did he look so worried? "Why did you go to her house for the work? Why did she not have a servant bring the cart to you?"

Peter Redditch licked his lips, as if pondering what to say. "They're the big house around here, if you know what I mean."

"I do."

"But not ones to spend money if they can avoid it." He looked awkward. "I would notice that their wheels needed repair and they just kept using them anyway. Dragging that old cart to town and lumbering back home loaded with milk churns and great cheeses. It'll destroy a wheel altogether if you do that long enough." He looked at her hopefully.

"So you thought you could prevent the ruin of their wheels—and make yourself a few pence—by approaching them at their home?"

He nodded furiously. "That's just it, missus. I've done it before and the lady of the house is a sensible one. If you point out a problem she wants to fix it and she paid what I asked."

"Do you have any idea why I'm here asking you about that?" She watched him closely.

"I suppose it's because one of them died that night," he said slowly. "I don't know nothing about that."

"Did you know the young man who died?"

He frowned. "I did. Everyone in the village knew him. Would be odd if they didn't, given he grew up just down the road."

"And what was your opinion of him?" Did she imagine it or did his hair cling more closely to his damp, pale forehead?

"I don't suppose it's my business to have opinions of my betters," he mumbled.

Now Ela frowned. "It's my business—as Sheriff of Wiltshire—to ask your opinion, and your business to give it to me when I do."

He blinked rapidly. "He was a big lad. Sturdy. The kind of boy any family would be proud of. But—"

"Father!" a girl's high voice peeled out from the back of the workshop. "Who's in there—" A door creaked open and a girl of about sixteen with bright blonde hair poked her head in. "What is going on in here?" she asked again, looking rather dazed by the phalanx of guards standing at the open doors to her father's dimly lit workshop.

"Mind your business Della. Go back upstairs and tend to your mother." He spoke sternly, but Ela heard the worry in his voice.

"No, wait!" called Ela. With her knowledge of Charibert she could suddenly envisage a scenario in which even timid and obsequious Peter Redditch might have a bone to pick with the lad. "Come here. I'm Ela, Countess of Salisbury and Sheriff of Wiltshire."

"A lady sheriff?" said the girl in disbelief.

Ela did not dignify the question with a response. "Are you familiar with a young man called Charibert d'Albiac?"

"He's dead, isn't he?" she asked boldly.

"Della!" cried her father. "M-m-mind your manners."

"He is dead," said Ela. "Did you meet him while he was alive?"

"You mean in secret? Like Polly Witton? Never! I'm not a fool. If I saw him coming I'd run and hide."

Ela frowned in confusion. "Who's Polly Witton?"

Della looked taken aback. "Everyone knows Polly."

This child was not conspicuous for intelligence. Unless she was lying to cover up her own misdeeds and prevent her father from being accused of defending her honor.

Ela drew in a steadying breath. "Why would you run and hide from Charibert d'Albiac?"

The girl had the natural pink cheeks and sparkling blue eyes of extreme youth. Combined with her bright hair her beauty might well be an attractive nuisance to a young man of low morals.

"He was very cheeky." She smiled, showing dimples. "And bold with it! Of course he was a noble and felt like he could do whatever he wanted."

"Did he take advantage of you?"

"Never! I'm too quick for him."

"He was a handsome man," said Ela, trying another tack. "A skilled rider and fighter. I'd have thought girls would admire and whisper about him rather than running for cover."

"Village girls like me know that one of his type would only use us and throw us aside. We're not stupid enough to think we'd end up living in his big house if we let him kiss us. We're better off waiting for a nice farmer's son to make eyes at us."

Ela glanced at her father, who looked like he was moments from dying of embarrassment.

"Very sensible," said Ela. "But did Charibert d'Albiac manage to—foist himself—on any other girls in the village?"

"I couldn't say, my lady. I dare say he tried with everyone. Well, except maybe Margaret Rudd because she's simple and only has one arm. But my mother warned me about the men of that family even when I was little. They're known in these parts as wastrels who'll ruin a young girl's life as soon as look at her."

"But you mentioned a girl called Polly, who…welcomed his attentions."

"I don't know that she welcomed them but she didn't fight him off, if that's what you mean."

Ela pictured the scene with Gertrude Wimberley. "Where can I find her?"

Della looked at her father, who stared blankly back at her. "I'm not sure, my lady," she said flatly.

"Does she live in the village?"

"Not in the village. On a farm outside it."

"It's down the track to the left of the great oak just past my workshop," said her father, suddenly wakening from his stupor. Maybe he was animated by the prospect of getting rid of her. "The farm's about half a mile down the track."

"I shall inquire there," said Ela, looking from father to daughter. *They know something.* Still, she didn't think Peter Redditch had murdered Charibert and his daughter probably hadn't either. Until she had more information herself, she wasn't sure how to pry more from them. "Please point me in the right direction."

CHAPTER 12

The spreading oak loomed over the road, its gnarled branches as thick as a man's waist. It had likely been a sapling when the ancient Romans were building their straight roads across Britain. But they'd missed this part. The track which started by roots of the oak wound through the landscape like a river, weaving its way around each bulge and hollow in the landscape like a living thing.

"This is pretty country," Ela heard one of her guards say to the other. "I'd fancy living in a place like this one day." She turned around to get a look at the speaker but saw only four straight faces behind her.

"It is lovely," she said brightly. She didn't want them to think they couldn't utter a word in her presence. "An ancient landscape. This track feels like it was made by sheep rather than man."

"No doubt it was, my lady," said one middle-aged guard named George. "And there they are." He gestured to a good-sized flock grazing on a hillock that rose to one side of the track. We should ask them where we can find Miss Polly Witton."

Ela chuckled. "If only we could. But I see smoke rising ahead."

Around a bend and past a knot of hawthorn bushes, they saw a low-slung cottage with a thatched roof. Outside it, a woman with a white kerchief tied over her hair was bent down picking an egg up off the ground and putting it in a small basket. She looked up in alarm at the sound of their hooves.

"Good day, mistress," called Ela. "Are you Polly Whitton?"

"No, my lady," said the woman, eyes wide. "I'm her mother. She's out gathering faggots."

"Can you send for her? I am Countess Ela of Salisbury, Sheriff of Wiltshire, and I wish to speak with her."

The woman all but dropped her basket on the step of the cottage and ran off into a copse of pollarded trees. Ela dismounted and a guard, also dismounted, took her horse. She could hear children's laughter coming from behind the house, probably younger siblings of Polly.

A crashing sound heralded Polly and her mother coming back through the woods. Her mother's kerchief was coming untied and her face wore a look of panic. "I found Polly, but would you please tell me what's amiss?"

Polly, bright-eyed with curiosity, followed close behind her. She stared at Ela, taking her in from head to toe as if an apparition had materialized in her garden. "May I speak with Polly alone?" asked Ela pleasantly of her mother.

"Well…" The woman wrung her hands in her apron. "I suppose so. If you must." She snatched up her basket of eggs and disappeared through the doorway into the dim interior of the cottage, then closed the scarred wooden door behind her. Ela felt sure she'd be watching them through a crack in the doorway, for the cottage had no windows.

Ela ushered Polly over to a shady spot behind the woven

bee skeps. The girl's round face shone with the rosy beauty of youth that would one day fade into careworn, weather-beaten plainness, but right now it shimmered like a jewel. A jewel that Charibert d'Albiac may have added to his collection of stolen treasures. "Did you know Charibert d'Albiac?"

The girl's face flushed red. "No."

The violent blush argued with her answer. Ela watched her in silence.

Her lips now reddened. "I mean, I knew of him. He's the nobility."

"Did you see him in the village?"

"Yes. When I brought eggs to sell."

"Did he ever speak to you?"

Polly looked at the ground, her face red as a beet.

"Your blush is answering my question," said Ela softly. "I know he was a forceful young man. Not easy to say no to."

Tears welled up in Polly's eyes. "He made me feel like such a fool," she rasped.

"What did he do to you?"

Polly wiped her nose with the back of her hand. "Flattered me with pretty words. Told me I had a neat figure and a bright smile and that I was the loveliest girl in all Wiltshire." Tears rolled over her rosy cheeks. Her chest heaved with emotion.

"And you let him kiss you?" asked Ela, after a long wait.

Polly nodded. "And I enjoyed it. He made my heart beat faster. I even fell in love with him." She looked at Ela, eyes wide. "I'm so stupid."

Ela's heart clenched. It wouldn't console Polly to know that she was just one of many conquests by Charibert. "Did he…fornicate with you?" Such a thing would be a terrible crime among two nobles, requiring one to marry the other to make amends. Among the common people, it was not so unusual and such illicit romances often led to marriage and a long happy life together. Such a dalliance between a noble and a village girl was sadly far more one-sided and never—at least not to her knowledge—led to anything other than the girl's prospects being blighted. A girl used so cruelly had every right to be angry.

But angry enough to kill?

Polly's lips quivered. "I don't know what that word means."

"Did he...bed you?"

Polly nodded. "Not in a bed, but in the hayloft of old Peter's barn that's far off the road. He said he loved me too and that I'd be his bride and come live in a castle and dress like a queen." She sobbed. "Like I said, I was so stupid. I don't know what came over me."

"You're young and falling in love is the most natural thing in the world. It's just a shame that a cold-hearted scoundrel like Charibert d'Albiac preyed on your affections rather than some more suitable boy." Sadly, at least Della Redditch knew about her indiscretions. That meant others probably did, too. It would be worse if she was with child. Not many prospective husbands were magnanimous enough to offer a home to a bride bringing a little cuckoo to their nest. "Are you with child?"

Polly shook her head. "I've bled since then."

"Thank God for that, at least," said Ela. "You're a beautiful girl and I'm sure some lucky man will marry you soon enough." Polly didn't seem like the type to kill anyone. She seemed angrier with herself than with Charibert. "Do you know of any other girls whom he wronged?"

"No. Just myself." Her eyes had dried and she looked more astonished than sorrowful. She rubbed at her red nose. "My mother says I'd better mind my chores and fill my head with prayers and not foolish fancies."

"Your mother sounds very sensible." And kind not to turn her daughter out into the street for her foolish mistake. She'd quite understand if Polly's mother or father wanted to teach Charibert d'Albiac a lesson—but were they motivated to kill him? She realized Polly hadn't mentioned one thing.

Ela drew in a breath. "Are you aware that Charibert d'Albiac is dead?"

"I didn't kill him," Polly said quickly.

"I didn't accuse you of killing him." Ela watched the girl closely. "Though you certainly had reason to be angry with him. Do you know how he was killed?"

"They said he was found dead in his bed. Maybe someone strangled him."

"Can you think of anyone who'd want him dead?"

Polly looked at the floor. "He ruffled a lot of people's feathers, one way or another. When I was swooning over him I found myself arguing with them and making excuses for him. Idiot!" Again, she seemed to be cursing herself rather than him. "He didn't seem to care if people liked him. I'm not sure he even thought of us as people. Looking back, I think he treated us all more like sheep, barking orders and chivvying us around. I suppose a lot of nobles are like that so I didn't think much of it." She poked at the ground with her foot. "Maybe I'd be like that myself if I was a fine lady riding around on a white horse."

Ela grew vaguely conscious that her white horse, Freya, stood waiting patiently nearby. "I'd like to speak with your mother."

"Can I go back to gathering wood now?"

Ela nodded. "Thank you for your help, and for being so honest."

"I hope you catch whoever did it. I don't know why, but I do feel sad that he's dead. He was very handsome."

"I shall do my best to find his killer and bring that person to justice." And to make sure that the wrong one doesn't hang for his murder.

The door to the cottage opened as soon as she knocked, confirming to Ela that Polly's mother had likely stood behind it, listening, the whole time. The inside of the dim, windowless room smelled like rancid bacon grease and cabbage. A boy of twelve or thirteen sat in the corner whittling at a piece of wood with a small knife.

"Where is your husband, Mistress?" asked Ela. A man might feel it his duty to avenge his fallen daughter's honor.

"My Ned's been dead these last four years, my lady." In the half light, Ela could see that woman had a sorrowful look etched into her features with finely drawn lines. "He stepped on a scythe blade and the wound festered. It killed him in the end."

Ela crossed herself as the gruesome image sank in. "May God grant you solace in your suffering."

"He's not granted me much of that. Not with my Polly having the wits of a chicken."

"Polly was very gracious with me just now. Many a girl has had her head turned by a callous young man. I'm glad there's no permanent harm done."

"It is a mercy that he didn't leave her with child, but who'll marry her now?"

"She's a pretty girl."

"Much good it does her. Makes the wrong sort of men hover around her like flies over a cowpat and frightens off the good ones. And she's not clever enough to know one from the other."

"I pray the Lord will bring her a suitable husband in his own time."

"Bless you, my lady, for your kind words."

~

BACK AT THE CASTLE, Ela said a prayer for poor Mathilde d'Albiac, locked up down below in the castle dungeon. She also had Elsie take a bowl of soup and a piece of bread to the jailer to give to her. Ela hoped the warm food would fortify her.

"I don't think there's a single person in that village who'd shed a tear for Charibert d'Albiac," said Ela to Bill. She sat by the fire, embroidering a small square of linen to use as a handkerchief.

"So everyone's a suspect?"

"None of them is a compelling suspect. Which doesn't bode well for Mathilde. I fear for her children, who might soon be orphans."

"Are they above suspicion? Their brother wished to turn them all out of their home."

Ela sighed. "They're young, but as my interview today reminded me, the young are foolish and rash enough to make life-changing mistakes. I shall visit them again tomorrow. Perhaps Petronella will have unearthed some new information from her immersion in their midst.

Truth be told, she was anxious about Petronella living among strangers in the wake of a murder, even with two guards and a maid that she'd sent along with her. "Do you think I should bring her illuminated prayer book? I told her not to bring it for fear it might be lost or damaged, but now I fear I've left her without that familiar comfort."

"Petronella is tough," said Bill. "I suspect she'll have solved the murder and reorganized the household by the time you arrive tomorrow."

"God willing," said Ela. "I think I shall retire early to prepare for—" They both turned as a blast sounded from the trumpet of Albert the Porter.

"It's a bit late at night for a fanfare, don't you think?" she muttered under her breath. "Whoever can be arriving in the dark?"

"Sir William Longespée!" cried Albert's hoary voice.

Ela's heart almost stopped at the name.

Sir William Longespée was one man alone—her beloved husband. But her son was recently knighted and now also bore the title of Sir before his name. "Will? Why would he arrive unannounced in the dead of night? I hope nothing's amiss." She peered at the door. She saw her tall, lanky son enter, blond hair hatless and disheveled, handing his gloves and cloak to a boy. She rose to her feet. "William, dear. What a surprise."

Will's brothers were already falling on him. They hadn't seen each other for some time since Will now spent most of his time up in Lincolnshire near his wife's family.

"Hail, good sir knight!" cried Stephen. Will beamed. His knighthood was still new enough to bring them all a burst of pride.

"Don't worry, it'll be your turn soon enough," he said, ruffling his brother's hair.

"Richard fought in two tournaments already!" said Stephen. "Bill said he's not half bad."

"Not half bad?" Richard cried. "I won a sword, and a suit of armor and I could have had his horse as well if I had the heart of a fox."

"You don't have the heart of a fox?" asked William. "To kill all the chickens and leave them uneaten just for sport?"

Richard smiled wryly. "No. Fighting doesn't come naturally to me like it does to you and Stephen, but I'm doing my best not to dishonor the family name."

"He's a champion," exclaimed Bill. "And far too self-deprecating if you ask me. But to what do we owe this great pleasure, and at so late an hour?"

Will looked around and smiled. It was an odd smile and produced a strange sensation in Ela's chest. "Would you like something to eat?" she asked, looking around for Elsie.

"No thanks. We dined at an inn near Marlborough. Very fine roast pig in a honey glaze. I'm stuffed. We had to stop because Ralph's horse threw a shoe and we had to wait for the farrier to put on a new one."

"Did you bring your wife?" Ela looked around for Idonea, the granddaughter of her dear friend Nicola de la Haye, who had died the previous year.

"I left her at home this time. I need to have a private audience with you, Mother, but it can wait until tomorrow." His youngest sister Ellie stood shyly to one side, waiting for a ray of her big brother's attention to fall in her direction. Will turned his beaming smile on her and lifted her up, even though she was now tall as some adults.

A private audience. A tiny chill crept up Ela's spine. This drama in the d'Albiac household had stirred up a lot of talk about when and how a son should inherit his family estates. She hoped that news of it hadn't blown up to Lincolnshire and stirred up a nest of hornets.

But she could find that out tomorrow. "Come, Will. Let us share a jug of spiced wine and you shall tell us all about the adventures of your journey."

"Can I sleep in Father's old chamber?" Will's bright gaze shone at her.

Ela froze. "Uh, no. The linens are all stored. They'd need to be aired. You can sleep in your old room."

No one had slept in her late husband's chamber, directly next to her solar, since he'd suffered a gruesome, protracted and painful death in there. Sometimes she went in, hoping to catch a whiff of his scent in the air or a stray memory of happier times before he'd sickened and died.

And if Will wanted to lay his head where his father slept, she was likely right that he hoped to step into his boots in other ways as well.

CHAPTER 13

*T*he next morning Ela did her round of chores and breakfasted early. Even while she walked around the gardens and watched the boy throwing scraps to the pigs, her mind sizzled with anxiety.

He's my son.

Her firstborn, that sweet, needy baby with his downy pale hair and chubby cheeks, had grown into a great giant of a man, but he was still her baby.

She wondered how he'd approach the matter. She could make things easy on him by bringing up the issue herself. She could then take the reins and steer the discussion from the start.

But she didn't want to make it easy on him. If he'd come here to challenge her authority…

If he had the *raw nerve* to demand that she relinquish her title—he'd have to pluck up the courage to speak first.

Still, the hair on the back of her neck prickled when he came down to break his fast—late as usual—surrounded by adoring dogs and his younger siblings. Already making plans for a possible hunt with Bill and the two older boys, he seemed barely to notice her as she sat reading her prayer book by the fire.

He ate slowly and copiously, asking for more and larger helpings of eggs and fruit and oatcakes, and she'd almost resolved to abandon the hall and head for Tierce service, when he rose and approached her.

"Mother, may we speak alone?"

"What about?" she tried to look unconcerned, leaving a finger to mark her place in her prayer book.

"Something important. We can talk in the armory."

Her back stiffened. *He's telling me where I can and can't talk in my own castle.* She half wanted to stiffly respond that the armory was in use and they could meet in the confines of her study—but then he might suddenly demand to look at ledgers or rifle through documents he had no business seeing.

She rose to her feet, drawing in a steadying breath. On impulse, she kept her prayer book in her hand. Humility is a virtue! Show forbearance! Her unfortunate natural tendency to pride and arrogance sometimes stood her in good stead in a castle full of boisterous soldiers, but she had to remind herself that this was her own tender son, not an enemy trying to besiege her castle.

Small windows high in the armory walls cast rays of light that glinted off the polished weapons arranged on the walls.

"The armory at Lincoln is far less impressive," observed William.

"This is the king's garrison. Even this is something of a token display. There are many more weapons kept under lock and key. But you didn't bring me here to talk about armaments."

"No." He shifted his weight, looking uncomfortable in his deep blue tunic. "I came to ask when I might expect to become Earl of Salisbury."

Ela watched, wondering if he'd continue. An odd silence hung in the air among the shining swords and spears and halberds.

William puffed up his chest. "I'm a married man and a knight now. Bill Talbot has educated me in both the finer and rougher points of being a man, and I've learned a great deal since I moved out from under your roof." He pushed his shoulders back and looked at her. If she didn't know him so well she might not have noticed the fear in his eyes. "I'm ready to follow in Father's footsteps as Earl of Salisbury."

Ela's chest tightened. She knew the courage it must have taken for him to come here and speak his piece. Or did her muscles constrict with fear for her own future? If William became Earl then she'd no longer be castellan of Salisbury or Sheriff of Wiltshire. He'd take over those roles and she'd be shuffled off to embroider beside the fire.

"You've always said you wanted to retire to a convent, Mother." Will could see his plea wasn't falling on receptive ears. "You could be an abbess."

"Have you failed to remember that you have younger siblings that are not yet in their majority, William?"

William sagged. "They will be soon enough. Nicholas is almost as tall as you."

"He's twelve. Sadly, height does not equate to maturity." Will had always had a greater abundance of height than maturity.

"My wife and I could finish their education," continued Will. "And Bill Talbot, of course. We'd be like their parents."

Ela now stared in astonishment. "Why would that be an improvement on my dear children being raised by their actual parent?"

"It's just that…at this rate, it'll be donkeys' years before I become Earl of Salisbury."

"Does ten short years seem like an eternity to you?" It

gave a twinge of actual physical pain to put a timeline on when she might quit dear Salisbury Castle—place of her birth and home to the happiest years of her youth—and shut herself up in a cloister for the rest of her life.

"It does, yes."

"Then perhaps you should question how mature you truly are. You have much wisdom to gain before you're ready to be castellan of the King's garrison."

"Dad was barely older than me when he became Earl."

"He only became Earl because he married me. I was already Countess in my own right."

"So you were countess when you were a small child. You can hardly have possessed the maturity to manage a castle when your father died. Why didn't your mother become countess?"

He had a point. "I was countess by right of succession, because my father was Earl and he died. My mother is from the de Vitre family and did not assume a right to the title on her marriage."

"But my father did." William seemed to be trying to puzzle it out.

"Your father was the King's son. If the King wanted him to be Earl of Salisbury he could have changed every law in the land to make it so. Luckily it was enough for him to marry me."

"So you became countess when your father died because you were the next in line." He peered at her.

"Yes."

"My father has died and therefore I am the next in line." He glared at her with considerable force. She didn't remember seeing such determination in him before.

"Your father has died but the title is still mine *suo jure*, as it was on the day my father died."

"And you're not going to pass it on to me, even though I'm a knight?"

Ela felt her breathing grow shallow. "All in good time. First, let your siblings grow to maturity and fly the nest into their own marriages."

"What if I'm dead by then?" Now his voice had a plaintive whine to it.

"Do you expect to die before age thirty?" She lifted a brow.

"No, but I might. Your father died young and my father died young."

"If the Lord calls you to his side, then you must go. God willing you shall enjoy many more years here on earth with your wife and family."

"But not at Salisbury Castle." Now he sounded like the petulant teen who'd whined about having to memorize passages in Latin when he'd rather be out hunting boar. "I do feel like you're being a dog in the manger."

Anger flashed through her. "Do you really think that my main purpose here at Salisbury Castle is to prevent you from becoming earl?"

"No, but..."

"But what? I take my role as castellan very seriously. The king's garrison is ready for a siege or an assault at any moment. I also take great pride in my work as sheriff. Many sheriffs take the opportunity to enrich themselves at the expense of their subjects and allow crime to flourish where it suits them. I put effort into pursuing the guilty and delivering them to their just reward."

"I would do that."

Would you, though? Ela couldn't see Will sitting on a dais all morning—and sometimes most of the afternoon—hearing the tiresome business of suppliants with their boundary disputes and accusations of cheating. Her son Richard, steady, fair-minded and philosophical, would manage the day-to-day affairs of Wiltshire far better than his older brother.

"You'd be surprised by how dull the official duties of the sheriff can be."

"If I find the work too dull, then I shall have a co-sheriff to attend to the tasks, just as you do." He squared his shoulders. Ela had found it necessary to accept the presence of a co-sheriff as a sop to the prevailing opinions that a woman in the role was astonishing and unthinkable. She'd been delighted to find that John Dacus was able when needed, but happy to fade into the background when he wasn't required. His support allowed her to do the job of sheriff without the constant tongue-wagging and backbiting that would have occurred if she'd assumed the role entirely alone.

"John Dacus assists me when required, but the lion's share of work falls to me and I tackle it gladly. Don't think I sit on my dais all day sipping wine and absorbing pleasantries." She felt a swell of indignation at the thought. "I am grateful for a chance to do God's work here in Salisbury and in Wiltshire. I can seek justice for widows and orphans and right the wrongs of a powerful neighbor against a weaker one. I've found stolen children and solved savage murders and unmasked a charlatan who duped the faithful for his own gain."

William looked skeptical. "How do you find the time to do all that while attending to the affairs of the household and your children? You must feel torn in several directions."

"Not in the least. As you've observed, your siblings are old enough to be busy with their tutors. I have undertaken the running of this household my entire life and it is now a finely wrought instrument that only needs tuning and waxing to keep singing smoothly. How are you proceeding with the management of your properties up north?"

"Well, my wife has the management of the household, naturally."

Ela sighed. Idonea was a very capable woman. "And how do you occupy your time?"

"Well, that's just it. I'm bored. One can only hunt so many days of the year."

Ela felt herself deflate. "Bill Talbot didn't raise you to be an idle wastrel looking to fill his hours with amusements. Surely you can find useful work to do. Can you not put yourself forward as Earl of Lincoln? The current Earl has no issue so that earldom will soon become vacant."

"He's pledged to name his sister Hawise of Chester as his heiress with the king's permission. And I belong here in Salisbury." Again, she heard a note of distress in his voice. This time it touched her heart.

"I understand the longing for your home as I felt it myself during my years of youthful exile. But you must look upon these years as a time for learning and growing. My work here in Salisbury is unfinished. In time it shall be, and you shall take up the mantle of Earl of Salisbury. But that time has not yet come."

"I'm a man! I'm older than King Henry who rules our entire land. How can you still treat me like a child who's bored with his rattle?" Now she heard anger in his voice, and red blotches appeared around his jaw.

"King Henry is surrounded by advisors whose years of wisdom make up for his lack of experience. Also, he's been king for fifteen years at this point so he's had the opportunity to learn his duties before reaching majority."

William stared down at her from his impressive height, obviously fuming. "I shall take my cause to King Henry. He's my cousin! He's not your cousin. He'll understand my frustration and listen to my grievances."

Ela felt panic flare in her chest. *Could he? Would he?* Such an outrage—a deliberate attempt by her own flesh and blood to undermine her authority—would be a grievous blow to her pride. The king would be shocked. And would he decide in her favor?

She tried to calm herself and respond in a way that would kill this idea before he could act on it. "My role here as castellan of Salisbury and sheriff of Wiltshire is by explicit agreement with King Henry III himself. I paid him two hundred pounds for shrievalty of this castle that we stand in, and a further five hundred pounds to retain the earldom and its offices for my entire life, should I choose to keep it." She spoke slowly, and even she could hear the edge of steel in her voice. "And currently, I choose to keep it."

"Seven hundred pounds?" William's eyes bulged. "Where did you find such a tremendous sum? Didn't father die leaving great debts?"

"I've taken great pains to raise profits from my manors." She deliberately chose the word *my* rather than our. "I have borrowed sums and repaid them and the estates are now in firmer financial condition than they were before your dear father's death. All this while you were out hunting boar or begging the cook for fresh spice cakes. Have you ever shown an interest in the finances of our estates?"

"You've spent hours going over those books with me."

"Against your will and over your protests. If you were listening to me at all you'd know the economies I've made and the profits we've enjoyed. But you were always in a rush to get back to your archery practice or try out a new horse."

William looked slightly chastened. "I was young. I'm mature now. And this is not an idea that just formed in my head like a bubble. It was suggested by a very prominent person."

Ela froze. "Who?"

Will hesitated. "I promised not to say."

"Why is it a secret? I wish to know who'd like to see me removed as castellan and sheriff of Salisbury?"

"It's not a secret, exactly."

"Is it someone I know?" Blood pounded in her ears. Who was this enemy?

"Everyone knows him. He's one of the king's closest advisers." William looked smug.

Of course. "Is it Hubert de Burgh?"

His face paled. His mouth worked for a moment like a fish. Then she held up her hand. "I don't need you to speak. I have my answer."

"He said King Henry would be glad to see me take up the mantle of Earl."

"Since King Henry has made other arrangements with me —very expensive arrangements that were the result of detailed negotiations—I very much doubt he said that. I suspect it is rather de Burgh's wish to see me banished from the scene."

Will did look surprised. "Is that because he's still angry that you refused his nephew's proposal?" Everyone in England now knew of the scandalous proposal and that her husband was still alive at the time that he made it.

"Perhaps." She hadn't told William of her full suspicions about Hubert de Burgh.

"Or because Papa was furious with him and complained to the king and forced him to apologize?"

"I suspect he is still smarting over that."

"He did apologize though, and gave my father a fine horse and entertained him in his house to make amends."

"Indeed he did." *And then your father returned home ill and was dead within the week.*

"I'm sure Papa and he would have been great friends if Papa hadn't grown ill."

Ela's frustration got the better of her. "Hubert de Burgh

141

and your father were never friends. De Burgh sided with King John against your father when they fell out. They were at odds even before then."

"I didn't know that."

"As I've noted, you have a lot to learn." Would William ever put two and two together and realize that Hubert de Burgh had likely poisoned his father? The temptation to put the idea in his head right now was almost overwhelming. But that was too great of a burden for her son to carry.

William blinked as if struggling to understand all this.

Ela hoped he wouldn't go right to de Burgh and tell him everything she'd said. Not that any of it would be fresh news to him. "Naturally you are mature and wise enough to keep this information to yourself, but you should keep it at the back of your mind. His motives regarding me are not so pure as he would have you believe."

She leaned in and looked directly into William's blue eyes. "De Burgh is a man who enjoys wielding power for its own sake. He rose from humble origins and is now married to the daughter of the king of Scotland. If he could find a route to become king himself I feel confident that he'd take it. Happily, his modest ancestry allows no such claims."

She leaned back but kept her gaze fixed on his. "But don't assume that he doesn't have designs upon the earldom of Salisbury and its assets. It takes a wise and powerful man—or woman—to wield such power in the kingdom of England. One day—God willing—you will be that man. As I've revealed to you today, I fought hard and paid dearly for the privilege and I do not take it lightly. I also do not plan to give it up until I'm confident that you are ready to field such great responsibility."

Will stared. "This is a lot of new information."

"Perhaps it's my fault for not telling you sooner. I suppose I was waiting for you to be wise and mature enough to carry this knowledge. Now I believe that you are."

"Do you think that de Burgh hates you?"

Ela stiffened. "Let's not use such strong language. I'm not his enemy. We're on the same side—the side of King Henry III and England. Let's just say that he dislikes me and resents my access to the king, whom I admire and respect and hold dear."

"Does the king dislike you? Why did you have to pay so much money to retain rights that are yours by birth?"

"Nothing is ever yours by birth unless the present or future king agrees for you to retain it. Learn that and remember it well. No man is above a charge of treason and a long stint in the tower, or even a short one on the chopping block." Her words had an icy edge to them and she saw him shudder slightly as if his knees buckled. "While I do believe that the current king likes me, and I like him, I still had to convince him that it was in his interests as well as my own for me to be castellan here."

"How did you do that? I mean, besides the money."

"Money speaks a language of its own, a powerful language that reaches straight into the hearts of men. Kings are always in need of money to fund wars or live the lavish lifestyle expected of them. If you have money, you have power. Remember that well, too." She sighed. "And in the years since I bought my way into my positions, I'm confident that I've proven myself a capable castellan and a sheriff committed to peace and justice in Wiltshire."

"Do you think that if you weren't a good castellan and sheriff that he'd rip the castle away from you despite the money?"

Ela hesitated, contemplating this. The truth burned her even as she uttered it. "Probably."

It could still happen even if she triumphed in her roles.

She wasn't foolish enough to believe herself entirely safe. Perhaps this was why William's rash aspirations troubled her —especially if he had Hubert de Burgh egging him on.

No one was ever truly safe from an enemy's accusations. If she didn't end up imprisoned or hanged, she could still be accused of insanity or witchcraft and locked up in a nunnery. Or even inside her own castle, like poor Eleanor of Aquitaine —once the most powerful woman in the world, wife of two kings and mother of three more—reduced to a life of solitude and isolation right here in Salisbury Castle while Ela was a child. "Do not grasp power unless you have the wit and wisdom to hold tight to it."

Will ran a hand through his hair. "I admit I do have a greater appreciation for your hesitation in passing the Earldom to me."

"It shall be yours when the time is right."

Will seemed rather deflated by their discussion, his broad shoulders drooping somewhat. He'd charged into battle and suffered a wound to his pride and his confidence.

"In the meantime, build your skills. Learn to lead and to both take advice and give it. Study who to trust and who to avoid. Learn how to navigate the king's court and keep your friends close and your enemies closer. Then when you are Earl of Salisbury, you'll be prepared for the dangers as well as the privileges."

"I shall." His expression seemed shuttered.

"Will you wait patiently?"

His gaze focused and he peered right into her eyes. "We shall find out, won't we?"

CHAPTER 14

The following day, Ela made the journey to Neversend. She wished to visit Petronella and see how she was managing, and she also wanted to spend time interviewing the girls again.

Helene, the elder, must have heard the horses arriving outside their manor house and hurried out the door as she arrived. "How fares our mother? Is she well?"

"As well as can be under the circumstances." Poor Mathilde had already lost weight and much of the color in her face despite Ela sending her food from her own table to supplement the meager rations in the dungeon. She looked ten years older after just a few days of confinement.

"How long will she be in prison?"

"Until the assizes. The date has not yet been set. It depends on the traveling justice who moves about the country trying serious crimes. We will have at least a few days' notice and I will send word to you as soon as we find the date."

"She would never kill Charibert. Never! And she didn't kill my father, either. She wouldn't hurt a fly."

"May we sit down and talk?"

Before they could take a seat, Petronella appeared. With a large key around her neck, her hair tucked under a crisp veil and a stern expression on her face, she looked more like a seasoned abbess than a young girl. "Welcome, Mother. May God go with you."

"Indeed I pray that he does." Ela tried not to be amused by her daughter's officious air. "What does that key unlock?"

Petronella looked down and fingered the big brass key hanging from a plain ribbon. "The cellar. With the mistress away I found that the servants were pilfering, especially the young boys that manage the animals. It's important to be frugal and careful in a difficult time like this."

"Very sensible. What does the housekeeper think of you taking command of the key?"

"She wasn't happy about it, since those boys are her sons, but she grudgingly gave it to me." Petronella smoothed the front of her gown. "I think you'll also find the house cleaner and tidier than it was. The chimneys are brushed out and the hearths swept clean, and one of the girls is in the process of scrubbing the floors with lye soap to lift a century's grime."

Ela looked down at her feet, where the clay tile floor did indeed appear to be an entirely different color than she remembered from her last visit. "I'm grateful for your care in managing the household."

"Mathilde was not a strict steward, I'm afraid. Many things have fallen into disrepair. But we shall mend them."

Poor Mathilde must have had her hands full with managing Charibert, let alone the household and her other children, all in the absence of a husband. A mild-mannered woman like Mathilde often had trouble compelling the servants to do tiresome tasks that could be pushed off to another day. Apparently, Petronella was troubled by no such weakness.

Petronella's mouth pursed with satisfaction. Her cheeks glowed pinker than usual. "Would you like refreshments after your ride?"

"No, thank you. I wish to speak with each of the girls alone, and then perhaps with other members of the household."

Last time she was here the interviews had been fairly haphazard, conducted in a parlor off the hall where anyone could overhear if they wished. The girls had been stunned and tearful in the wake of their brother's death. And she herself had been distracted by news that Sir Godfrey Wimberly had visited on the night of Charibert's death, so she'd been less suspicious of others than perhaps was wise.

Now that the girls had had some time to sit with the grim news, she hoped they might provide more insight into what happened.

"Most of the rooms in the house are rather on top of each other, and fan off the hall," said Petronella. She gestured at a gallery on the second floor that led into what must be quite small bedrooms. "But there's a sort of annex behind the kitchen and the pantry. I think it used to be a dairy, but it's just used to store baskets and such. It has thick walls of stone and is quiet as a cloister. I've gone there to pray when I need to quiet my mind amidst the bustle of the household."

Ela couldn't imagine this household of quiet females, even with the addition of a boisterous young boy, could seem very bustling after the furor of the castle, but the house was a lot smaller, and thus it must be harder to tuck yourself away in a corner. "Please, lead the way and let Helene come first."

The storage room had a small, high window that shone light down on its rather dusty contents. There was nowhere to sit, so they stood. "Helene, now that you've had time to reflect on your brother's death, what are your thoughts about who killed him?"

Helene looked down at the floor—not yet scrubbed—then at a pile of baskets in various states of disrepair, then at Ela. "It seems so hard to believe that someone killed him. Perhaps he just died. Sometimes people have a hidden ailment of the heart, where it just stops." She looked oddly hopeful.

Ela frowned inwardly. Giles Haughton did not doubt that Charibert had been poisoned.

Helene shifted and plucked at the sides of her dress. She looked...nervous. Was she anxious because her mother sat in the castle dungeon...or did she suffer from guilt?

Ela watched her face closely. "What was your relationship with Charibert?"

"He's my brother," she said quickly.

"I know that," snapped Ela, wanting to put some pressure on her. "Were you close? Or was he difficult to get along with?"

Helene knotted her hands into the front of her dress. "We were close when we were younger. He was far behind his brothers in age and would get left behind at home when they went hunting with our father. He always loved to play games with us outside and he used to gather herbs for the kitchen and even help the cook with preparing dinner. I used to retell some of the Bible stories we'd heard in church and he liked to hear them over and over, especially the ones with wars and disasters." Her face took on a fond expression. "He loved the story of Jonah and the great fish most of all."

"Did he change as you both got older?"

A muscle twitched almost imperceptibly in Helene's pale cheek. "As he spent more time with our father he grew embarrassed at doing anything our father considered girlish, which included spending time with Joan and me, and even with our mother. He even stopped him going to church with us on Sunday after his brothers were killed. He said God had deserted the kingdom of England and that no man should waste time in church when he could be out hunting instead on a Sunday morning. Though in truth he did more drinking and gambling than hunting."

"Those were your father's idea of manly pursuits?" Ela shuddered inwardly at the thought.

"He had no compunction about his habits. He always said that a man who can fight can take anything he wants, a man who can drink can enjoy the longest, darkest night, and a man who can gamble can command a king's ransom."

"Did Charibert believe him?"

"I don't know if Charibert was foolish enough to take those statements for fact but he did look up to him in his boyish way."

"Do you believe that your father is dead?"

"I don't know. I always assumed he was alive and overseas, since that's what Mother always said. Now I'm not so sure."

"You don't believe your mother?" Ela wondered how much Mathilde had shared her own troubles with her daughters.

Helene looked at the ground. "It's not that I don't believe her. I know she thinks he's alive. I'm just not sure that she's right. He's been gone a long time. Perhaps he got into a fight with the wrong person or drank too much and fell into a river. He sometimes drank so much that he tumbled off his horse. Mama always said he was made of wood and could bounce back from any tribulation."

Ela peered directly into Helene's gray eyes. "Did your mother get tired of your father's antics? I think almost any sane woman would."

Again Helene's lashes flickered. "If she did, then she never breathed a word of it to us girls. My mother never complains. If you ask me she's a saint walking on the face of the earth." Helene spoke with surprising passion. "She

149

certainly didn't kill anyone. Not her husband and not her son. The idea that she's accused of that is agonizing to me."

Ela felt Helene's pain echo in her own heart. She also thought that Mathilde was falsely accused. "The only way to ensure that your mother is found innocent at the assizes is to find the person who murdered Charibert."

"But what if no one murdered Charibert?" said Helene, her voice rising.

"Are you suggesting that he drank the poison of his own accord?" Ela didn't believe that for a moment.

"No," said Helene quietly. "Not on purpose. But maybe he thought he was reaching for wine and—" She tailed off. "Perhaps that Sir Godfrey person killed him." She looked at the floor again while she said it. "He spent time with him on the night that he died. And I heard him raise his voice to Charibert."

"Sir Godfrey had good reason to raise his voice to your brother. He did it because I saw—with my own eyes—your brother attempting to seduce his daughter during the tournament at Brackley. However, Sir Godfrey Wimberley appeared before the jury and ably convinced them that he had no interest in killing your brother. I believed him. His daughter was mercifully unharmed by your brother, partly due to my timely intervention. Sir Godfrey is a well-respected man, known to possess both intelligence and a moderate temperament. He stated, convincingly, that he came here to Neversend simply to warn Charibert against similar misadventures. He assured the jury that he had no reason to wish your brother dead and certainly not to risk his own life and liberty by killing him."

"I see." The words came out as a whisper. "The wheelwright also came that day." She looked up hopefully.

"I spoke with him and his daughter and I see no reason to

believe that he did anything other than fix your wheels. Did he even come into the house?"

"No," admitted Helene.

"Did Charibert speak to him as he went about his business?"

"Not that I know of." Helene seemed deflated. Ela didn't much appreciate her trying to pin the blame on an innocent tradesman. Was she hiding something? "Who in the household might have had the opportunity to slip poison into Charibert's wine?"

"Anyone, I suppose," she said quietly. "But none of us would." She spoke the last part with force.

"Has he troubled any of your servant girls?"

"No," she said quickly. "My mother warned him about that regularly. She said we couldn't afford to keep losing them as none of the local people wanted to come work in the house." She looked at the floor again. "Apparently they say it's cursed."

"Why would they say that?"

Helene stared at her as if she was dimwitted. "My father is dead or missing, my three brothers are dead—all before their time and by foul means. My dear sweet mother is locked up in your dungeon. Even I must wonder if my family is cursed."

Sometimes families did seem to be cursed, if only by a quirk of temperament that led its members down the road to ruin. Ela felt a pinch of sympathy for Helene. But she couldn't shake a feeling that she knew more than she was letting on. She inhaled slowly. "Did Charibert ever interfere with either you or Joan?"

"No! He's our brother."

"Such a thing, while reprehensible, is not unheard of. A jury might even be understanding if a murder was committed to prevent such a foul crime being committed in perpetuity."

"Charibert never laid a hand on us, I swear it! He was foolish and feckless but not a monster."

"What about Agnes?"

"What about her?" asked Helene quickly.

"Did Charibert make advances to her?"

"She's a mother! Her son follows her everywhere and sleeps in her bed. Even if he wanted to he'd never have the opportunity."

Ela narrowed her eyes. "That wouldn't likely stop a determined and lusty young man, which we know your brother to be."

"He always knew she was off limits. Our mother warned him, years ago when he was still quite young, that if he laid a hand on Agnes she'd take him over her knee and spank him."

Ela's eyes widened again. "Why did your mother feel the need to warn him?"

"I suppose because my brother Alain had already made that mistake. Agnes was known to be a fallen woman and as such might present a temptation to a man with low morals."

"I hardly think Agnes being raped by Alain makes her a fallen woman."

"Oh, Alain didn't rape her. She was in love with him."

Ela stared at her for a moment. She decided to reserve judgment until she could hear Agnes's account of the matter. "She must have been almost a child when he lay with her."

"She was young."

"So he took advantage of her and the blame for her fall—if we must call it that—lies with him."

"He wasn't much older than her, but I see what you mean. He was the oldest living son—the heir—at that time and she was the lowliest servant."

"Exactly. She may not have felt that she had a choice but to submit to his attentions. It was sensible of your mother to warn Charibert away from her." Lusty young sons becoming enamored of unsuitable women—servants or not—was always a worry for a mother. Ela wondered if Charibert ever listened to his mother, though. She wouldn't put it past him to make unwelcome advances to a pretty young woman, even one with a baby at her breast.

"I'd like to speak to Agnes next."

～

AT FIRST AGNES took Charley by the hand and tried to bring him back into the store room, but Ela asked Petronella to keep an eye on the boy so she could speak to his mother alone. She wanted her candid responses, which would likely be unsuitable for a child's ears.

Ela closed the door. Agnes looked around the shadowy room, with its baskets and jars and coils of old rope and string. She plucked at her dress anxiously.

"Were you in love with Alain, the father of your child?" She couldn't resist asking the question that now burned in her mind.

Agnes looked surprised, clearly not expecting to be asked about Alain rather than Charibert. "Does it sound terrible if I say I wasn't?"

"I'm not sure what does and doesn't sound terrible. I want the truth. From my perspective, Alain seduced a young and innocent girl against her best interests. Regardless of whether you liked him or not, he took advantage of you and jeopardized your future. I see no compunction for you to have any feelings for him other than disgust and possibly anger at how ill he used you." The fervor of her response surprised her.

Agnes stared. "I'd never say that to the mistress. Or his sisters."

"Because they loved him?"

"Yes. And he's dead. You should never speak ill of the dead."

"Oh, but you should, if you're before the sheriff or a jury, and there's ill to be spoken about them." She didn't want Agnes thinking she needed to honey her accounts of any d'Albiac male. "The truth is the only thing that matters."

Agnes's rosy cheeks looked taut like she was clenching her teeth. "Alain took my innocence against my will. He did it for a long time and no one knew. I couldn't say anything as I had nowhere else to go. My family was too poor to take care of me because my father was crippled by a kick from a cow and I was the youngest of five. That's how I ended up working here by the time I was eight years old."

Ela's chest tightened. Poor Agnes had lived subject to the whims of the d'Albiac family for most of her young life. "Was there any suggestion of him marrying you when you became pregnant?" Again, Ela asked out of curiosity, since this bore little relevance to her current investigation. Perhaps she wanted to get a greater sense of Mathilde's commitment to morality and fairness.

"He died only two weeks after I found out I was pregnant. He was off in far-away place called Bedford—besieging the castle alongside his father, in the pay of someone or other. It ended in a battle where many were killed and injured."

"So he never knew you were pregnant?"

"No, and marriage was never discussed."

Ela was curious to know Mathilde's thoughts on the matter. She had to admit that if one of her sons had the misfortune to get a servant girl pregnant, she would do everything possible to get the girl and her child well settled in life, and married to someone else, but she wouldn't consider blighting her children's bright prospects by forcing them to marry someone of low birth. On reflection, this was probably immoral, but she knew how the world worked and her sons each had an important role to play in the future of England.

"Did Mathilde ever try to arrange a marriage to another man of more suitable status?" That's what Ela had done when her maid Hilda became pregnant by a visiting knight. The girl was now happily married to a kind and hard-working miller's son.

"No. At least not that I know of." Agnes seemed to have trouble meeting her gaze. The girl's big brown eyes always seemed to be looking just past her. "I was relieved they let me stay under their roof. I don't think the mistress would like me to leave and take Charley away. He's her grandson."

"Indeed he is."

"And I'd never want to leave Charley here to go off and marry someone." Agnes now looked at her in a panic. "I'd rather die."

"No one is trying to take you away from him," she said quickly. Though she had no idea what would happen to Agnes and Charley if Mathilde was hanged. Her fate would rest in the hands of Charibert's sisters. And their fates would likely rest in the hands of whatever husbands—if any—could be found for them. "Does Charley know who his father was?"

"Yes, of course. Why shouldn't he?" Agnes looked curious.

Ela wasn't sure how to respond. A craftier family might have come up with a story about a dead husband of more suitable background, but then likely everyone local to Neversend would have guessed the true story anyway.

"Are you happy, living here in this household?" Ela peered at her, trying to see past her distant expression.

"Yes, I am," she blurted. "Why wouldn't I be? I mean, at least until the mistress was taken away. I hate to see her accused as she never killed her own son. She loved him."

"What about Charibert's sisters? Did they love him?"

Agnes looked away awkwardly. "Naturally. They're his sisters."

"But he was a brash and thoughtless youth, at least from what I've learned of him. He seems the type of boy who might be difficult to live with at least some of the time."

"He was no better and no worse than his brothers," said Agnes flatly. "Or his father."

"Some say the family is cursed." Ela knew this was nonsense and she felt a twinge of guilt at talking such rubbish, but she was curious to hear Agnes's take on the idea. "Do you think it's true?"

CHAPTER 15

"Cursed?" Agnes's forehead furrowed. "I suppose they might be. None of the men ever prayed, but Mathilde and her daughters pray every day. Maybe that's why the men are dead and the women are alive." She looked down at the floor. "I pray every day too. I pray for the mistress to be released from prison." Then she looked up at Ela, her eyes suddenly wet with tears. "Could she really hang?"

"I'm afraid she could," said Ela with a sigh. "Unless we can find the true killer. Do you have any suspicions about who it could be?"

"I don't know," she muttered, looking hard at the floor. "But it wasn't the mistress."

"You don't think it was one of Charibert's sisters?" They had opportunity, being at home with him and with access to his food and drink. Given Charibert's caustic nature—and active intent to banish them from the family estate—Ela suspected that they had at least some motive.

"No!" Agnes's answer came with force. "They'd never do such a thing."

And what about you? Ela was having trouble summoning the words to lay an accusation at the feet of this girl—a young mother who'd had no control over her own life from start to finish. "Was Charibert cruel to you?"

"No." She looked directly at Ela.

"That surprises me. Given his character I'd expect him to tease you and even torment you."

"No more than he did to anyone else. I'm just a servant." Her lips tightened into a thin line. "I didn't matter to him."

"What about the other servants? Did he interfere with any of the girls? Or did he browbeat any of the boys?"

"No," she said quickly. "A least not that I know of."

Ela found this surprising given Charibert's considerable energy for mischief. "Was he kind to Charley?"

"Yes." Her eyes darted to Ela's. "He was."

I don't believe her. "I'm seeing another side of Charibert in these conversations. It's wonderful that he was kinder to his family and the household than he was to strangers at a tournament or tradesman in the town."

"Yes." Her voice had a mechanical quality, like a tolling bell.

Ela watched her face closely. "Will you miss Charibert?"

Her lip twitched slightly. "I don't know if I'll miss him or not miss him. I'm just a servant and he was my master."

"Some servants grow attached to their master and mistress."

"I care deeply for Mistress Mathilde. She's shown such kindness to me and I love her almost like a mother, even though of course she isn't a mother to me. My heart breaks to think of her suffering."

"True. A double loss. The loss of her freedom as well as the loss of her only surviving son."

Agnes's lip quivered again. "Yes. It's terrible."

"But you don't know of anyone who could have killed Charibert?"

"No."

～

JOAN, the youngest, looked nervous as Ela closed the door behind her in the store room. Ela's eyes had adjusted to the light well enough to see a small spider building a web in one corner, between a broken basket handle and the plastered wall.

"I'd like to visit my mother," said Joan.

"I'm afraid the dungeon doesn't permit visitors." It was underground, with no stairs, to prevent prisoners from escaping. Now that Mathilde was accused of two murders, Ela had been left no choice but to confine her in its damp and unwholesome depths.

"So I won't see her except at the assizes?" Joan looked panicky.

"I'm afraid not."

"And if she's convicted, how long will it be before they hang her?"

Ela swallowed. She wanted to cross herself as if it might provide protection from such an eventuality. She kept her hands by her sides. "Hangings usually take place at dawn the next day."

A sob burst out of Joan, followed by a high-pitched keening sound. "She's going to hang, isn't she?"

"I'm doing my best to gather evidence so she can receive a fair trial. My hope is to present the true killer and absolve her of the crime."

Joan swiped at the tears wetting her cheeks. "It's not fair. Charibert did nothing but hurt people and our mother did nothing but help people, and now she's going to die because of him?"

Alarm bells rang in Ela's mind. Did Joan hate her brother enough to kill him?

"What did he do to hurt people?" she asked innocently.

Joan stared at her as if she might be simple. "You've met him! He was banned from all tournaments for breaking the rules. You yourself stopped him in the act of seducing a young woman. He was rude and loud and had to come first in everything. He treated us all like his servants and lately he'd been talking about taking control of Neversend and turning us all out of it—" Joan stopped. Perhaps she realized she might be going too far. "I mean, of course I loved him. He was my brother." Her words lacked conviction.

Ela remembered her mistrust of Agnes's mild feelings about him. "Did he ever do anything…inappropriate with Agnes?"

Joan gasped. "Did she say that?"

"No. She didn't. I'm just wondering as it seems like it might be in his character to make advances to her just as his older brother did."

"She has her child with her all the time. I think she wears him like a talisman of protection."

"Was Charibert kind to Charley?"

Now Joan hesitated. "No." Her gaze flicked around the room as if she were hunting for signs of how much information she should reveal.

"How did he treat him?"

"He scolded him for being loud and running and making a mess with his food. But they're all things he did himself at that age, some of which he still does—I mean did."

"Did he ever beat him?"

"Not that I saw. I doubt he'd have taken that much trouble with him." She paused and drew in a breath, then looked right at Ela. "He did call him "you little bastard," though. To his face."

Ela winced at the cruelty of it. "I suppose Charley was too young to understand the full meaning of that phrase."

"Oh no, he understood it. Charibert took great pains to explain it to him. He even used to torment him about his father being dead."

"How awful." Why had Agnes not mentioned any of this? "Did anyone try to stop him?"

"Yes. Our mother used to scold him terribly but he thought it was funny. He had a cruel streak."

Ela despised Charibert even more now that he was dead, if that was possible. She hated the idea that he could reach from beyond the grave to somehow destroy his mother's life. If anything, he deserved to die and the person that killed him was a sort of hero.

But she was the sheriff, not the justice at the assizes, and such determinations were not hers to make. "Will you testify at the trial?"

"Testify about what?"

"That your brother was very difficult to live with."

"What if they think I killed him?"

Such a thing was never impossible. What if the jury somehow found Mathilde sympathetic, with her gray-streaked hair and careworn face, and took against Joan with her confident manner and outspoken criticism of her brother?

"Who do you think killed him?"

Joan's gaze flickered, darting to the side. "If I only knew."

"If you only knew, then what?"

"Why, I'd bring him before you to take the punishment that might be meted out on my own dear mother!"

"It's important that you and Helene and Agnes are all

there to testify to her character. It's her best chance of escaping a conviction."

"You don't think Mother killed him, do you?"

No. But then who did?

ELA SPOKE TO THE SERVANTS, who were a motley assortment of the very young and the very old, as often found in a household where the pay was paltry and the prospects for improvement slim. None of them would breathe a word against Mathilde, and they could barely be persuaded to mutter a criticism of Charibert, either. They'd learned to hold their tongues and keep their heads down.

Ela suspected that anyone in the household had at least an iota of motive to wish the world rid of Charibert d'Albiac, but no one would admit to killing him and none of them stooped to point their finger at another.

WHEN A MESSENGER ANNOUNCED the date for the assizes, Ela wasn't sure whether to welcome the possibility of Mathilde's release from her grim dungeon or dread the awful possibility that it might be her last day on earth. No further evidence had emerged. Based on how the jury had reacted last time, she thought that there was a very real possibility Mathilde would find her neck in a noose.

The judge and his entourage arrived at the castle the day before the trial. The justice, Sir Michael de Braose, was settled into a comfortable chamber and his men billeted about the castle, some of them sleeping in the great hall. Ela knew little of Sir Michael except that he hailed from York-shire and that he'd fought with her husband in France at one point. He probably knew or cared little about the affairs of Wiltshire, let alone the events at remote and quiet Neversend.

She'd sent a carriage to Neversend to bring Petronella and Mathilde's daughters to the trial. Ela had asked her to bring Agnes as well, leaving Charley in the care of servants, but Petronella arrived with only Joan and Helene.

"Where's Agnes?" asked Ela, as Petronella bustled into the castle, shepherding her charges even though they were both almost grown women.

"She said Charley didn't feel well and she couldn't bear to leave him behind. I tried to convince her to bring him but she said he'd be a nuisance in the hall and I can't help but think she was right. He can be quite a boisterous young one. I suspect he has more than a dash of the d'Albiac spirit." She shot Ela a knowing glance.

"I do pray that you're wrong. The d'Albiac men seem to be doomed by their own hubris. It seems terrible to even imagine the same fate for an innocent boy."

"I pray for him nightly," said Petronella primly. "And all the rest of the household as well. There's a sense of impending doom there, as if the very walls of the house might crumble to dust. Mathilde is still alive to stand trial?"

Ela crossed herself. "Mind your tongue. I've taken special care that she receives proper food and warm clothing. She's bearing her ordeal bravely."

Elsie had led Mathilde's daughters across the hall and seated them to take some food after their journey. Petronella looked over at them and leaned in close to Ela. "What will happen to Joan and Helene if their mother is hanged tomorrow?"

"I suppose they shall be made wards," said Ela quietly. "Though since Neversend is not a profitable manor, I don't suppose nobles will be lining up to compete for the privilege." A wardship entitled the person granted it to collect all profits from the estate in exchange for providing the orphan or orphans care and sustenance of whatever kind was considered appropriate until their majority. Ela's husband had enjoyed several profitable wardships that Ela had swiftly transformed into marriages—to her own children—upon her husband's death. Her son William's bride Idonea was one of these former wards.

Already heaving with people, including the arriving jurors and curious villagers as well as the usual soldiers and staff, the hall grew louder as the time for the trial drew near. Still, a trumpet blast rose above the din and made Ela turn to face the door. Who was arriving now? Had her son William come to preside over the trial to see what happened to a woman who wished to keep control of her son's inheritance?

"Sir Hubert de Burgh!" announced Albert the porter.

Ela felt her mouth drop open. If only it were just her son William. Had de Burgh come for the same purpose? To make sure that Mathilde would hang for daring to maintain control over her own estate until she felt her son was ready to assume control? And to make sure that Ela watched it happen?

Her heart beat faster as de Burgh swept into the room, his green cloak flying out behind him and a cadre of well-dressed young men hurrying at his heels. He looked directly at Ela and a smirk tugged at his mouth. "My lady! I'm so glad I've arrived in time."

"Are you?" She said, forcing an icy smile. "Why, pray, does this small matter of the d'Albiac family feature on your crowded calendar?"

"It's a matter of principle, my dear," he said in his deep, rather menacing voice. "Of making sure that justice is done. A double murder, no less!"

"There's no evidence that she killed her husband—there's

not even a shred of evidence that he's actually dead. And no one in the household thinks that Mathilde d'Albiac killed her son. I interviewed all of them."

"Ah well, we shall see what the judge and jury have to make of the matter, shan't we?" He pulled off his great leather gloves and handed them to a page, then he took an offered cup of wine. "I look forward to watching the proceedings."

CHAPTER 16

*E*la had arranged for Elsie to attend to Mathilde to make her presentable for the jury. She wore a clean gown and fresh barbette and fillet that Petronella had brought for her from Neversend, and Ela could see that Elsie had pinched her cheeks to add some false color to her prison pallor.

The guards led Mathilde to the chair in the middle of the tables set up for the judge and jury. Another guard came forward carrying a heavy manacle with its clanking chain.

"That won't be necessary," said Ela.

"But my lady, the defendant is a double murderer!" exclaimed de Burgh, who watched from one side.

"An *accused* double murderer," she reminded him. "She has not been convicted of any crime and may be entirely innocent of the charges laid against her." Ela looked at the jury to see how this approach sat with them.

Their row of grim faces peered at Mathilde with suspicion that made Ela's heart sink. She had intended to introduce the case, to familiarize the judge with the charges and evidence at hand, but once de Burgh arrived she suspected it was best to pass the torch to Bill Talbot.

If de Burgh was indeed there to cast aspersions on her own attempts to hold onto her property in her husband's absence, she did not intend to help him hold up a lantern to her face. She'd tried to apprise Bill of the situation as thoroughly as she could, and prayed that he could remember the salient details well enough.

Bill rose to his feet. "Mathilde d'Albiac has presided over a series of misfortunes that would fell most of us. Her two oldest sons were killed at the siege of Bedford Castle and now her youngest, Charibert, was found dead—apparently poisoned—in his bed at home. Her husband has been missing for six years, during which time she's heard no word from him. Under these trying conditions, and with no great resources, Mathilde d'Albiac has managed to maintain the roof over the heads of her and her children and to produce a living from their manor. She's known locally as a pious and industrious mistress and lady of the manor, and is admired by all who speak of her."

Hubert de Burgh now stood. Ela felt a frown forming on her face and quickly endeavored to banish it. She didn't wish to let de Burgh know how much his presence irked her. He leaned forward. "Am I right in understanding that the suspicion exists that her husband has been missing without any word for six years because she may have killed him and buried him six years ago?"

"That suspicion has been raised," said Bill, with an expression of jovial disinterest. "Mostly in the absence of any reasonable explanation for his disappearance and long absence. It is odd indeed that the records of the king's garrison contain no notes on him being sent abroad to fight or on any other business."

"And he was known to be a gambler and a wastrel?" said

de Burgh. Ela cheered inwardly. She was glad that these unpleasant facts about Montaigu d'Albiac should enter into the record and the judge's ears.

"He was indeed known to be profligate and given to wagers," said Bill.

"And it's been said that he encouraged an attitude of rashness in his sons, such as they might be likely to risk their lives in battle at a young age?"

Bill stared at him, clearly wondering where he was going with this. "All men who fight for the king, or for their liege lord, are prepared to risk their life in battle." She didn't remember hearing his voice so deep.

"Of course, but perhaps Sir Montaigu did not prepare his sons as well as another father might have?" said de Burgh, with an odd little smile on his mouth. "Would you say this is true, mistress?" He turned his challenging gaze on Mathilde.

She shrank under it. "I couldn't say, my lord."

"But you might have cause to think, as you sit alone at night in the solitude of your manor house, that your husband might bear responsibility for the death of your two oldest sons?"

Mathilde's chest rose. "I never blamed him for their deaths. Any noble mother raises her sons to be ready to fight. If it's God's will that they shall rise to join him from the battlefield, then it is a mother's lot to accept it."

Good answer, thought Ela. She knew Mathilde wasn't stupid, despite her mild manner. Her measured response, spoken with calm and clarity, seemed to disarm de Burgh, who leaned back in his chair and looked toward Justice de Braose.

Ela turned her attention to the justice, whose salt-and-pepper brows lowered over his dark eyes. "My lady, I wish to give you the benefit of the doubt." An odd half-smile tightened his skin over his prominent cheekbones. "Where did you think that your husband had gone?"

"He traveled frequently on business of one kind or another. He liked to go into London to meet with friends."

"To drink and gamble and perhaps enjoy the company of whores?" The judge didn't change his tone at all for the last word, which tugged a gasp from Mathilde's lips. Ela's heart started pounding.

"I cannot say for certain what he did when he was away from home," she said more quietly than before.

"At what point did you become concerned about your husband's disappearance?"

Mathilde seemed to steel herself, straightening her back in the chair. "It was not unusual for him to be gone for two or three months at a time. Especially over the Christmas season when there were many amusements to be enjoyed in the city, or in the summer when there were tournaments and games of various kinds to draw his attention. When he did not return after four or five months I wrote to the address of one of his friends in London."

"Who was that?"

"Sir Garamond de Witt. He did not reply. I later learned that he had died in a horse-riding accident and that his house and its chattels had been sold to pay his debts and his remaining family had scattered."

"How sad!" said the justice, with odd emphasis. "Did this unhappy news perhaps frighten you into picturing such a terrible fate for your own small family?"

"I did not think of such things." Mathilde pressed her lips together. "I simply wondered what had become of my husband, since there was no news of him to be gleaned from his usual associates. One of them suggested that he may have traveled to Paris."

"Was he in the habit of visiting Paris?" asked the justice, with a raised eyebrow.

Mathilde shook her head. "Though he did enjoy travel and adventure, so it wasn't difficult to believe."

Ela glanced at the jury, who—almost to a man—wore doubtful expressions. She had to admit Mathilde did seem willfully simple to accept that her husband had gone into town and vanished for six years but that nothing was wrong and she should quietly wait for his return.

"At what point did you report your husband's disappearance to the sheriff?" asked the justice.

"I didn't. It was my son Charibert who told the sheriff about it."

"Because he believed his father was dead," cut in de Burgh briskly. "Having attained his majority, the younger d'Albiac wished to claim his inheritance."

Ela bristled. She would have preferred for Bill to explain that part of the case, as he no doubt planned to, but de Burgh had rudely interrupted the proceedings before he had the chance.

Justice de Braose peered at Mathilde as if she were some strange creature that had crawled into his courtroom. "So, you never—in all six years of his disappearance—thought to report that your husband was missing and launch an official inquiry into his whereabouts?"

"No." Mathilde's whisper had an undertone of guilt. Even Ela could see that such deliberate ignorance was inappropriate. If Mathilde had cared about her husband even one whit, she would have raised an alarm after a year or so of his absence.

"Sir Hubert suggested that your husband was a gambler and a wastrel—I believe those were his words. Is this true?"

Mathilde nodded.

"Did he also drink to excess?"

"Yes," she said quietly.

"Was he a careful steward of his manor and its inhabitants and its flocks and fields?"

"No." Mathilde spoke so softly that Ela could barely hear her.

"Did you perhaps live in fear that he might wager the roof over your heads in a drunken game of dice?"

Mathilde brightened. "I did sometimes worry that he would lose everything. He gambled away two smaller manors that his mother had left him."

"How have you managed in his absence? Did you hire a steward?"

"There wasn't enough money to pay a man's wage, so I learned myself as best I could. I consulted with the shepherds and the wool tradesman and spoke to the village farmers about which crops to grow and the best times to sow seed and harvest." Ela could tell that Mathilde was proud of her accomplishments. As well she might be. Ela had done the same despite considerable difficulties in persuading men to share their valuable hard-earned knowledge with a mere woman.

"Ah," the justice smiled. "So you found yourself to be a better steward of your husband's estate than he had ever been."

"After some time, yes, I did."

"And no doubt you preferred a peaceful and profitable existence, enjoying his manor in his absence, without any of his drunken nonsense?" He was encouraging her.

Ela's gut clenched. She prayed Mathilde wouldn't fall into his trap.

She didn't. Her brightness faded as she realized what the justice was up to. "I simply wished to keep a roof over my children's heads."

De Burgh looked around the room. "Naturally one

wonders if Mistress d'Albiac grew so tired of her husband's poor management and drunken wastefulness, that she decided to send him away on a long journey—to meet his Maker."

Mathilde's eyes widened. Ela half hoped she'd cry out in the process, but she didn't have a demonstrative temperament.

"How did you kill him?" asked de Burgh. "Poison, I'd suspect, as it's a woman's wont to kill without violence and bloodshed."

Is that why you poisoned my husband? Ela's chest filled with rage toward de Burgh. Her husband William's agonizing death still haunted her nightmares…slow and painful and filled with remorse and desperate pleadings to a God he'd ignored many times over the years. *My William would have killed you within moments in hand-to-hand combat.*

"I didn't kill my husband! I'd never kill anyone."

One of the jurors observed that they'd searched the grounds of Neversend for his body and not found it. He did mention that they had found the body of a woman, who turned out to be a serving girl.

"Was this missing serving girl's absence reported to the sheriff?" asked the justice of Mathilde.

Mathilde swallowed. "No. We all thought she'd gone home to her family."

The justice let out a snort of derision. "As a mistress, you seem remarkably careless of those in your care. Three sons dead, a murdered servant and your husband missing for years?"

Tears filled Mathilde's eyes. As well they might. This was going very badly for her.

"My two eldest sons died fighting with great courage in the siege of Bedford Castle," she protested.

"Fighting for our king or against him?"

Two tears rolled over Mathilde's cheeks. "They were on the side of Falkes de Breauté, an old associate of their father's. I realize now it was the wrong side, but neither I nor they knew that at the time. My husband insisted they were ready to fight."

"I'm afraid such a miscalculation on his part only strengthens your motivation for ridding the world of him."

"I'd never kill my husband! I don't wish to suffer the eternal torment of hellfire." Mathilde sobbed. Ela glanced at her daughters, who stared open-mouthed, too horror-struck even for tears.

THE BRUTAL QUESTIONING by both the judge and de Burgh had tipped the scales against Mathilde. The jurors now regarded her with derision, and as the judge questioned them about the case they seemed unwilling to utter a word in her defense.

"Let us not forget that her son had raised a suit against her, insisting that he was in his majority and should inherit the estate since his father was almost certainly dead," said de Burgh. Silver shone in his dark hair. "I can't say I blame him. How long should a son be forced to wait for his mother to decide that it's time to step aside?" The question might be considered rhetorical, but he asked it of the judge as if it were a genuine inquiry.

Justice de Braose peered down at Mathilde. "It's customary for a son to inherit when he attains his majority. For what reason did you withhold his rights?"

Mathilde, now something of a quivering wreck, dabbed at her face with her handkerchief. "He was impulsive, my lord," she stammered. "He possessed the chief fault of his father, and of his brothers—that of wanting to rush in unprepared despite the risk."

"I dare say that, as his mother, you bear some blame for his shortcomings. Could you not have trained him in forbearance and discipline?" The justice gazed along the length of his nose.

Mathilde's lips moved and Ela suspected that if she could find words she might have agreed with him. "Perhaps I should have been firmer with him...with all of them..." she blurted eventually. "I have many regrets. I hoped to prevent Charibert from losing the estate or ruining it with the rash impetuousness of youth."

"From the sound of it, your husband never grew out of such follies," said de Burgh. "Would you have continued to withhold the estate until he was forty, perhaps? Or fifty?"

I would, thought Ela. Why should a foolish man of any age imperil the fortunes of his family when a perfectly capable woman could manage them in his stead?

"Ela," said de Burgh, turning his grim smile on her. "I know your son William rankles similarly in his wish to assume the mantle of Earl of Salisbury and to take command of this castle. Why do you keep him from his patrimony?"

Perhaps he hoped that she'd openly identify with Mathilde—which she certainly did privately—but she had no wish to put her head in a noose even by proxy. "The situation is rather different in my case, my lord. I am countess *suo jure* as I inherited the title directly from my father. It is thus mine —by right—to keep until I see fit to relinquish it." She fought to keep her voice from trembling, even though it was with rage rather than terror. "As you are aware, I made arrange-ments with the king that confirm the matter."

At this moment, Ela hated de Burgh with such force that the heat of it might even condemn her soul to hell. She craved the solitude of the chapel to beg forgiveness for her sins of pride and anger.

"Mathilde, did you inherit Neversend from your father?" asked de Braose.

"I did not," said Mathilde quietly. "My husband inherited it from his father."

"How old was he at that time?"

"I believe he was twenty-four. We'd been married for three years."

"Was his mother living at that time?" asked de Braose.

"Yes, she lived with us until her death."

"So such an arrangement—typical and appropriate—did not occur to you?"

"I still have two daughters who are in their minority." Mathilde gestured toward Joan and Helene. Their faces were now crumpled and wet with tears. "Their brother said on more than one occasion that he would be sure to turn us all out into the street at his first opportunity."

De Braose's eyes widened. "Surely not! Were there any witnesses to such a statement?"

Mathilde shook her head. "He said it only to me."

"That's not true, Mother," said Helene, in a broken voice. "I heard him say it."

"Don't speak out of turn!" cried de Braose. "Who is this girl?"

"She is Helene d'Albiac, Charibert's sister," said Ela. "Let us call her as a witness." She prayed that Helene could somehow stem the tide that was sweeping Mathilde's prospects of survival out to sea.

"It hardly seems relevant," scoffed de Burgh. "A daughter is always going to speak up for her mother even if she's seen her commit an act of murder with her own eyes."

A sob escaped from Helene's mouth.

"I'm interested to hear what she has to say," said de Braose. "Come forward, girl!"

Helene shuffled forward until she was standing just a few feet from her mother, in between the tables of jurors.

"Do you believe your father is still alive?" he asked. "Answer the truth in the sight of God."

Helene hesitated, then shook her head. "No. He's been gone too long. I suspect he's perished."

"Do you think your mother might have killed him to wrest control of the estate from his poor management?"

"No, my lord," said Helene quickly. "She would never hurt a soul."

"Do you not find it remarkable that your father died mysteriously and now your brother is dead as well?"

"All three of my brothers are dead," said Helene. "The villagers say my family is cursed."

"Cursed?" de Braose exclaimed the word so loud that Ela jumped in her chair. "Do you believe in such witchery and suspicion?"

"No." Ela heaved a sigh of relief that Helene had said the sensible thing. "I think it's terribly bad luck."

"You think it's bad luck that your brother was poisoned?" de Braose looked astonished. "I consider a poisoning to be a lot more than bad luck." He turned to Giles Haughton, who sat off to one side. "You are sure it was a poisoning, are you not?"

"Indeed I am," said Sir Giles. "The sudden demise of a man in perfect health always raises the specter of poison. Add to that the vomitus on the pillow and a post mortem examination that showed his heart to be structurally normal in every way."

"Was your brother a difficult young man?" asked de Braose.

"He could be selfish," she said quietly. "As many young men his age are."

"Are they indeed?" de Braose raised a brow. "Countess Ela, you have several sons, I believe. Do you find them to be selfish louts?"

"No, my lord." There was no other answer she could give under the circumstances. "But her brother committed an outrage against my son at the tournament at Wilton, and was subsequently banned from fighting in any more tournaments this year." She was tempted to mention the incident with the Wimberley girl and Sir Godfrey, but she suspected it would just confuse the issues at hand without providing relief for Mathilde.

"Were you concerned that your brother was pursuing a suit to wrest the estate from his mother and to throw all the womenfolk out of the manor?"

"I did pray that he wouldn't succeed," admitted Helene.

"You prayed for his failure?" again de Braose seemed astonished at her audacity. "Did you perhaps ensure his failure and safeguard your own place in your home by poisoning him yourself?"

"No!" cried Mathilde. "She never did."

Helene was too shocked to respond. Her lips quivered and tears fell from her eyes.

"How can you be so sure?" asked de Braose of Mathilde. "Are you certain she is innocent because you yourself are guilty?"

Mathilde didn't say anything. Her face took on a blank look of resignation. Maybe she realized that if she went to the gallows, at least her daughters would be spared that fate.

Did one of them kill Charibert? It was hard to imagine who else might have poisoned him.

As a mother, Ela could imagine making the difficult but brave choice to save your child's life when your own was already half over. She found it hard to imagine covering up for someone who'd committed the crime of murder, even if that person was her own child, but perhaps if the reason for the killing was good enough...

De Braose questioned Joan and asked the jury to share any further information they might have on the matter. The jurors unfortunately persisted in their suspicion of Mathilde, perhaps deepened by the aspersions de Burgh cast on her.

Ela wanted to speak up, to remind them that she was considered blameless and faultless by all those who knew her well. But this would require sticking her own neck out and she felt sure that de Burgh would waste no time fashioning a noose around it if she gave him half a chance.

"In the absence of any other suspects, and considering the motivation that Mathilde d'Albiac had to keep control of the family estates, and on the evidence and opinions of these jurors who've taken the time to acquaint themselves with the case, I must find Mathilde d'Albiac guilty of the murders of her husband, Montaigu d'Albiac, and her son, Charibert d'Albiac." De Braose paused for breath. "She shall hang by the neck until she is dead."

Joan and Helene sent up terrible moans that echoed off the stone walls of the hall.

Ela's heart pounded. She felt sure that this was a terrible miscarriage of justice, but she had no evidence to present in support of that claim.

"Do you have anything to say to the court before you are taken away?"

"Could I see my grandson one last time?"

"Your grandson?" de Braose furrowed his brows. "I

thought all your sons died unmarried and your daughters are still children."

"Charley is my grandson. He's the child of my maid Agnes. My son Alain lay with her before he was killed."

De Braose made a sound of disgust. "Does this family have no sense of common decency?" Even the jurors muttered among themselves.

"He's just a little boy, protested Ela. "And the girl, his mother, was an innocent party cruelly used by a callous youth." If word must be sent to Neversend, then Agnes and Charley brought to Salisbury, that could delay Mathilde's execution by a day or more. Ela still prayed for a miracle to intervene and save Mathilde—and by extension her two surviving daughters, not to mention Agnes and Charley— from being abandoned to the cursed fate of being related to a double murderess. If they did even manage to hold onto the estate in the face of inevitable legal challenges by distant male relatives, they'd lack the experience to keep it from falling into ruin without their mother's guidance.

"If the boy is bastard-born he's not your real grandson," said de Braose dismissively.

Fury spiked in Ela. "Many a fine man is bastard-born and claimed by his relatives no matter how great," she said, almost under her breath. "I believe you knew my late husband, Sir William Longespée?"

De Braose's eyes widened. "Your husband was a great man, my lady."

Everyone knew her husband was King Henry II's bastard…which, admittedly was not quite the same as being the unwed offspring of any Tom, Dick or Harry, but the principle remained the same.

The justice hesitated, probably fearing to offend Ela by insulting her late husband's memory. "All right, I agree to let the grandson visit if he can be brought here tomorrow. He can spend time with her, but she will be hanged before the end of the day whether he arrives here or not."

Ela let out a breath she didn't realize she'd been holding. A reprieve of one day—what did it matter? But her gut told her it did. She turned to the guard standing nearest. "Send our fastest messenger to Neversend and tell him to return with the girl and her son at speed."

CHAPTER 17

*E*la made arrangements for Helene and Joan to share a chamber in the castle overnight. Petronella took charge of the weeping girls and prayed with them in the chapel. Ela admired the way she didn't shrink from the difficult task of attempting to console them in the face of disaster.

Ela spent most of the evening on her knees in the chapel, praying for guidance. After all her children had gone to their rooms for the night, Ela summoned Bill to join her in the hall for a cup of wine. "What is to be done, Bill? I feel sure that a terrible miscarriage of justice will take place when Mathilde is hanged."

She didn't add that her prayers had gone unanswered. Bill observed the ordinary rituals of the church but she'd observed over the years that he wasn't a deeply religious man. She didn't want to shake his already questionable faith.

"You've done everything you could. It's in the hands of the Lord, now."

Ela stared in surprise at his unusually pious answer.

"Surely the Lord can't want an innocent woman to hang in front of her young daughters?"

"It's not our lot to know what the Lord does and doesn't want, my lady. Perhaps he wishes to call her to his side."

"Like he called my dear William to his side." She said prayers daily in the hope that William was indeed in God's kingdom and not in some darker place. He'd repented his sins in terror during his final days, knowing that he'd lived a life with the seven deadly sins as part of its daily fabric. She prayed that the monastery built in his name, where monks would pray daily for the passage of his soul to Heaven, would provide the relief he sought.

Bill's fatalistic attitude should have soothed her, but it didn't. "And now little Charley will have to say goodbye to his dear grandmother. I will make sure that he is kept in the castle and under Elsie's care during the hanging. No child should witness such a terrible sight."

IT WAS ALMOST midday before Agnes and Charley arrived, seated tandem on a horse being led by a guard. Ela rushed out into the courtyard at the announcement of their arrival. Another guard lifted them down one by one and apologized profusely for the delay.

"I'm sorry it took so long, my lady." He was a brusque man in his thirties with a deep groove between his dark brows. "We set out in the cart, but an axle broke near Dinton. We were unable to get it repaired in time, so we left it by the side of the road. The girl and her child sat on the horse while we walked alongside it. The journey took a lot longer than anticipated."

"I understand," said Ela. She glanced at Charley, who played with a small wooden object he'd brought. It looked like a homemade horse or donkey. He seemed barely aware of the busy castle courtyard.

Agnes on the other hand, looked like she'd been struck by lightning and barely survived. Her face was white except for red-rimmed eyes and unnaturally red lips as if she'd been biting or chewing at them. "I need to speak to you alone," she rasped, staring at Ela with eyes that looked like they'd seen the dead.

"Perhaps we should visit Mathilde first," said Ela, knowing how anxious Mathilde was to lay eyes on Charley. She'd hoped they could at least spend some time together before Mathilde was taken away to the gallows.

"No! Please, no. Let me speak with you."

Ela looked around at the courtyard, where two men were unloading a cartload of small barrels—possibly ale—and soldiers stood around in groups. Where was Elsie? "Come into the castle."

She bustled Agnes and Charley in through the great door —they'd brought no baggage at all—and she handed Charley into the care of her youngest daughter Ellie, telling her not to take her eyes off him for an instant as young boys could get into mischief in the blink of an eye. Then she led Agnes into the armory and closed the door.

Agnes looked around at all the sharp weapons gleaming on the walls and burst into tears.

"You've heard that Mathilde will hang today," said Ela softly. "She wanted to say goodbye to Charley, and you, of course."

"You must kill me instead!" cried Agnes, so loud that Ela started.

"Why?" An uneasy sensation stirred inside her.

"Because I killed Charibert. I poisoned him with stalks and leaves of wolfsbane that I found in the woods and ground up with the cook's pestle." She stopped and looked at

Ela as if waiting to see if she believed her. "I scrubbed the pestle and mortar clean afterward and buried the unused leaves under a bush in the garden."

"If this is true, why didn't you confess when I interviewed you at the house?"

"I never thought that they'd find Mathilde guilty! How could they? Look at how she's taken care of me and my boy when many would have turned us out to starve. No normal woman could have suffered the harsh whims of fate the way she has. I was sure she'd be let off and I didn't want my boy to be left motherless."

At first Ela wondered if this wasn't some misguided attempt to save Mathilde by claiming a crime she didn't commit. But she thought it very unlikely that Agnes would choose to abandon her child. "But why would you kill Charibert?"

"Why?" Agnes almost screamed it. "He was a loathsome piece of scum. He abused me and Charley daily—calling my son a bastard day and night and explaining exactly what it meant. And then last year he started raping me. He's strong and quick and I tried to fight him off but I couldn't."

Ela's heart sank. "Helene and Joan swore that he hadn't harmed you or them. I did ask as I know from personal experience what kind of character Charibert possessed."

"I didn't tell them or Mathilde. I couldn't! Who would they turn out of the house? They couldn't throw Charibert out because it was *his house*! Instead, he hoped to shove all the rest of us out onto the street."

Her skin stretched taut across her face and her eyes glowed like a person possessed. "After he came back from making his suit at the castle, to claim his rights—as he said— he gloated over all of us and said it was only a matter of time before our few possessions would be piled onto a cart and that he'd personally drag it off the manor and erect a high fence to keep us out!"

Ela wondered if the jury would be inclined to clemency if they knew Charibert had raped her. "How many times did he force himself on you?" she asked softly.

"Countless," said Agnes through quivering lips. "A hundred or more. He even did it with Charley right there in the room some nights." Tears rolled down her pale cheeks. "I'm pregnant with his child."

Ela glanced at her waist and noticed—for the first time—that the folds of her robe gathered around a more-than-slightly distended belly. With her years of experience, Ela guessed that she was about six months along. "Did no one notice that you're with child?"

Agnes shook her head. "My belly never went back to being flat after Charley. It's only just starting to swell more than usual and I think they've had too much else to worry about."

Something occurred to Ela. "Do any of the others—Mathilde or Helene or Joan—know that you murdered Charibert?"

Agnes hesitated. "I don't know if they guessed it. I didn't tell them. They never accused me."

"You'll have to come in front of the jury and say all of this or Mathilde will be hanged today."

"I know." She swayed slightly. "I was sure they'd let her go. Now I will hang and I suppose I deserve it. I've already condemned my soul to hell."

Sorrow pinched at Ela's heart. She might well hang before the week was out, if not before today's sunset. A confessed murderer was an easy target. "I pray the justice will see that you were provoked beyond reason."

"I doubt it. I'm a servant and Charibert d'Albiac was my

master. I'm supposed to quietly submit to his attentions. I know that because I did it before, seven years ago."

"That's not true! What he did was wrong and reprehensible. And his cruelty to your son only twisted the knife he'd already stuck in you."

"What will become of Charley?" Agnes's voice sounded thin. "Mathilde will hate him now that I've murdered her son."

Ela inhaled slowly. While she didn't think Mathilde would take her anger out on the child, it was possible that she wouldn't want to show any more clemency to Agnes. Mathilde had indeed loved her wayward youngest son despite all his faults. Ela had no doubt of that.

"The Lord shall determine his fate, along with all of ours. Will you say a prayer with me?"

A tear rolled over Agnes's cheek and she nodded silently.

MATHILDE WAS FREED IMMEDIATELY after Agnes's confession before the jury. Her innocence in Charibert's death somehow absolved her of suspicion in Montaigu's disappearance as well. She rushed into the arms of her weeping daughters. Ela had instructed Elsie to look after Charley for the time being, and she kept him busy and distracted while his mother was put into the chains that Mathilde had worn.

"Mathilde d'Albiac," called the justice. Mathilde, barely out of her rusty irons, twitched as if she might be put back in them. "Please come before the jury and share your opinion of this girl who freely admits to killing your son."

Mathilde blinked and pushed back a stray lock of hair that had fallen in front of her eyes. She came forward, walking woodenly as if she wasn't quite sure of her footing. She glanced at Agnes and sorrow filled her gaze. "Agnes is like a daughter to me. As you know, her son Charley is my grandson. I'm devastated to learn that two of my sons have taken advantage of her but filled with hope that she carries another grandchild who will bring joy into our household."

Ela looked at the justice's face. Mathilde was suggesting that Agnes should live to bear this child, instead of being hanged before dusk.

"Are you not angry with her for killing your only surviving son?" asked de Braose, a deep furrow between his heavy brows.

"I feel deep sadness, not anger. I'm sad to lose my son and sad that Agnes has suffered so much at his hands. I don't think she deserves to die." Mathilde said the last part quietly. "I pray that she will be spared and that I shall meet my new grandchild."

De Braose sat silent for a long while. "The girl shall remain alive, but under arrest, until she is delivered of the child. At that time we shall convene again to decide her fate."

"The dungeon is no place for a pregnant woman," said Ela, feeling a spark of hope. "She shall stay under lock and key in a room in the castle. We have several such fortified chambers. Her young son can stay with her."

Mathilde looked relieved that Ela had taken on the responsibility. No doubt she needed time to recover from her imprisonment and the shocking revelation that Agnes had killed her son.

"Mathilde d'Albiac, it seems that the Lord has offered you a reprieve from a fate that seemed certain." De Braose didn't look particularly happy about this. "You may now return to your manor and govern it in the manner you see fit, at least until any further male claimants press their suit."

Ela bristled at his last words. Why should some distant male cousin have any claim at all over the estate that

Mathilde had nurtured? Still, she was alive and might well get to live there unmolested for the rest of her life.

"I'm glad that Agnes's confession has prevented what might have been a tragic miscarriage of justice," said Ela, looking hard at the jurors. The justice only knew what they and Ela told him of the case, and what he discovered by his questioning. It was often the opinion of the jurors that decided a case, and they had taken against Mathilde almost from the start.

Though she had herself to blame as well. She had questioned all of them and had never even seriously considered the possibility that Agnes had killed Charibert.

"May I say something, my lord?" asked Mathilde, in a tremulous voice.

"You may." He regarded her with some surprise, as if a child had suddenly spoken up.

"I am mortified to learn that my son Charibert has taken advantage of Agnes. I want you to know that I don't blame her for what she did. I blame myself for not realizing that such an atrocity was occurring under my roof for a second time. I am sure that he provoked her beyond reason and that his death was in part earned by his brutal and unwarranted actions."

A murmur rose from the jury. Even Ela was shocked by this statement. She knew that Mathilde cared for Agnes, but this suggested that she valued her life even above that of her son.

"Even though she is a mother-to-be, she is still a murderer," said Justice de Braose curtly. "And look to your own safety before you worry about that of others. I'm sure the jury has not forgotten about your husband's disappearance. While there exists no evidence that you killed him, there is also no proof that you didn't."

~

LESS THAN A MONTH LATER, Mathilde appeared in Ela's hall one midday, with her daughter Helene in tow. "My husband is returned, my lady."

Ela stared at her for some moments, trying to fathom this unexpected turn of events. "Such good news," she finally said, knowing it wasn't. Perhaps Montaigu d'Albiac's taste for gambling and dissipation had altered during the years of his absence.

"I suppose I can't be accused of killing him now," said Mathilde. "So that, at least, is good news." Her white face and wide eyes did not suggest jubilation at his return. "But he's brought a foreign woman with him and installed her in my house!"

Ela's heart sank. "Who is this woman?"

"Her name is Bricea, or something like that anyway, and she doesn't speak a word of English. She's barely older than my daughters."

"Is she a servant of some kind?" asked Ela hopefully.

Mathilde hesitated and her lips quivered. "No, my lady. He touches her with familiarity, and she returns his affections. It's clear that their relationship is...immoral."

"Oh dear."

"Is there something I can do?" Mathilde looked at her imploringly. "To make her go away?"

Ela suddenly remembered the Greek legend of Agamemnon who'd brought a foreign mistress home to his wife after many years away at war. She'd heard it sung by a minstrel some years ago, in King John's court. She couldn't remember the exact details of what happened in the tale, except that everyone ended up dead. "Perhaps your local priest could have a word with your husband and remind him of his marriage vows."

"Montaigu would never let a priest pass the entrance to the property. He calls them thieves and scoundrels for the tithes they demand every year."

Ela racked her brain for any similar situation that might suggest a course of action. "I suppose you could bring a suit for abandonment and seek a divorce, but then he'd almost certainly retain the estate. He'd likely be ordered to pay you a sum to keep you and I'm sure he'd make the process as diffi-cult as possible so I can't say I'd recommend it." In addition to financial difficulties with the meager estate and her awful husband, Mathilde would find that the world did not look kindly on a divorced woman.

"Am I supposed to accept this…adulterous relationship taking place under my roof?"

"No." Ela was still blindsided by Montaigu's reappearance after six years. "I shall come speak with him myself and, in the meantime, I shall consult with legal experts about what might be done to compel him to send her away."

"I didn't think things could get worse," wailed Mathilde softly. "But this is so much worse. He seems to have money. He brought with him cartloads of possessions that he has brought back from the continent. But his habits haven't changed. He's drinking himself into a stupor nightly and I'm sure it's only a matter of time before he'll find some gambling partners and wager his way into penury again."

"Did he say how he acquired his newfound wealth?"

"He only said that it's none of my business."

"He will find that it's the king's business, as taxes will be owed on his riches. And tithes to the church as well!" Ela suddenly relished sharing this information with the infa-mous Montaigu d'Albiac. And she intended to bring Bill and a good number of guards with her when she did.

CHAPTER 18

*E*la set out early the next day, riding Freya with her entourage in tow. It was a warm sunny day and a pleasure to trot along the firm, dry roads. Wildflowers bloomed in the hedgerows and bees buzzed about gathering pollen.

Bill was glad of the opportunity to enjoy the countryside on his fine bay palfrey. "I can scarcely believe the man is alive. Six years is a long time to disappear from civilization."

"I'd hardly believe it myself except that my own dear husband was missing, and presumed by many to be dead, for a full year himself."

"But he was injured and unable to communicate with you."

"Perhaps Montaigu was similarly incapacitated. Though I suspect it more likely that he found himself enjoying a life of debauchery in a foreign city and found no need to alert anyone to his whereabouts."

"Then why would he come back now?" asked Bill.

"Well, his youngest son did just reach his majority. Perhaps Montaigu suspected—correctly as it turns out—that his son would try to have him declared dead so he could inherit and do as he pleased with the manor and all its chattels."

"Ah, that makes sense," said Bill. "And instead of abandoning his illicit pleasures he simply brought them back to England with him. Is there really nothing that can be done to compel him to remove this woman from the house?"

"It's a difficult situation. I'm sure the queens of England would no doubt have preferred their royal husbands not to stray and produce so many illegitimate children with their many mistresses, but their lack of success is evident. If a husband chooses indecent behavior, there's little that his wife can do but leave and return to her parents or attempt to divorce her husband—which often ends in suffering and blame for her."

"Divorce might be the best course of action for Mathilde d'Albiac," said Bill.

"Peasant women sue and win divorces from their wayward or useless husbands so they can marry again," said Ela. She'd presided over two divorces herself. "But, in such cases, there's no property involved and if there was they'd have to leave the marriage without it. Poor Mathilde is not likely to find another husband if she has no property—and the Neversend property is too small to divide appropriately —so a divorce might guarantee her destitution. I want to lay eyes on this Montaigu d'Albiac who's been the subject of so much discussion in his absence. I shall see what I make of him."

~

NEVERSEND HAD A MORE chaotic air to it than usual. Even the chickens clucking around the house flapped their wings and scratched at the ground as if harried by fresh cares. The squat manor house bore the air of semi-neglect that Ela had learned to respect as frugality. While she took pride in the bright whitewashed walls of her properties, such a display was not always the best expenditure from a smaller purse.

Mathilde appeared in the doorway as their horses clip-clopped up the lane. She glanced behind her nervously, then hurried outside. "I'm afraid of how he'll respond when he sees you."

Ela was more worried about how he'd treat Mathilde after they left. "Where is he?"

"He's upstairs in the bedchamber. He was up late drinking and carousing last night and sleeps through most of the morning."

"Shall we surprise him there?" asked Ela, hoping she wouldn't be subject to a spectacle of debauchery.

"What's all that noise out there?" A rough male voice above their heads tugged their gaze to an upper window. A man stuck out a tousled head of black and gray hair.

"I am Ela Longespée, High Sheriff of Wiltshire, and I wish to speak with you. You've been a subject of much discussion in my hall, due to your long disappearance and the death of your son Charibert."

"Go away," he growled.

"Not until you've spoken with me."

"Will you arrest me if I don't?" he sneered.

"Perhaps I shall," said Ela, as calmly as she could.

"You'd better get your shackles ready then," he said. He slammed the wooden shutter.

"Oh dear," whispered Mathilde. "He's always difficult."

But he came downstairs before they had a chance to discuss arresting him. He'd dressed in haste and his hair stuck out from his head, but his clothes were fine and with a foreign flair. The decorative ribbon around the neck and hem of his dark gray tunic had a pattern unlike any Ela had seen before. His shoes were new, of neat, dark leather with decorative stitching. With his dark hair and slightly beaky features, he didn't look anything like his son Charibert, but his eyes did have the same insolent glare to them.

"Your long absence led many to presume you were dead. Where were you for the last six years?"

"Here and there." His rough voice contained no hint of the nervousness some men might feel at being roused from their bed by the sheriff.

"For what purpose did you originally go abroad? The king's clerk consulted his records and we found no record of you traveling with an army."

"I went away on my own business." He stared hard at her, his gaze growing ruder. Ela suspected that it had just sunk in that he was being cross-questioned by a woman, and he was not used to treating women with respect, let alone courtesy.

"And what business was that?"

"None of your business." He lifted his chin, which bore a salt and pepper stubble.

"Ah, but it is. I am the king's representative and it is very much my business to know what his subjects are doing and what goods and chattels and riches they have returned, with —that King Henry III may collect his fair share of them."

"Over my dead body," he sneered.

That can be arranged. Fury welled in Ela's chest, at this man's arrogance and the immense amount of suffering that he'd caused—so far—during his few decades of life.

"And tithes will be due to the abbey," she said with a half-smile. "But for now I have a more pressing concern. I hear that you have brought a woman back with you and are keeping her in your house as if she were a second wife."

He burst out laughing, a bone-chilling guffaw that made Mathilde shiver. "A second wife? Would that such a thing were allowed in dear old England. I should move to the

Barbary Coast where rumor has it a man can keep as many wives as he pleases."

"Perhaps you should, but in the meantime, you are in Wiltshire and must abide by the laws and customs of this county."

"I think you'll find I'm hardly the only man in Wiltshire who warms his bed with someone other than his wife." His gaze challenged her to argue with him.

She couldn't. Her own husband had cheated on her—more than once—and she knew it. "How do you think your long-suffering wife feels about this callous behavior?"

"Long-suffering? She's been living in the lap of luxury from what I see here."

"You should be grateful that she's made such fine work of running the estate. You might have come back to find the roof fallen in and the land waist-high in weeds."

"You're right." A slow smile crept across his mouth. His casual expression unleashed an eerie feeling inside her. "I am grateful that now I can sell the estate for an even prettier penny than I had imagined."

"Sell it?" Ela glanced at Mathilde, whose mouth fell open. "Why would you sell it?"

"I find moveable goods more convenient. I shall sell up and return to the continent where the weather and the manner of living are more to my liking."

"But you can't!" bleated Mathilde. "What will become of me and the girls?"

"Apparently you're more resourceful than I'd reckoned. I'm sure you'll all find yourselves husbands in no time."

"I can't marry anyone else when I'm still married to you."

"I won't divorce you," he said calmly. "Or the judge would order me to pay you a king's ransom to buy my freedom."

"Where were you living on the continent?" Ela had a

feeling she'd be sending envoys out to hunt him down there in the near future.

"Wouldn't you like to know," he said, his eyes crinkling with twisted delight. "But no. I shall keep my little paradise to myself."

"The girls need their father," said Mathilde weakly.

"No, they don't. They're better off without me." He looked pleased by the idea.

His brazen carelessness infuriated Ela. "Are you not saddened by the death of your son Charibert?"

"Can't say I am. I came to take back the estate and sell it before he could claim it for himself. If he were here I might even have to fight him for it." He looked amused by the prospect.

"You're a monster," hissed Ela. She couldn't contain her contempt for this man. "Did you kill Cathy Cross?"

"Who?" He flicked at an imaginary mote on his sleeve.

"Cathy Cross. A servant girl whose body we found buried in your grounds." Ela could hear the edge in her voice. "You are taking pains to demonstrate to me that you are heartless and cruel with no compunction for youth or frailty. Your daughters said that the girl's demeanor changed and she became agitated and distant. Perhaps you had your way with her then disposed of her like a dog that will no longer hunt?"

Did his expression betray surprise or guilt? It was hard to tell. She'd certainly caught him off guard.

"I don't even remember her."

"Don't think that doesn't mean I can't prosecute you for killing her if I choose to." She glared back at him.

He returned her gaze without flinching. "You wouldn't dare."

Ela considered this a thrown gauntlet, but knew she had to gather evidence and warm up a jury before making the accusation. "Did you know that your son Charibert impregnated the girl Agnes, who already bore a son for your son Alain?"

"How could I not? The news is all over the south of England. She killed him. She should hang for her crime."

She probably will. Though Ela was still building a case for clemency. "She's been given a reprieve until the birth."

"And the boy will come to me and Mathilde?" He lifted a brow.

"I suppose so," she said reluctantly. "You are his closest relatives." That poor babe, especially if his mother were to hang. "But how can that be if you mean to sell the estate and abandon your wife and children?"

"My plans are not yet final," he said slowly, as if weighing his options.

What horrible scheme is he concocting?

"I could take care of the babe," said Mathilde. "I could hire a wet nurse, if Agnes—is gone."

"Yes, that would be the most sensible course," said Ela "And I hope you would raise little Charley to adulthood as well."

"Oh yes," said Mathilde earnestly. "He's my grandson."

Montaigu snorted. "Little bastard. I've never even laid eyes on him."

"I'm surprised at your disdain," said Ela. "He's all that's left of your dead son."

"Like father, like son," he said, more gleeful than rueful. "I always was a lusty lad myself. Some things never change, I suppose."

Ela's stomach couldn't take much more of this. Short of arresting him there was nothing she could do to stop him ranting and cursing and making outrageous statements. And, at least for now, she didn't have grounds to arrest him.

"Mathilde, take heart, I shall return. And I shall ask a local priest to come pray with you."

Mathilde's expression showed alarm rather than comfort.

"I'll strangle him with his own cincture," snarled Montaigu. "Don't send any prayers or praters to my house or you'll regret it."

Ela wished she could take Mathilde with her. It pained her to think of leaving her vulnerable young daughters in the house with such a man and his strumpet. But again, she had no legal grounds to do so. "God be with you, Mathilde, for you will surely need Him."

ELA SUMMONED a small jury the following morning and attempted to drum up their support for arresting Montaigu on a charge of almost any kind.

"Is there a law against a man taking a mistress?" asked Paul Dunstan, the miller.

"God's law," said Ela. "Thou shalt not commit adultery."

"There's some space between God's law and man's law, for better or worse," mumbled farmer Peter Hogg. "His wife should lodge a complaint."

"She did. She came to my hall for that purpose two days ago."

"Is she seeking a divorce?"

"I couldn't recommend that course of action, but perhaps that would be for the best." If Montaigu intended to sell the manor and flee the country again, Mathilde might at least be left holding a small part of the pie.

"It's possible, even likely, that he killed the servant we found buried in their demesne." Ela clutched at straws. "You heard the coroner speculate that her body was cut to pieces with swift blows from a sharp sword, like one wielded by a trained knight. Though he displays no knightly valor or values, Sir Montaigu has a knight's training. Cathy Cross has no family left. She has no one to speak up for her except you, the jury of the hundred."

After some discussion, the jurors finally agreed that Montaigu should be brought in for questioning. Ela suspected that such a thing would be easier said than done.

CHAPTER 19

"*F*resh linens on the beds at once!" Ela had just received word that her son William was on his way back, this time with his wife Idonea. Ela felt a rush of sadness that Idonea wouldn't be in the company of her grandmother, who had died the previous year. Nicola de la Haye was a formidable character who'd been sheriff of Lincoln and defended the castle against a siege. She was one of the few people in England that Ela both feared and admired in equal measure.

"Petronella, can you see to it that interesting books from my collection are placed in Idonea's room? Perhaps that pretty book of Psalms with full-page decorations. And something by one of the Greeks. Aristophanes, perhaps. Her grandmother liked his dark humor. Idonea's an intelligent girl."

Ela had been delighted to make the match between William and Idonea. She prayed nightly for the success of the marriage and that they would be blessed with children.

But her delight at seeing Idonea and her son was tempered by worry that he might once again press his suit for the title of earl. And he'd said he was already in Wiltshire and only a short distance from the castle. Why had he come down here—again—without telling her in advance?

～

"Sir William Longespée and his wife, the lady Idonea!" announced Jake the young porter.

Ela hurried to Idonea and kissed her on both cheeks. "God be with you, my daughter." A lovely girl in the full bloom of her beauty, she carried herself with grace and dignity. William had also grown into his tall rangy frame, and no longer looked like a juvenile roe deer about to stumble over the furniture. But why did he look so anxious?

"William, my dear. I'm surprised to see you at such short notice. Why didn't you tell me you were coming to Wiltshire?"

He licked his lips quickly. "We had other business in the county."

Ela glanced at Idonea, now making a fuss over young Ellie who'd arrived with the dogs in tow.

"What business is that?" asked Ela, wondering why he hadn't volunteered the information.

"We've been to visit the king at Clarendon," said William. He attempted a smile but it didn't reach his eyes. "He is my cousin, after all."

Ela stood stunned into silence for a brief moment. "Yes, indeed he is. Did he invite you?" Ela wasn't aware that William had a personal relationship with King Henry, despite their being close in age.

"No." He drew in a breath. "I visited him to discuss my future prospects."

Ela saw Idonea glance up at her, then quickly snatch her gaze away and back to Ellie and Nicky, who'd just arrived.

She tried to keep her expression pleasant. "Did you discuss a position at court?" Such a thing would be entirely appropriate, though still bold of her son to pursue when still so young and inexperienced in the ways of the world.

"More or less. I spoke to him about my prospects for becoming Earl of Salisbury." His cheek twitched.

"I see." Ela heard the ice form on her words. "I did tell you about the nature of my arrangement with the king."

"Yes, Mother, you did." William looked around. As usual, the hall bristled with soldiers and servants and townspeople there on some business or other. "Goodness, there are a lot of people around. Shall we save this discussion for later?"

"No, I'd like to hear what the king said." She looked hard at him. He'd openly defied her! Her mind raced, scenarios unfurling like ribbons at a tournament. Would King Henry stand by their bargain? And what would she do if he didn't?

"He said that he'd have to consult with his lawyers."

"His lawyers? About what?"

She watched William shrink under her hard stare. "About whether his arrangement with you prevents me from becoming earl." He looked around the hall, up at the high stone walls with their ancient tapestries. "This is my father's castle, and his father was the king of England. It is my birthright to command the castle, Mother."

"I know." His rebuke stung. He was right. But it was her castle too and she had the wisdom and strength required to run it while William still lacked them. "And in time it shall be yours."

"Possibly not that much time, depending on what the lawyers say." William's eyes flashed a glint of steel she didn't remember seeing in them before.

"I shall await the opinion of his lawyers with bated breath."

Seven hundred pounds. Surely the king wouldn't accept

such a tremendous sum—provided for a very specific purpose—and renege on his promise? Only five years had passed since their charter was signed and she still hadn't repaid the debts she'd raised to make the payment.

Ela leaned in close. "And what, pray, would you have me do if the king grants you your dearest wish?"

"Your convent at Lacock will soon be built," he said calmly. "And you've stated your intention to retire there."

Ela stiffened as her own promise was thrown back in her face. She looked forward to retiring to the cloister...once she was old and frail and ready to quit the world and its cares. That time had not yet come.

"And shall I leave your young siblings to be raised by wolves?" She glanced at Ellie and Nicky, now showing Idonea a trick they'd taught to the little terrier. He could stand on his back legs and swat a ball dangling on a ribbon.

"I'd hardly call Bill Talbot a wolf, Mother." Now William's mouth did tilt into a smile.

"Will Bill Talbot teach Ellie how to run a household? Will he teach her how to make conversation with her mother-in-law and discipline a pilfering servant girl?"

"I daresay he could."

Now Ela smiled. "He'd probably make a very good job of it as well." Then she sighed. "You've gone behind my back William, and I won't soon forget it."

Perhaps as early as next year she'd find herself cloistered in a tiny monastic cell at Lacock, with nothing to do but pray from dawn to dusk and all the hours in between. If she were truly the woman of God that she wished she was, such a fate would fill her with joy and longing—as it did for Petronella, whose deep and unshakeable faith filled Ela with admiration.

Instead, the prospect of quitting her beloved home, her children, her dogs and her horse Freya, dearest Bill and young Elsie—of leaving them all for four whitewashed walls and a book of prayer—filled her with dread.

I'm here to seek justice for the voiceless.

Conviction roared inside her.

My time here is not yet over. The Lord has stoked this fire inside me to be sheriff and castellan at Salisbury. When he wishes me to quit, he will relieve me of this longing.

She schooled her face into a pleasant expression. "The cook is making pheasant for supper. She promised to prepare that sauce of almonds and nutmeg that you like so much."

Will didn't smile cheerily as she would have expected. "I'm not a child, Mother, to be mollified with a fig pudding and a pat on the cheek. I'm a man and a knight and I'll soon be a father."

"A father?"

Idonea heard the word and looked over again. She glanced at Ela, then at Will, then at Ela. "Did you tell her?" she mouthed.

Will nodded. "Idonea's expecting a baby this November, according to the doctor."

"God be praised!" Sheer joy filled Ela's heart. She rushed to Idonea and pressed the girl to her bosom. "Tonight's meal must be a feast of celebration."

Will smiled at Idonea, whose face beamed with pride.

"I do wish our baby could be born here in Salisbury Castle," said Will, his expression still uncharacteristically serious.

"He can. Or she...you're always welcome here." An uncomfortable feeling of apprehension disturbed her. But this was William's ancestral home, just as it was hers, and she would have to find the generosity in her heart to welcome him and his family here—even as he was trying to take it from her.

~

MONTAIGU D'ALBIAC ARRIVED, scowling and cursing, his hands bound behind his back, at midday the next day.

William and Idonea had just left, over Ela's rather luke-warm protests. She wasn't entirely sad to see them go, since she was both curious and anxious to find out the king's response to William's petition for the earldom. She wasted no time in writing a letter to Henry, reminding him of their arrangement and explaining that while she had great respect and love for her son, it was not yet his time to be the earl.

She avoided the vicinity of Montaigu, where he sat chained to a chair, because he kept calling out to those around him and trying to engage them in talk. Even threats to put him in the dungeon had no effect, and that would have been an inconvenience since the jurors had already been summoned to question him. He seemed to know just how far he could go in teasing and cajoling and tormenting those around him, stopping short of any behavior that might have justified violent censure. He knew that as a noble and a knight he could not simply be clapped around the head for speaking out of turn.

If I were Mathilde I'd be sorely tempted to slip some poison into his spiced wine. Ela asked for God's guidance in seeking justice for this man who tried her patience so sorely.

When the jurors arrived, Ela reminded them that they were gathering information to discover whether Montaigu should be tried at the next assizes, for the murder of Cathy Cross, whom he was suspected of killing and dismembering with his sword sometime before he disappeared for six years.

Ela had felt sure that with his odd foreign clothes and his insolent expression, Montaigu would rub the jurors the wrong way, and—for once—she wasn't opposed to them bearing some prejudice against the man. She found him reprehensible at every turn and considered him at least half responsible for the untimely deaths of all three of his sons.

"What have you to say for yourself? Did you kill her?" asked juror Will Dyer of Montaigu, when she opened the floor to them.

"I did not," said Montaigu without a moment's hesitation. "And given the passage of many years and the dearth of any evidence whatsoever, I find it hard to imagine that any justice would even consider the idea." He spoke calmly and sounded reasonable for once. "Why would I kill a servant girl? Any man displeased with her service or tired of her company would simply send her away."

A murmur of agreement showed that he'd already bought some sympathy on the jury. Ela stifled an inward groan.

"Let me remind the jury that the coroner is convinced that she was dismembered with a sharp sword, so the perpetrator was either Sir Montaigu or one of his older sons, who were but youngsters at the likely time of the girl's death."

"Far be it from me to point the finger of blame at a youngster, especially one who died on the battlefield, but they were both strapping lads and of a lusty temperament." He spoke as if wistful.

This man has no shame!

At every turn, Montaigu observed that there was no possible way they could prove him the killer so many years after the event. He took every opportunity to throw his dead sons under the mill-wheels of justice, lamenting over how wild and willful they were. While she suspected that last part might be entirely true, given her acquaintance of Charibert, Ela found his conduct reprehensible.

Still, she could see that if she took a vote, the jurors would likely err on the side of "caution" and not recommend detaining Montaigu for trial.

Fed up, she stood. "Good men of Salisbury, might I

remind you that you had little difficulty in accusing Mathilde d'Albiac—a long-suffering woman of gentle character—of murdering her husband and son on no more evidence than has been presented today. A great deal less, in fact, in that she was accused of killing her husband in the absence of his body, which we see before us—alive and well—today. Her husband is known throughout Wiltshire and beyond to be a drinker, a gambler and a fighter. He has installed a foreign mistress under his roof, in front of his wife and young daughters. Why, might I ask, are you so much more willing to believe in Montaigu d'Albiac's innocence than in that of his wife?"

There was some awkward shifting and grunting and one of the oldest jurors leaned forward. "There's something unnatural about a woman running a manor in her husband's absence for so long and never coming forward to declare that he's missing." Murmurs of agreement rose from those around him. "It just seemed as if she didn't want him to come back."

"Her daughters made it clear that she was sure he'd return. She never doubted for a moment that he'd be back. She was a careful steward of the manor in her husband's absence. Other women would have made haste to remarry but she demonstrated patience and forbearance."

They can't stand the idea of a woman being in charge of her own existence. She knew her command of the castle and the sheriffdom irked the men around her. She'd had to unravel a plot against her by the commander of the garrison troops not long ago. But that had no bearing on today's proceedings. "All I ask is that you consider him at least as likely to be guilty of the crime of killing Cathy Cross, as you considered Mathilde to be of killing her husband and her son."

"I take your meaning my lady, but let me present it this way," said John the Tanner, a younger member of the jury and often a rather probing questioner. "Mathilde d'Albiac's husband is alive and her son's true murderer has confessed. She is innocent of the crimes she was accused of. Should we not consider Montaigu d'Albiac to be just as likely to be innocent of the crime for which he stands accused?"

Ela felt the air drain out of her. She glanced at Giles Haughton, who shot her a sympathetic glance. With all the jurors apparently on Montaigu's side, she couldn't even justify holding him in the dungeon until the assizes.

Montaigu looked smug and had the good sense to sit quietly. Ela had no choice but to thank the jurors and dismiss them. Then she turned to Montaigu. "I would ask that you do not leave the county of Wiltshire for any reason. You are still under suspicion of murder and if more evidence should be found you will be back to appear before the judge at the assizes."

Montaigu said nothing, but the slight tilt of his mouth told her that he intended to do exactly as he pleased.

THE INTERVAL between the past assizes and the next one seemed to stretch on interminably. News came in that Montaigu had returned to his gambling habits and was borrowing money again. Agnes's belly kept growing and Ela contemplated allowing her outside into the herb garden for fresh air, but reflecting that the garden contained several potent toxins and her prisoner was a confessed poisoner, she kept the girl confined.

"I know I shall hang, but what will happen to my baby?" Agnes asked the question with little emotion. Petronella had taken pains to pray with the girl daily, and to help her navigate her feelings about her fate. Agnes seemed to have accepted it to a disconcerting degree.

"You might not hang," said Ela cautiously.

"I think I will, though. And I shall burn in hell, too. I broke the worst of the ten commandments."

"The Lord looks with mercy on those who find themselves in a desperate situation." Ela was still hoping for clemency here on earth as well, though she knew it was a long shot.

"Job found himself in a desperate situation, and he didn't kill anyone." Agnes stroked her belly. "I should have shown more forbearance. That's what Petronella says."

"I suppose she's right, but there are times when forbearance allows an enemy to triumph. Jael and Judith are two women in the Bible who killed to save their people in time of war."

"This isn't a time of war," said Agnes quietly.

"Perhaps not a war between nations, but one could argue that you were under siege in your own home. And you had a natural mother's instinct to protect your child from insult and injury. Who knows what horrors Charibert might have inflicted on you or Charley if he hadn't died when he did."

Charley was downstairs being entertained by Ellie and Nicky, who still took pleasure in childish games.

"What will happen to Charley?" Now Agnes's voice did reveal an edge of fear.

"I shall ensure that he is taken care of. He can stay here in the castle if needed."

"Will he be put to work in the kitchens?"

"Something like that, when he's old enough." Ela didn't much like children under ten doing any serious work, though it was common enough in large households. Even in a peasant family, a child of his age might well be expected to perform small labors like plucking weeds in his family's vegetable beds or gathering kindling for their fire. "But don't give up hope that you shall yet see him grow up and get married."

"Get married?" Agnes's voice rasped. "Who would marry the bastard son of a murderer?"

Ela stilled. She had a good point. Even if Agnes survived the trial, the stigma of her crime would follow her—and likely her children too—for the rest of her life.

"I feel almost as if Charibert is reaching from beyond the grave to blight my life in punishment for taking his." Her eyes filled with tears.

It was hard to comfort someone whose prospects were so bleak, especially when two tender young lives depended on her. "You're only about two months away from giving birth. Have you thought of names for the baby?"

"What does it matter? I might as well call him Charibert as that's all anyone will think about when they see him."

"This one might be a girl," reasoned Ela.

"A girl?" Agnes stared at her curiously. Then tears dripped from her eyes. "I always hoped I'd have a little girl. This was long ago, before I grew up and realized that nothing in life works the way you expect it to."

Suddenly the girl doubled over and let out a gasp.

"What's wrong?"

Agnes looked up at her, eyes wide, and let out a tiny cry. "Something's tearing inside me!" She bent over and let out an agonized groan.

Panic jerked Ela to her feet and she ran to the door. "Guards! Fetch the doctor at once." This boded very ill.

"Am I going to die?" asked Agnes, still bent double, in the same emotionless voice she'd used earlier.

"No, but you might be about to give birth."

"I can't be. The baby's not due for weeks. Two months at least."

"We were just guessing when you are due based on how

you look. You said that Charibert was using you at least once a week for months. You might be at full term."

Agnes grimaced in pain. "I was a lot bigger with Charley."

She didn't look to be more than about seven months along. Ela thought it was likely that her placenta had ruptured or some other horrible event that might indeed lead to her death and that of her baby—hence her call for the doctor rather than a midwife. Would death in childbirth be merciful under the circumstances?

Elsie came running, along with Petronella. "What's amiss?" asked Petronella. "The guards have gone for the doctor?"

"I think Agnes might be having the baby."

Petronella's eyes widened. "Already?"

"Remember how when Hilda was having her baby, you prayed continuously? And a dangerous situation turned out fine."

"Yes, the baby was breech and I prayed for it to turn."

"Would you mind praying for the safe delivery of Agnes's baby?" Ela tried to sound quite matter-of-fact about it, as if she needed someone to pray in the corner as much as she needed clean linens and warm water.

"I shall start at once."

CHAPTER 20

*E*la sent Elsie to the kitchen to fetch warm water and bring Cook with her if possible. Cook was experienced with deliveries and a reassuring voice of calm in a crisis. Despite careful study of the medical texts of Trota of Salerno, which dealt extensively with labor and delivery, Ela's experience was limited as much by her nobility as anything else. She'd attended precious few births outside of her own, which had each been relatively uncomplicated.

White-faced and trembling, Agnes was clearly in tremendous pain. Worse yet, blood now soaked her undyed wool tunic. If she didn't deliver soon she might die from loss of blood, whether the baby lived or not.

"Let's undress you and lay you on the bed. I can take a look and see if the baby's head is crowning." Ela tried to sound reassuring. They struggled to get Agnes's tunic off over her head.

"The doctor will see me in my shift," gasped Agnes with horror.

"Don't worry. He's seen people in all states of undress. It's his job to tend to the body, not its outer garments." A red stain spread across Agnes's shift. "Lie down."

"I can't," Agnes stared at the bed. "I'll stain the sheets."

"The sheets can be washed."

Agnes bent over, gasping, again.

"Lie down, I want to feel your belly. I might be able to tell where the baby is."

With considerable difficulty, Agnes lowered herself onto the bed and crouched there in a fetal position.

"Stretch out your legs and arms." Agnes pulled her shaking limbs away from her torso, and Ela placed her hands on the girl's belly, touching her through her thin shift.

Is the baby alive? She held her hands very still and felt a small kick. She pushed and prodded, trying to determine the position of the baby's head and limbs. "I think it's head down. Let me take a look and see if the head is crowning."

Agnes cried out as a wave of pain came over her, and she rolled back into the fetal position, that she almost knocked Ela in the head with her knee. "This hurts so much worse than when I had Charley," she gasped, once the racking pains had passed.

Something's wrong. There shouldn't be this much blood. "Lie still and let me look between your legs." She peered as best she could in the gloom. Agnes had started to dilate but had a long way to go.

Cook arrived and Ela asked her to go brew up a cup of soothing chamomile tea and a paste of the softening herb marsh mallow, which would help Agnes to dilate faster.

"Are they going to take my baby away from me when I give birth?" In between contractions, Agnes asked this in a calm voice that must have taken considerable effort. Her hair hung in damp tendrils around her pale face and her eyes were wide with both pain and fear.

"No," said Ela. "The justice said he would deliberate your

fate at the next assizes, so you shall keep your baby until then at least, and hopefully long past it." She thought it a good sign that the judge had let her live to deliver. And Mathilde wasn't calling for her death.

"Where's Charley?"

"He's in the hall with Ellie. She'll take care of him and keep him entertained."

"What if I'm dying? Will she bring him to say goodbye?"

Her question froze Ela's blood. Every expectant mother knew someone who'd died in childbirth. "You're not going to die." She glanced over at Petronella, who stood in the corner, head bent and lips fluttering with prayer. "Soon you'll be holding your baby."

Cook brought tea, cooled enough to drink, and they tried to get Agnes to sip it, but she couldn't do more than wet her lips with it.

The doctor arrived and was—unsurprisingly—very alarmed at the amount of blood Agnes had shed. The girl's face was almost as pale as the plain linen sheets she lay on. Even her lips were bloodless and her whole aspect was frightening.

"We should deliver this baby as fast as possible," he said. "If the cord or the placenta are ruptured and bleeding, we won't be able to stop them until the baby is out."

Poor Agnes's agony stretched on for hours as they hovered and whispered words of soothing encouragement. Agnes was now too weak even to express fear, and the doctor tried again to get her to drink the tea. He wanted Agnes up and walking around, to encourage the weight of the baby to open her uterus. Agnes found it next to impossible to stay upright as she was in so much pain.

As they day stretched into night, the doctor took Ela aside. "I may have to cut her open to save the baby. She won't survive it."

Ela crossed herself, heart aching. She trusted Doctor Goodwin's judgment. "When will you have to decide?"

"If the head doesn't come down by the time your daughter Petronella has reached the end of ten more Hail Marys."

"May her words reach the Lord's ears before then," said Ela softly. Agnes's suffering was terrible to behold, and it would be far worse if the doctor had to cut her baby from her.

Ela held Agnes's hand. "Can you feel the baby pushing, wanting to come out?"

"I don't know. It hurts too much." Agnes gasped each word. Her grip grew weaker and Ela could feel her slipping away.

"Imagine the baby pushing its way out, coming out into the world, ready to greet you." Ela tried to conjure the scenario in her mind.

Agnes closed her eyes, and a low moan slid from her mouth.

"Can we check her?" Ela asked the doctor. He nodded, his low voice reassuring as he helped Agnes up onto the high bed. Ela helped to lift her shift and watched closely as the doctor examined her.

"The head is crowning," he said, matter of fact. "Push as hard as you can and let's see if we can get the little one out."

Ela took Agnes's hand again and squeezed it. Now almost too weak to move, Agnes couldn't seem to summon the energy to push. "You must push—the baby's right there!"

Agnes's lashes fluttered and Ela watched her face tense as she made a fierce effort.

"That's it, the baby's coming," said the doctor. "Push with all your might!"

Ela squeezed Agnes's hand and urged her to push. Agnes

tensed every muscle in her exhausted body, the doctor stood ready to catch the infant…and the baby stayed put.

Petronella's gone past ten Hail Marys, thought Ela. She muttered a silent prayer of her own.

"Get ready to push again," said the doctor. "Your life and your baby's life depend on your efforts."

Ela had never heard him use such language. A man in late middle age, who must have delivered a thousand or more babies, as well as treating ailments from broken bones to suppurating ulcers, he'd seen everything the human body could produce. Fear gripped her heart at the thought that Agnes could die—along with her baby—if she couldn't summon the last shreds of her strength to push it out.

"Come on Agnes. Give it everything you've got," urged Ela. Once again, Agnes gritted her teeth and her face tensed into a rictus. This time—as she let out a heart-rending moan —the baby emerged in a rush of fluids and the doctor caught the slippery body in his arms. He used a finger to clear its mouth and immediately held it out to Ela. "I must work on Agnes."

Shocked, Ela took the baby. Small, but still almost full-sized and perfect in shape, the limp form hadn't made a sound. "Give me a linen cloth," cried Ela to Elsie, who rushed over with a pile of them. "Help me rub her." She looked at Agnes, who now lay on the bed, eyes closed as if she were already dead. "It's a girl!"

"A girl?" Agnes's eyes fluttered open.

"She's beautiful." Ela rubbed at the baby's face and chest and arms, which reddened under her touch. The baby stirred to life and soon emitted a cough and then a hearty cry. "What's her name?" Ela wanted to keep talking to Agnes. The girl appeared to hover on the threshold between life and death. She couldn't tell exactly what the doctor was doing between her legs but she suspected it involved trying to deliver the placenta and stop the bleeding before the last dregs of her lifeblood ran from her body.

"Mathilde," gasped Agnes. "For she's shown me more kindness and forbearance than I deserve."

"That's a wonderful choice. She'll be so happy to meet her namesake. I shall send a messenger to bring her here as soon as she'd able."

"I'm going to die, aren't I?"

"No! Of course not," said Ela, hoping the doctor would chime in to agree with her. He didn't. "You're going to be fine. The worst is over and now you need to rest."

Should she call a priest? If the girl really was going to die she needed last rites. Especially given that she had a murder —even a well-motivated one—on her conscience.

"Can I stop praying now?" asked Petronella, who'd now risen and was peering at the baby. Ela remembered how sweet Petronella had been with Hilda's baby when it was first born. She'd hoped the experience might ignite maternal feelings in Petronella that would encourage her to consider marriage and a family of her own. It didn't. Nothing seemed to shake Petronella's quest to lock herself up in a cloister at the earliest possible opportunity.

"More prayers can never go amiss," said Ela cautiously. "How are things looking?" she asked the doctor. "Do I need to send for...anyone?" She hoped he would catch her meaning.

Doctor Goodwin looked directly at her, his frank gaze saying more than his words. "The placenta is out. There was a large piece of it torn off. If I can remove it, then I hope all shall be well."

Ela took his meaning. She turned to Elsie and whispered in her ear for her to go send for Father Thomas, but not to say anything to alarm anyone.

Father Thomas arrived not long after, as he was always

somewhere about the castle. Ela hurried up to him and told him not to alarm Agnes if he could avoid it. He walked slowly over to her, keeping his eyes on her face not on whatever Dr. Goodwin was doing to her. "Dear Agnes, I am here to offer prayers for your full and speedy recovery."

He anointed her with oil and muttered the words of Extreme Unction in Latin, which Agnes mercifully didn't understand. He then anointed her infant and blessed it. He then said another long prayer in Latin that didn't seem entirely relevant but Ela suspected that, much like herself, he didn't really know what to do in this situation.

Agnes seemed to be beyond pain, her expression unchanging and her eyes closed as if in sleep. Alarmed, Ela approached her. The doctor still sat between her legs but his efforts were hidden by a blanket that he'd draped there for her modesty. Ela felt a rush of relief to find Agnes's skin still warm to the touch.

"Am I going to die," asked Agnes calmly. "Is that why the priest is here?"

Ela drew in a steadying breath. She didn't want to lie to Agnes in this moment. "It's just a precaution. Dr. Goodwin is making sure you're safe and healthy."

"It doesn't hurt anymore. I don't feel any pain," said Agnes peacefully.

Ela glanced at the doctor in alarm. Such lack of sensation didn't seem normal or natural. She wondered if this relief from pain was in fact death creeping over Agnes. Her husband William had stilled and calmed as death overtook him after days of agony.

"All is well, my ladies," said the Doctor, looking up. "Some cleaning and stitching were required and Agnes will need to rest very quietly during her lying-in period. He stood, wiping his hands on a cloth. Elsie hurried over with a copper bowl filled with fresh water that she'd just brought from downstairs. He washed his hands and forearms with practiced care.

"You're a brave girl, Agnes. May God grant you many happy years with your new daughter."

Ela crossed herself, praying for the same. The doctor had no idea that Agnes might be ripped from her child by the justice at the assizes, and even expelled out of this world and into the next one by his judgment.

Agnes's daughter Mathilde, now known to all as Tilda, had reached almost six weeks of age by the time of the next assizes. Tilda was a round, bonny girl with rosy red cheeks and tufts of red-gold hair that recalled her late and utterly unlamented father. Agnes recovered rapidly, at least in body, but remained quiet and distant, as if waiting for the hand of God to come pluck her happiness away.

Mathilde came to visit her and the baby twice, and Ela noticed that she seemed to be cultivating a distance between her and Agnes, who had, after all, murdered her last surviving son.

Ela drew Mathilde aside after her second visit. "Do you think it would be best if Agnes didn't return to your household?"

Mathilde's relief was obvious. "I didn't know how to put it. I don't entirely blame the girl for what she did, and I don't want her to die. But Charibert was my own dear son that I gave birth to and raised and nurtured from infancy. I miss him every day."

"I understand." Ela knew if that if one of her sons made some foolish mistakes, even quite terrible ones, she wouldn't cease loving him. Her husband had done things that would cause a seasoned priest, who'd heard decades of confessions, to blush. While she'd chastised him on more than one occasion, she hadn't ceased caring for him. "I shall find another home for her and her daughter."

"I could provide a home for her daughter, who is, after all, my granddaughter and my dead son's child."

Ela's heart sank. Mathilde was asking her to separate mother and son.

"And I could provide a home for Charley, as well. He's my dear dead son Alain's only child."

Your sons are both rapists who wreaked violence upon an innocent young woman, and now you plan to destroy her by taking both her children away? She couldn't think of a way to phrase this delicately. Mathilde was a victim, too. And for all she knew, the judge would sentence Agnes to hang for poisoning Charibert. At least then her children would have a home to go to, even if it had the reprehensible Montaigu d'Albiac in it....

MONTAIGU WAS SUMMONED before the justice at the assizes at Ela's request, to face trial for the murder of Cathy Cross. To Ela's dismay, the evidence against Montaigu for killing Cross was dismissed as circumstantial. The crime was distant in time, no one reported it, Montaigu was never under suspicion at the time, etc, etc. The justice then wasted no time in granting custody of Agnes's children to Mathilde and Montaigu. It seems that Montaigu had written him a letter—presumably at Mathilde's bidding—requesting this.

He did, however, spare Agnes's life on the condition that she forsake her children utterly and not go within five miles of Neversend for the rest of her life. Limp with exhaustion and devastation, rather than relief, Agnes agreed.

"What will become of me?" she said, between bouts of

sobbing, after her children had left with Mathilde and Montaigu.

"You're still young," said Ela, rubbing her arm gently. "You have your whole life ahead of you." She knew better than to suggest that Agnes could have more children and forget her first two. That was likely her best course of action, though. It would certainly be easier to find a husband without two other men's children in tow and Agnes was still youthful and pretty despite her years of suffering.

She carried a great deal of baggage, though. "It wasn't murder," Ela reassured her. "You killed Charibert in self-defense. The judge even said it. His tormenting you and your son weighed so heavily on you that you can't be judged too harshly for trying to escape from more abuse.

"And now my dear Charley is in the same house with that brute...and his foreign woman! How Mathilde manages to live without poisoning him I don't know. I suppose it's good that I shall never see him again. At least I dearly hope not. But the thought of life without my babes makes me wish to lie down in my grave right now. Perhaps it would have been better if they hung me."

"The Lord has other plans for you."

"I wonder what they are. Have I not suffered enough?" Her question had an edge of desperation. "Who will hire a maid that has killed her master?"

No one, thought Ela. She wasn't even sure either of her married daughters would be willing to take Agnes into their household, not unless she pleaded with them. "How is your sewing?"

"It's passable," said Agnes dispiritedly. "Mathilde taught me to hem and mend and do a neat seam. I can even embroider a simple pattern."

"Then you might find work as a seamstress or dressmaker in a town where no one knows you. And in the meantime, I know there is work here mending clothes for the soldiers of the king's garrison."

"I don't think the king will want a poisoner under his roof."

"You've been sheltered from the comings and goings of the castle in your locked room, so you may not be aware that the king's garrison is stationed under my roof."

Agnes's eyes widened. "I wondered why there were so many soldiers here… Will they rape me?" She asked the question with alarming frankness.

"If any of them so much as looks at you sideways, come to me immediately and I shall have him disciplined by his superior. I don't blame you for being wary of young men after what you've been through."

"I do hope Montaigu won't be cruel to Charley," she said, her voice cracking.

"I don't think Mathilde will let him."

"She did stop Alain or Charibert from being cruel to me."

"I shall give them a chance to settle, but in about two weeks I will pay a call on them and report back to you."

"Would you really?" Agnes's face brightened. "It would mean so much to me to hear news of them."

"I will indeed."

TRUE TO HER WORD, ten days later Ela set out for Neversend, bringing Bill and Petronella with her. "It's lovely to see you out riding, Petronella," said Bill, after he'd helped her mount a speckled gray palfrey.

"I wish to visit Joan and Helene and offer them succor. I taught them several prayers that might bring them solace in their time of need, and I wish to make sure they remember the words."

"That's very thoughtful of you. And your prayers for Agnes have certainly proven effective. The doctor didn't know if she would live or die during the delivery. She's almost back to normal now."

"I admit that I fear for her children in this household. Neither Joan nor Helene has a much stronger character than their mother. If their father is as cruel as their brother, it may well be a dreadful and godless place."

Ela didn't think she'd even mentioned Montaigu's foreign mistress to Petronella. She decided now was not the time to start. Let Montaigu read the shock and disgust on her face as she discovered his shame for herself.

But when they arrived at Neversend shortly after the bells for Nones, both Ela and Petronella suffered a far greater shock.

CHAPTER 21

a dismal aspect had settled over the manor of Neversend. Leaves fallen from the trees dusted the road and no one hurried out to sweep them away. The thatch had rotted above one of the eaves and Ela wondered if Montaigu would ever part with the money to repair it now that he was back and in charge of the family purse strings.

"Hello!" called one of Ela's guards from outside the front door. "Is anyone home?"

Montaigu stuck his head out the same upper window as before. "You failed in your efforts to hang me, now go to hell!"

"I'm here to check on the children," said Ela calmly.

"They're none of your damn business," said Montaigu. "So turn around and trot back to your castle."

Still, no one had come to the door.

"Mathilde, are you here?" called Ela. No sound. And no sign of Joan or Helene, either. Unease roamed through her. She dismounted, handed her horse to the guard, and approached the door. She raised her hand and was about to knock when the door opened to reveal Mathilde standing behind it.

Ela smiled, relieved she was alive and not buried in the garden somewhere. "How are you?"

"Fine." Mathilde's tight smile belied her reply. "We are all well. Can I help you with something?"

"I'd like to see Charley and little Tilda. It would cheer Agnes to hear news of them."

"They're both down for a nap right now." Mathilde spoke quickly, and her eyes darted over Ela's shoulder to her entourage behind her. "I would invite you in but we're all very busy."

"Refreshments would be most welcome after our long ride," said Ela. Mathilde's manner struck her as strange. And why would Charley, a boy of seven, be napping in the middle of the day?"

"I'm afraid I can't ask you in. My husband…he…." She ran out of words. Mathilde was not an inventive liar.

"He what?" asked Ela quietly. "I know he's no saint. Does he still have the woman here?"

Mathilde glanced over her shoulder quickly before nodding. "We're getting used to her. I suppose she'll be like another daughter to me." Her flat tone further jangled Ela's nerves.

"Where are Helen and Joan?"

"In their rooms."

"May I see them? Petronella is here and would like to test their recollection of a prayer she taught them."

"I'm afraid I can't ask you in." Her voice had dropped to a near whisper. "My husband hates visitors."

"I'm not a visitor. I'm the sheriff of Wiltshire," said Ela with a tight smile. "And I would like to see your children."

Panicked, Mathilde glanced behind her again. "I'll fetch Joan and Helene for a moment. Wait here."

Mathilde closed the door in her face. Ela glanced behind her and made eye contact with Petronella and Bill, who both dismounted. In a few moments the door opened and Mathilde shoved Helene and Joan outside in front of her and closed the door, The girls greeted Petronella stiffly and made polite chatter, then recited the prayer with perfect recall.

"The little ones both had a fever. They're recovering well but may still be contagious," said Mathilde.

"Why didn't you say that before?" asked Ela, deeply suspicious. Charley was a boisterous lad and could usually be heard in some way, either his laugh or his feet pounding down the stairs. He'd been quite a handful to keep track of at the castle while Agnes was confined to her chamber. "Do they still have the fever?"

"They're a little hot but they'll be fine." Agnes kept glancing behind her like she expected Montaigu to appear with his hand raised to beat her.

"Is Montaigu abusing you?" Ela whispered.

Mathilde shook her head. "We're fine. But please leave. He does have a temper and will rage and storm if he gets angry."

"I'll return a week from today," said Ela. She could see that Mathilde was desperate to be rid of them and she didn't want to make the poor woman's life more difficult. There was at least a chance that the story about the fever was true. There had been a stomach ailment going around that particularly seemed to affect children but luckily wasn't dangerous. "And at that time I will expect to see the little ones."

Mathilde swallowed. "Of course. I'll see you then."

Petronella bade farewell to the girls and they both mounted.

"It was rude of her not to invite us in," said Petronella quietly, as they rode up the drive.

"It was. And she seemed awfully anxious. And I'm not

sure I believe her story about Charley and Tilda being in bed. I admit I'm anxious for their safety."

"Mathilde wouldn't let anything happen to them, would she?" asked Petronella.

"I don't think so, but she is weak and her husband is a brute and a bully."

They rode along the nearby lane, leaves drifting down from the trees overhanging both sides. Suddenly a girl ran out into the road in front of them.

"Joan?" Ela stopped her horse.

"They're gone," gasped Joan. She was panting as if she'd just run fast. "Charley and the baby. I haven't seen them since the day before yesterday."

Terror clutched at Ela. "They're not in the house?"

"No, I searched everywhere after I didn't see or hear them yesterday."

"Why did your mother lie to me just now?"

"I don't know." Joan's face was white, her breath coming in unsteady gasps. "But I think my father has taken them somewhere. What would he do with them?"

"We're going back there right now," said Ela. "And unless I get a good answer I'm going to arrest him."

ELA ALLOWED time for Joan to make her way back to the house, so she wouldn't be missed and her treachery discovered. Then, guards on alert and ready to take action, they rode back up the overgrown drive.

"We must see Charley and Tilda at once," called Bill. "Bring them outside."

"Leave my property," called Montaigu from his upper window, without even bothering to stick his head out.

"If they're not produced before I count to twenty, I shall

arrest you," replied Bill, in his deep, sonorous voice. "And don't try to leave as we've sent guards around the back."

Silence stretched for a moment, then Ela heard Mathilde's voice say, "But where are they?"

"None of your damn business," replied Montaigu. Ela couldn't see either of them but could hear them clearly. "Get out of my chamber, woman!"

"Draw your swords," said Bill, quietly, to the guards. "Get ready to make the arrest."

"How will we fetch him back to the castle without a cart," asked Petronella.

"He can walk with two guards as an escort. Or they can throw him across the back of one of their horses. The guards know how to transport a prisoner." Ela crossed her arms over her chest. She already knew that the children weren't coming out. "Go take him now," she cried, after a reasonable interval.

The guards marched toward the door and Ela tried to sit quietly on her horse as she heard them storm upstairs.

"Unhand me, you brutes!" Montaigu's voice carried outside. A woman's screams followed, and what sounded like pleading in a foreign language. "What are you arresting me for?"

The guards, who knew better than to bargain with a prisoner, kept their mouths shut. Soon Montaigu d'Albiac appeared in the doorway, scowling and cursing, with his hands tied behind his back. "You'll regret this!" he snarled at Ela. "What I do with my own brats is none of your business."

"Where are they?" said Ela, trying to conceal the urgency she felt. "Your punishment will be less if they are recovered quickly."

"Their whereabouts is none of your business."

"Did you sell them?" Her maid Elsie had been rescued from child slavers after being sold by her uncle.

"What if I did? It's not illegal to sell my own child."

"They're not your children. They're the children of your former servant Agnes and the judge granted you custody of them to provide them with a safe upbringing. He didn't give them to you as goods and chattels that you can take to market."

Montaigu didn't argue, partly because a guard now tied a kerchief tightly across his mouth, parting his jaw with it, so that all he could do was grunt and groan.

"Guards, please remove that for a moment so I can determine where the children are. It's a matter of great urgency to find them." Since selling children was considered morally repugnant in England, the slavers usually took them out of the country. She looked right at Montaigu. "Where did you take them?"

"I'm not going to tell you."

"Children's lives are at stake, including a helpless infant," said Ela. "Guards, cut off his nose at once!"

One guard looked at her in horror but drew his dagger from its sheath. Before he could raise his arm, her ruse worked and Montaigu spat out a name and location in a small nearby village.

"Spare him. For now. If the children aren't where you say or if we can't recover them, then I will be back for it."

Ela turned her horse and trotted away, with Petronella, Bill, and one of the guards following at her heels. Powerful emotions rocked her. How could anyone be so heartless as to sell a child into bondage, let alone a tiny baby!

"Mama, did you really intend to cut his nose off?" asked Petronella, once they were out of earshot.

"I would feel no compunction whatsoever about it, God forgive me," she said. "That man makes me so angry I could do it myself. I'm furious with Mathilde for pretending the children were still there. Why would she do that? But, for now, I care about nothing except retrieving those helpless babes from whatever hellhole they're being kept in."

"My lady, we should send for more guards before approaching such a dangerous person as a child slaver," warned Bill.

"We can't. We don't have the luxury of time. The baby is only a few weeks old and will sicken and die without mother's milk. Do you think they'll have made such a provision?"

"I suspect a newborn baby would be a valuable treasure for a childless couple and worth a great deal to one in that trade."

"I realize the risks and accept them. I regret not learning the art of the sword and carrying my own. It is unfair that all the responsibility for fighting falls to you and one guard, but my faith in you is absolute."

"With God's Grace I shall be worthy of it," said Bill. She heard a tinge of reluctance in his voice. Being well into middle age made him less confident of his prowess, but she'd rather have him at her side than any man in the king's army.

The remaining guard was about thirty, with a jutting jaw and a serious expression. Ela told him that their goal was to retrieve the children by any means necessary. The boy could then ride in front of Bill. Ela, mounted on her trustworthy Freya, intended to hold the baby in the crook of her own arm while managing the reins with her other hand.

The village of Sprye was barely more than a crossroads and a ramshackle assortment of cottages. The remains of an ancient stone cross stood at the heart of the crossroads, its carved pattern worn almost smooth by wind and weather.

"Mill cottage, he said," muttered Ela as they rode through the town. "Let's ask someone where that is."

The guard cornered a villager, who pointed them toward a narrow lane. They followed the lane as it turned into a track, then came to a dead end next to a stream. The mill itself was clearly abandoned, its wheel rotten and the thatched roof fallen in, but a small wattle and daub cottage stood nearby.

The guard went and knocked on the door.

A round woman with a yellowed kerchief came out and slammed the door behind her. Her eyes widened as she looked at Ela and her party. "What do you want? The mill's been closed these ten years. Master Finney grinds the flour now over in Moss End."

"We have no flour to grind. We seek Bridie Haslop." She gave the name spat out by Montaigu d'Albiac.

"She's not here." The woman's face closed like a portcullis lowering.

"May I come in?" Ela wondered if the children were inside the cottage. She had no intention of leaving without entering it.

"No, my babe is asleep."

Ela's heart leaped. "How old is your infant?"

"Eight months."

Ela's excitement faded somewhat. Tilda was only about six weeks and there was no way to confuse her with an eight-month-old. But this woman looked old to be the mother of an infant, so perhaps she could rescue another child from bondage. "Do you have other children within?"

"What's it to you?" the woman's tone turned hostile.

"I'm the High Sheriff of Wiltshire," said Ela. "And I seek two children of the d'Albiac family. They would have been brought here two days ago."

"I don't know what you're talking about, and I need to beat my washing." The woman turned to walk around the house.

"What was that?" Ela could swear she'd heard a small voice from inside the house. "Is there someone in there?"

"Help!" she heard.

"Charley, is that you?"

"Yes," cried the small voice. "Help me."

"Bill, open the door. Break it down if need be."

The woman darted for the riverbank, clutching the hem of her skirt in her hands. "Catch her!" called Ela to the guard. "Don't let her get away." The guard jumped from his horse and ran after her. Ela could see her now untying a small boat that sat at the edge of the water.

Bill kicked down the door and Ela expected Charley to run out, but he didn't. She and Petronella dismounted and hurried to the dark doorway. Ela always felt a frisson of unease at entering a strange cottage, especially if the owners were known to be of poor character, but Bill marched into its gloomy depths.

"Charley's tied up in the corner here," said Bill, already tugging at the boy's bonds.

"Is Tilda here, too?" Babies were noisy creatures, always fussing and sucking and squalling, especially if there was a commotion nearby. Ela didn't hear any noise at all inside the one-room cottage. The woman must have lied about having an eight-month-old.

"She isn't," said Charley, clearly near tears. "A woman came and got her yesterday. The mean lady said they were taking her far away where she'd never be found or know who she was."

Panic surged through Ela. It could prove almost impossible to find a missing infant. Extracting the information about who had her, by cruel means if necessary, from this woman would be the only way to find Tilda.

Ela could hear a great splashing outside, so she hurried out to see what was going on between the one remaining guard and the woman. She stood in the boat, which swayed and yawed as she used an oar to beat at the guard. He held fast to the gunwale, using his hands to prevent her from leaving the water's edge, but flinching under the rain of heavy blows.

"Bill, we need you!" He was still inside trying to free Charley. Ela rushed down to the water's edge and grabbed hold of the boat.

"Stand back, my lady, please! You mustn't get hurt!" cried the guard. The woman now swung her oar at Ela, who ducked as it flew toward her.

"Tip the boat," gasped Ela. She could see it was close to capsizing just from the woman's weight heaving about in it. "Down hard on this side in one, two, three!" They both leaned all their weight on the nearest side of the wooden boat and the woman and her oar crashed toward them. The woman fell out of the boat and onto Ela, knocking her to her knees at the water's edge.

"Grab her!" The woman flailed her oar, which she still held with a death grip, but the guard managed to grab it and seize hold of her arm. He wrestled her to the ground and Ela swept the oar—which proved surprisingly heavy—out of the way.

"Mama, are you hurt?" Petronella rushed out of the cottage holding the rope just removed from Charley's wrists.

Ela rose shakily to her feet. Her gown was wet and smudged with riverbank clay. "I'm fine."

Bill bound the woman's hands with the same crude homemade rope.

"Where's the baby?" hissed Ela. "Your life depends upon you giving us accurate information at once."

"I don't know." The woman didn't meet her eyes.

"I feel sure that you do. Who is your master? Where is he?"

"I don't know."

Ela was sorely tempted to threaten to cut off her nose—it had worked so well with Montaigu. But this woman might call her bluff and she didn't intend for empty threats to become a regular part of her arsenal. With what she knew about Montaigu she might just have gone through with it if needed. This woman was a stranger and perhaps a victim of sorts herself.

"Who is your husband?" asked Ela. The woman lay face down on the riverbank, her hands tied behind her back.

"I don't have one."

"Where do you live?"

The woman looked up at her as if she might be simple. "Right here."

"What did you intend to do with Charley?"

"Who's Charley?"

Ela stared at her. "The boy you had tied up in your own home. Did you not even learn his name?"

"What good would that do me or him?" she muttered. "And I bought him fair and square."

"Montaigu d'Albiac sold him to you?" Ela already knew the answer. "For how much?"

The woman hesitated. "Seven pounds."

"That's a great sum. What did you do with the money?"

Bridie Haslop glared at her. "I used it to eat and keep a good roof over my head. I'm a widow, and not all of us have dead husbands who leave us a castle and a pile of gold coins."

Ela felt her words as a stinging slap. Clearly this woman knew something about her. "Wiltshire is full of widows who find a way to survive without buying and selling innocent children."

"There's no law against it."

"It's against the laws of God and nature. And the Magna Carta states that no free man shall be seized or imprisoned or stripped of his rights or possessions—"

"Are you trying to suggest that this little baseborn bastard is a free man before the law?"

Ela drew in a steadying breath. In preserving the liberty and rights only of free men, the legal document had used language that excluded a great deal of the population if lawyers wanted to split hairs—women, children, those in any form of legal bondage including villeins or apprentices.... "The justice at the assizes gave Charley and his baby sister into the safekeeping of Montaigu d'Albiac and his lady wife. They did not hand them over as chattels to be bought and sold. They were sold to you illegally and must be returned at once." She leaned in and glared. "Where is the baby?"

"I told you I don't know." The woman's face was growing red. She appeared to be having trouble breathing after so long tied up on her stomach with her hands behind her.

"Get her up," said Ela. "Who bought the infant?"

"The woman who paid for her wouldn't give her name, for obvious reasons," said the woman, after she'd been heaved to her feet, panting and gasping. "But she was a fine lady. She wore a fur-trimmed cloak even in this warm weather—can you imagine?"

A noble, or a rich merchant's wife. That narrowed it down. "Was she local?"

"I don't know, but I don't think so. The man who sold me the children told me about her. He knew her, but, for some reason, she wouldn't buy the child direct from him. I didn't get much of a cut for my troubles, I'll tell you."

"So he had made arrangements for this woman to buy the baby even before he sold the children to you?"

"That's how I understood it. She came to me the same day and knew about him already."

"What color was her hair?" Ela wondered if she could deduce the woman's identity from a description.

"I don't know. It was all hidden under a white veil. The veil was pinned to hide most of her face as well, though she had pale blue eyes. Her eyebrows were plucked so I couldn't even tell you what color they were."

Montaigu will know her identity. "You shall enjoy discussing the terms of your trade with your recent client as you both rot in my dungeon. Throw her over the back of a horse."

Ela turned and left. She needed to confront Montaigu d'Albiac and force the noblewoman's identity out of him before the baby should suffer or even die in the hands of those not equipped to care for such a young infant.

Bill pulled Charley up onto his horse and told him to hold fast around his waist, and they made their way back to the castle.

When they got there Ela found that the king of England had issued an urgent invitation for her to attend him at his hunting lodge at once.

CHAPTER 22

"*W*hy must I attend the king at once?" Ela asked Bill, keeping her voice low. "This infant is in urgent danger and I daren't wait even a day before pursuing its whereabouts."

Bill made a sympathetic expression.

"But he's the king…I can't send my regrets. I still can't believe my son petitioned him to rip my castle and title away from me and bestow it on him. This must be what Henry wishes to talk to me about and I'd be a fool if I wasn't at least a little apprehensive."

Bill nodded silently, knowing that she didn't need or want any advice. "Would you like me to interview Montaigu?"

"Please do. And don't be afraid to actually cut his nose off if you think it will help."

Bill chuckled. "It might give me pleasure, but I will try to leave the course of justice to the judge at the assizes."

"That man needs to hang or he'll be a menace in the county of Wiltshire every day of his life. He's one of those people who sends out rippling waves of evil in all directions. And why on earth did his wife say nothing of the missing children? What has he done to her or threatened her with? She must be brought here at once. Though I'd rather cut off my right hand than give little Charley back into her care. He shall stay with me—and by extension with his unfortunate mother—for now. The justice and jury need be none the wiser about any of it."

~

DRESSED in a fine red gown with gold trim at the neck and cuffs, and with her hair smoothed under a fresh white veil, Ela set out for Clarendon within the hour. Normally she might have brought one of her children along, to let them get better acquainted with their cousin the king, but, under the circumstances, she thought it best to go alone.

She rode in a carriage—her silk gown being too delicate to risk on horseback—with a small phalanx of mounted guards. The sun sat high above the horizon on this late summer afternoon, promising several more hours of daylight. She hoped to have a brief and businesslike meeting with the king and return to her castle before dark.

Her hopes were dashed when she arrived to find the courtyard of the king's favorite hunting lodge jammed with carriages and horses and grooms and footmen milling about, and guests dismounting and dusting themselves off from their journey.

It appeared the king was hosting some kind of entertainment. Ela wondered why she hadn't been issued an invitation in advance. She suspected that she'd been invited at the last moment so the king could divest himself of some duty regarding her as quickly as possible and be swept away on a tide of revelry.

"Ela, my dear." The oily voice of Hubert de Burgh made her glance to her right.

Of course. This was likely all his idea.

"Sir Hubert." She offered her hand without attempting a smile or further words.

There was a moment of silence that de Burgh probably expected her to fill with harmless pleasantries. "The king wishes to resolve the issue regarding the succession of the house of Salisbury," he said quietly, watching her closely.

"I see he intends to do it before the fish course is served," she said, gesturing at the milling crowds of nobles and servants all around them.

"Quite so." De Burgh smirked. Or was that just his resting expression? "He's in his private chamber and awaiting your arrival. I shall take you there at once."

"I'm grateful for that, as I am in the middle of urgent county business."

"I'm sure your urgent business can wait until tomorrow morning."

"It will have to." She still hadn't smiled. De Burgh gestured for her to walk ahead of him. No doubt he knew that she was quite familiar with the layout of Clarendon and the location of the king's private rooms. The palace was a pet project of Henry's and he'd lavished money on painted murals, floors of colorful stone mosaics, and carved stone embellishments to rival Salisbury Cathedral.

Musicians plucked at stringed instruments in one corner of the room and ladies' laughter rose above the clinking of sparkling silver cups of wine. Ela marched on, down a short hallway, and paused before a tall carved wood door.

"I see that you know your way around," said de Burgh.

"The king is my husband's nephew." *The husband you killed in cold blood.*

"Yet you're not as close as you might be," said de Burgh. "Perhaps because you're too busy fussing over county business when you might be attending to the needs of your large and distinguished family."

Ela turned to glare at him. "Your opinion of my family affairs is both unasked for and unwelcome."

His eyes widened. He clearly hadn't expected outright rudeness. And since he was both ruthless and vindictive she knew she took a risk by offering it. But showing weakness or attempting to mollify such men had never gained her an inch of quarter so she didn't intend to do so tonight.

They still stood before the heavy wood door. "Your family affairs are the nation's business, my lady," his low voice dripped with malice. "And as such are my business, since I am the king's justiciar."

"Will you knock, or shall I?" asked Ela, keeping her voice and face utterly expressionless.

De Burgh grabbed the handle and pulled the door toward them. Despite its great size, it moved soundlessly on oiled hinges. Inside, Ela saw the king, seated on a dais, making conversation with a man she recognized as Richard, the second son of the late, great Sir William Marshall, whose eldest son William—married to the king's young sister—had died earlier that year under strange circumstances.

"Countess Ela," said the king. Normally his face would brighten with boyish enthusiasm, but this time his brow creased with worry. "Thank you for coming on such short notice and I apologize for the crush of guests. I do hope you will be able to join us for the entertainments."

Ela did now manage a smile and a polite bow of her head. The king excused his guest, who left at once. De Burgh closed the door, leaving them alone in the king's chamber but for two stone-faced guards on either side of the door.

"Perhaps you can surmise why I've asked you here today," said Henry, expression serious. He was no longer the awkward youth of even two years ago; he had gained assurance and dignity. "It concern's your son William's request that he be granted the hereditary title of Earl of Salisbury."

"I suspected as much," said Ela coolly. She could have gone on to remind him of his prior—very expensive—agreement with her, but she didn't wish to put words in his mouth or seem argumentative. He was the king after all.

"To be honest, I sympathize with young William," said Henry. "Though I've never had to wait to assume an inheritance since I was rather rushed into it prematurely by my father's untimely death."

Ela kept a polite smile on her mouth.

"At what time do you intend to pass the title and estates over to your eldest son?" he asked, looking curious rather than uncomfortable.

Ela took heart in this question, which seemed to imply that the title and estates were indeed hers to bestow at her leisure. "When both my son and I are ready," she said. "That occasion has not yet arrived, but in time it will."

"Your son is most definitely ready," cut in de Burgh, in a gruff voice. "And made his feelings on the subject most plain."

"I'm sure he did," said Ela politely.

"I advised the king that it was in the best interests of the kingdom for a trained knight, and the royal scion of a great and distinguished warrior, to take over his position as the head of such an ancient and powerful family.

Of course you did. Ela looked at the king.

Henry cleared his throat. "I…ah…my lawyers have reviewed the matter, including the fines paid by yourself to assume your role as castellan and to bear the hereditary title bestowed upon you by your father—"

Ela held her breath. The king's lawyers could change the law to suit the king's whim if they chose to. She had no illusions about the power of even a signed and sealed scroll over the might of the monarchy.

"And they have advised me that the title, estates, and all honors and positions associated with them are yours to wield for as long as you choose—your entire life if you will—as outlined in our second agreement made in the eleventh year of my reign."

Now Ela smiled with genuine relief. "I am sorry that my son has seen fit to throw our family business at your feet when I know you are burdened with the responsibilities of the kingdom. I appreciate your swift and unequivocal confirmation of the arrangements that we made following my husband's death." She shot a steely glance at de Burgh.

"It was a very unique arrangement," said the king.

"And one that I advised against at the time," said de Burgh, regarding Ela coolly. "But you made such a persuasive case for maintaining control that you swayed us all. It's just a shame that the consequences are depriving a proud young man of his patrimony."

Fury pricked Ela's skin. How dare he talk to her like this —and in front of the king! He was insulting the king's acceptance of her proposal as much as the arrangement itself.

"I feel called to do God's work in Salisbury, my lords," she said, struggling to keep her expression neutral. "Perhaps if that execrable villain Simon de Hal had not been made sheriff when my husband died, the need would not have been quite so urgent." She knew de Burgh had been instrumental in choosing an aggressive, violent and litigious man to install in her castle. He'd hoped de Hal's presence would intimidate her into silence. How little he understood her.

"I am grateful for your work as sheriff," said the king. "I hear nothing but good reports of your work to maintain peace and justice in the county."

A frown disturbed de Burgh's forehead. "Of course, it's

not possible to solve every crime in a great county such as Salisbury. The d'Albiac case springs to mind. A woman was fighting her son to gain control of her husband's estates and then that same son turned up dead."

If looks could have shot poisoned daggers, de Burgh would have dropped dead right then. Ela kept her voice steady. "The maid Agnes confessed to killing him."

"Perhaps his mother paid the maid to dispatch her own son to death?" De Burgh raised a salt and pepper brow. "And I hear the girl is not even to be hanged?"

"The girl was provoked and tormented by the son, who stole her virtue against her will and got her with child." *And now the baby has gone missing.* She doubted that de Burgh knew this and didn't intend to introduce the news now. It would only undermine the king's perception that she was adept in handling county matters.

De Burgh made a tut-tutting sound. "What a terrible family."

If you only knew. "But I'm sure the king has little interest in these small local matters," said Ela. "I'm grateful that we've been able to resolve the issue at hand."

"Indeed," said Henry, rising to his feet. "And now let us join my guests for an excellent dinner."

THE JURY CONVENED EARLY the next morning to examine Montaigu and Bridie Haslop about their roles in selling Agnes's children. Ela also sent out messengers to travel across Wiltshire and spread the news of the search for the baby. She knew they must recover the infant within days or they'd likely never see little Tilda again.

Bridie Haslop appeared first. She looked considerably the worse for wear after a night in the dungeon, her kerchief missing and her hair wild. She also responded to all questions in an insolent tone that quickly got the jurors' backs up.

"Who is your master?" asked Peter Howard the baker.

"I have no master," she snapped.

"So you bought these children yourself."

"I paid for them fair and square," she said firmly. "All above board and perfectly legal."

"Did you give Sir Montaigu a written bill of sale?" asked Stephen Hale the cordwainer. Ela was fairly sure this was some kind of sarcastic jab at her claims of legitimacy.

"I don't have letters. My word is my bond." Her lips settled into a wide, flat line

"I'm sure you know that there's nothing above board about buying and selling children," said Ela. "It's reprehensible in every way and condemned by church and state."

"I take them from a home that doesn't want them and find them a new place in a home that does. If I wasn't taking coin for it, it would be an act of charity."

The jurors shook their heads and muttered.

"You should be ashamed of yourself for taking an innocent baby from its mother," said Stephen Hale.

"I didn't," she said triumphantly. "The courts did that from what I hear. I took that babe from a very unpleasant man who wished to trade it for coin to pay his gambling debts and sold it to a well-dressed couple that had tried and failed to make their own child for years."

"What is their name?" said Ela.

"They were secretive. Wouldn't tell me the name. I suspect they intend to pass the babe off as their true issue. Their coin was good and that's all the name I need."

"For all you know they might have intended to roast the baby and eat it with chestnut stuffing and almond gravy!" cried old Matthew Hart who'd sat in horrified silence thus far. "How do you know they'll give it a good upbringing?"

"I don't," she said, her expression defiant as ever. "Much as none of us here knows if we'll even live to see tomorrow. I suspect I shall though, as you can't hang me for something there's no law against."

Trust me, we can find a law. Ela certainly had no intention of letting this woman continue to ply her trade in Wiltshire. On the other hand, she'd take no pleasure in hanging her, either. "What is your history? Are you a widow?"

"That I am, my lady. As a widow yourself you'll know that it's not always easy to make one's way in the world."

"I would starve before I'd sell a child," said Ela. "Either mine or anyone else's."

"Easy to say when you've got a big castle and a pantry overflowing with food and running with wine." The woman's mouth flattened out again. She had a big, square jaw that only added to her air of determination. "I doubt you've ever come close to starving."

Ela regretted offering her personal opinion. Far better to maintain a reserved distance. "I entrusted these two children to the care of the d'Albiac family. Their natural mother lives under my roof. If that baby isn't returned alive and unharmed there's an excellent chance that you will be charged as an accessory to murder."

"But—" She attempted to rise to her feet but the guards grabbed her arms and shoved her down in the chair.

"I've sent messengers to all the villages and towns hereabouts with the news that if the baby is delivered to the castle safe and sound there shall be no charges made against those who bring it."

"And in the meantime, I'm to rot here?"

"At least you won't starve," said Ela brightly.

Bridie Haslop was removed back to the dungeon and Montaigu was brought to sit in the chair in front of the jury. His insolent expression was undimmed by a night in the dungeon. Worse yet, a lawyer had arrived, intent on representing his interests.

Ela hardly knew where to start. He was such an execrable excuse for a human being. "If the babe dies, you too shall be an accessory to its murder."

"I never laid a hand on it."

"I entrusted it into your care."

"More fool you," said Montaigu under his breath.

Bill Talbot rose to his feet suddenly, chair scraping back. "Don't you dare speak to your countess like that!"

Ela reflected that d'Albiac was right. What on earth had possessed her to allow the judge to place two vulnerable infants in a house with this villain? "How did you threaten your wife that she didn't say a word when I asked her where the children were?"

"I told her I'd sell our two daughters along with them. They'd fetch a pretty penny at that age. Fruit ripe for plucking." He also insisted that he didn't know the name or whereabouts of the couple who'd bought Tilda. He swore that he'd sold her to Bridie Haslop and knew nothing more of the matter.

His bold-faced evil struck Ela speechless. Even his lawyer seemed non-plussed but jumped in with the expected argument about how children did not fit the legal definition of "free men" and were therefore not legally protected from being deprived of their liberty.

Ela listened to his ramblings for as long as she could stand them. "Does the jury have questions for Sir Montaigu?" She spat his name with disgust. He didn't deserve to be a knight.

The jurors spend some time admonishing him for his misdeeds, but, ultimately they determined—aided by outrageous arguments from d'Albiac's hired lawyer—that fault lay with his wife who should have sued him for a divorce based on his infidelity. Such an action might have protected the children from him.

Ela struggled to keep her expression neutral. "His wife is an innocent victim, browbeaten, lied to, and misused until she barely knows her own name. She managed the household alone for six years and has bravely borne the return of her disgraced husband. I fail to see how she is at fault for his cruelty and avarice."

Ela tried to argue for keeping Sir Montaigu in the dungeon along with Bridie Haslop, but his lawyer observed that as a noble and a knight, he was entitled to his freedom unless he was explicitly charged with a crime. Since the boy had been recovered and the baby was—as far as they knew— still alive and well, no law had been broken.

Ela was forced to release Sir Montaigu to continue his reign of terror against decency and propriety. "Rest assured, Sir Montaigu—" she half hissed his name. "That I shall be keeping a close eye on you. I shall also consider the prudence of fining you for the time and trouble you've already caused us with your misdeeds. I advise you to watch your step and choose your actions very carefully." She'd be delighted if he set out for the continent again. At least then he'd be someone else's problem.

She dismissed the jury and retreated to the chapel to pray for strength. She'd barely sunk to her knees on the prie-dieu when Elsie burst in. "My lady, a strange baby's been reported in Devizes!"

CHAPTER 23

"*I*s it Tilda?"

"They're not sure, since one baby looks much like another. But an old woman who cleans house for the doctor there said that he's been attending a sickly baby in the home of a wealthy merchant. And while the woman claims it's hers, no one in the town remembers her being pregnant and she's long in the tooth to have a baby."

"Sickly, you say?" Ela spray up from her prie-dieu. "I do hope her life isn't in serious danger. We must go to her at once."

Ela fetched Agnes to go with her. She knew she'd recognize Tilda herself, but she reckoned that if the baby was ill to death the smell and taste of her mother's breast might help her rally. Ela didn't want to waste time getting the carriage hitched up, so Agnes—who didn't know how to ride—was mounted on a quiet horse to be led by a mounted guard.

"Hold onto the horse's mane," urged Ela, as Agnes sat awkwardly atop the big bay mare. "She'll take care of you."

They arrived at Devises just as the bells for Nones were ringing, and followed directions to the doctor's house. It was a two-story building with steep gables and a smart black and white timber and plaster facade. A guard knocked while Ela stayed mounted on her horse. An old woman in a tight kerchief opened the door.

"Is the baby here?"

"No, my lady, it's at the big house three doors down. Right here on the main road!"

They followed her directions to a tall, narrow manor house with three gables overhanging the street below. At the door, the guard knocked again, and a servant answered.

"We've come to see the baby," called Ela.

The girl ran into the back of the house, then returned a few moments later, face white. "There's no baby here, my lady."

"I can hear it," said Ela. She could make out shuffling and rustling sounds and could almost swear she'd heard a muffled cry. "I'm the Sheriff of Wiltshire and I demand to see the infant at once."

The maid knotted her hands together. "It's not well."

Ela jumped down from her horse. "That's why I'm here. Agnes, come with me."

The guard helped Agnes awkwardly down from the big horse and they hurried into the house. The girl, who'd clearly been told to lie to them and get rid of them, hovered just inside the door.

"Countess Ela of Salisbury is within and demands to see the infant," called Ela, her voice bouncing off walls of paneled wood.

Again, the muffled cry of a baby pricked at Ela's ears.

"Tilda!" cried Agnes, running toward the sound. A door slammed in their faces as they turned the corner.

"This is a private home," said a shrill woman's voice from inside. "You have no right."

"I'm the sheriff of this county and I demand that you open the door at once or I shall have you arrested."

The door stayed close for a moment, during which Ela and Agnes could hear the baby attempting to squall. Then the door creaked open and an older man's face appeared. "I'm a doctor. My only interest is in the health of the baby."

Ela and Agnes rushed into the room. Little Tilda lay in a carved wood cradle, face scrunched in misery. Her cheeks sunken and her lips pale and thin, she looked barely recognizable from the bonny babe of a few days ago.

Tilda instinctively snatched her from the cradle.

"Put her to your breast," said Ela calmly.

"My milk has dried already," said Agnes, clearly panicked.

"Try anyway," said Ela, who knew from personal experience that milk could persist in the breast long past when it was wanted or needed.

Agnes looked around for a chair, then moved toward a stool in the corner. She sat down and unfastened the side of her gown, which was altered to allow for nursing. Almost immediately the baby latched on and started sucking.

"I'm dry," lamented Agnes, clearly in pain.

"Breathe and relax," said Ela. Not easy to do in the circumstances. She wanted to hurl questions at the woman who stood watching. "The milk will flow. Just give it time."

"It's coming," said Agnes with relief. "I can feel it. There you go, little one. Drink your fill. I thought I'd never see you again!"

The babe sucked with gusto and as time passed the color did return to her wasted cheeks.

"The poor mite was perishing of thirst," said the doctor. "They didn't hire a wet nurse for fear of discovery. Instead, they tried to feed it cow's milk with a sponge."

The woman, perhaps five to ten years older than Ela and

with high cheekbones, crossed her arms. "We fed it morsels of cheese and meat as well."

"An infant that's only a few weeks old can't eat solid food," hissed Ela. "Did no one tell you this? How much did you pay for her?"

The woman's face closed and her mouth settled into a sour expression. "Far too much judging from her poor health."

"This child was in perfect health before she fell into the hands of an evil man who saw fit to trade her for coin. Surely you knew that it was wrong to buy an infant?"

"How else is a childless woman supposed to have a child?" asked the woman.

"You could offer a home to an orphan."

"My husband is a good deal older than myself and was third in line to inherit this manor. We waited decades to get it and we've only been here four years. If my husband dies, it will pass into his younger brother's hands. If we had our own child, or a child that people believed was ours, we could stay here indefinitely."

Ela inhaled deeply and then sighed out the breath with force. "Our inheritance laws have much to answer for, but ultimately what happens or doesn't happen is the will of God. Where is your husband?"

"Upstairs, in his bed." The woman indicated the ceiling with her head.

"He's unable to walk," said the physician quietly. "He's suffered a palsy these last few months and gradually lost the use of his limbs."

"My sympathies are with you," said Ela. The woman's hard face had softened and Ela could see tears hovering in her eyes. She was about to lose her husband and her home. "But you must be able to see that this baby needs to be suckled."

"I wish the child seller had told me that. She just took my money and said she didn't need to know any names."

"She's imprisoned at the castle," said Ela.

"How will I get my money back?"

"You won't. Count yourself lucky that I don't intend to arrest you as well. I may yet change my mind about that." Ela stared at the woman. "A child cannot be bought and sold like a ewe or a hen. Consider the safety of your immortal soul before you look to your purse and even the roof over your head." She did feel some sympathy for the woman's predicament, and even an inkling of sympathy for the widowed child seller, but these women weren't empty-headed fools. They knew that what they'd done was wrong in man's eyes and in God's.

She looked at Agnes. "Come, we'll bring Tilda back to the castle."

THEY MADE slow progress back to Salisbury. Agnes didn't want to take the baby from her breast, and—considering Tilda's weakened condition—Ela didn't think it advisable, either. The mother and child sat astride the big mare, but since Agnes's arms were in use, a guard walked on foot, leading the horse at a slow and steady pace.

Agnes wept off and on throughout the journey, perhaps overcome by relief at holding her baby again. Tilda had rallied considerably and even made some babbling sounds in between nursing sessions. They made good progress and were within sight of Salisbury Castle when an arrow whistled through the air and knocked Ela's left rein out of her hand. The guards sprang into action, surrounding Ela and drawing their swords. Stunned, she searched herself for injury. Her rein had snapped from the force of the blow, and Freya danced uncertainly in place.

The guards wanted Ela to jump down from her horse, but she had no intention of being a sitting target. At moments like this, her heartbeat slowed, as if allowing her the time and space to focus rather than flooding her veins with energy to flee. One of the guards had pulled Agnes and the baby off her horse, and little Tilda, tugged from the breast in the tumult, let out a shriek.

"It came from those trees." Ela pointed to the left of the road, where three great oaks rose together into a single vast canopy. The hidden archer could shoot again at any moment. "Flush him out!" she cried.

Two bravely rode their horses toward the trees. "There he goes!" shouted one. "He's running across the field!" They burst into a gallop. As Ela rode up behind them she saw a man who'd deserted the trees and now hurried down a hill away from the road. Almost at once, the guards overtook him and one jumped on him and threw him to the ground.

Ela rode over, leaving poor Agnes sobbing, and looked down at the man now pinned to the ground. An older man, with a worn quiver of arrows and a much-used bow, he wore a faded tunic that looked like it hadn't been washed in a year.

"Who are you?" asked Ela.

He didn't reply. He closed his eyes as if somehow this might deliver him from his predicament.

"You could have killed me, so I can only assume that was your intent. I don't know you. Why did you shoot at me?"

The man's lips—surrounded by a bushy gray beard—moved, but he didn't utter a word.

The heated young guard who'd chased him now drew a sword. "We could bury him here and save ourselves the trouble of hauling him back to the castle."

"Attempted murder of the sheriff is a hanging offense," growled another, older guard. "He's a dead man for sure."

Finally, he groaned and shifted. "Please, I'm a poor old soldier trying to earn a penny for food."

"By killing your sheriff?" asked Ela, coldly. "That's a poor line of business to be in. I presume someone hired you to shoot at me. Let me guess, his name was d'Albiac."

The man peered at her with bloodshot eyes. "He didn't tell me his name but he said that if I get you off his back he'd make me a rich man. Said he's a noble with a manor and a chest of gold. One gold coin could keep me in comfort for a year or more."

"It'll keep you in the comfort of a dungeon now," snarled the young guard.

Ela lifted her hand to silence him. "Not necessarily. If you will testify in court against this same man, perhaps we can come to some understanding."

He brightened slightly but winced when he tried to move his leg. "I'll do it. And if you hang me at least I'm done with the trouble of living."

Ela shifted in her saddle. She needed to establish that Montaigu d'Albiac was the man who'd hired him. "Describe the man who told you to shoot an arrow into me."

The man inhaled slowly, obviously in pain, lying on the ground with a guard's foot on his chest. One of the other guards took his bow and snapped it across his knee. The old man coughed. "He had dark hair, with some gray in it. A tall man with dark eyes."

"That describes half the men in the kingdom," said Ela.

"He never said I'd be shooting at the sheriff," mumbled the first man. "He said I had to shoot the lady on a gray horse that rides out every day down this road."

"It's no difference if you kill a beggar or a sheriff," said

Ela. "It's still a murder. Truss him tight and throw him over the spare horse."

~

MONTAIGU D'ALBIAC WAS ARRESTED—THIS time on suspicion of hiring an assassin to kill the sheriff—and brought to the castle in chains. The old man who'd shot her swiftly identified him as the man who'd told him to shoot at Ela.

"I've never seen this man before in my life," said Montaigu.

Ela looked at the gathered jury with a raised brow. "Does anyone believe him? I'm convinced that Montaigu d'Albiac hired this man to shoot and kill me so that he'd be free to conduct his cruel and sinful business unchecked in the county of Wiltshire, since apparently no one but myself cares to stop him."

The jurors, cowed—and likely sheepish about the role they'd played in setting Montaigu d'Albiac free to sell his two grandchildren—shook their heads and mumbled no.

"Montaigu d'Albiac, you are accused of hiring an archer to kill the Sheriff of Wiltshire. You shall both rot in the dungeons until the next assizes. If you are still alive at that time, you shall face trial for murder."

"You said I'd get clemency if I told you who hired me," rasped the old man, who was sitting, in chains, off to one side.

"You tried to kill me. Do you think I should let you go free?"

The man's head drooped. She ignored the tiny flame of compassion that flickered inside her. No matter his sad story or the desperate circumstances that drove him to commit the crime, this man had attempted murder. It was her duty to preserve peace in the county of Wiltshire and to keep herself alive while doing it. "You shall be tried at the assizes and may God have mercy on your soul."

Is my heart growing hard in the course of my work? She did find herself thinking less like a mother and more like a soldier. She'd dealt with so many reprehensible villains that she sometimes found herself treating the criminals that crossed her path less like individual children of God and more like demons who'd found their way to earth.

She would need time to reflect and pray on this and ask herself if it was indeed perhaps time to retreat to a cloister before she became as ruthless as Hubert de Burgh.

ELA SUMMONED Mathilde d'Albiac to call on her at the castle the following morning.

The sight of the woman, pale and drawn beneath her white veil, filled her with a mixture of pity and loathing. "You lied to me." She stared down at Mathilde from her dais. Mathilde had the decency to look contrite to the point of mortification. "You told me the children were in your house, sick with a fever, when your husband had sold them to a child trader."

"He told me he'd sell Helen and Joan if I said a word about it."

"And you believed him?"

"Why wouldn't I? As you have seen yourself, he's capable of anything. He said they'd fetch good money as whores on the streets of London—" she broke off, in tears.

"I entrusted Charley and Tilda into your care. Little Mathilde—" she emphasized the name given to her in her grandmother's honor "—could easily have died from lack of sustenance. The child trader sold her to an older couple with no notion of how to care for and feed an infant. They were giving her meat!"

Mathilde stood there, sobbing, head in her hands. "I'm so ashamed. I don't deserve to live. If it wasn't for my daughters, I'd drown myself in the millrace."

"That wouldn't help anyone and would also be a mortal sin. Fortunately for Joan, who bravely spoke up in time, the children were saved and are both doing well. Tilda is back at her mother's breast and I fully intend for her to remain there, no matter what Justice de Braose has to say on the matter."

"I owe Agnes an apology," said Mathilde, through her tears. "I can see how desperation can drive one to do terrible things. I forgive her for killing Charibert. I know I can never forgive myself for letting my husband sell her children."

"You can tell her that yourself." Ela sent Elsie to fetch Agnes.

"Will my husband really hang this time?" asked Mathilde, a hint of hope in her broken voice.

What a thing for a wife to wish for. "Without a doubt. His attempt on my life by a hired man was witnessed by four guards and Agnes herself. The fool who fired the arrow will stand witness to his criminal intent. Any justice in the kingdom would hang him for an attempt on the life of the sheriff."

"I suppose it's wrong for me to be relieved. But how do I get rid of his woman?"

"Turn her out into the street." Again, Ela wondered at her lack of compassion for this strange, foreign woman, who was likely as much a victim as Agnes and Mathilde. But she couldn't find room in her heart to care about the fate of one who'd entered another woman's home on her husband's arm. "I'm sure she'll find a way to survive."

Mathilde nodded. "If she won't go?"

"Then you will have to make her go." Ela found herself

impatient with Mathilde. "You must look inside yourself for the strength to be head of your family and make the right choices for yourself and your daughters. Let Joan's courage be an inspiration to you. I'm sure your daughters will be as glad to see the back of her as you are."

Elsie appeared with Agnes, who held Tilda in her arms. Little Charley stuck close behind her as if he wanted to hide in her skirts.

Mathilde burst into tears again at the sight of them. She threw herself to her knees and begged Agnes to forgive her for the worst mistake of her life.

Agnes, dignified as a queen, spoke softly. "I do forgive you. I know you were driven to a state of madness by the cruelty of a d'Albiac man, as I was myself. I committed a far graver sin that's been the cause of great suffering for you."

Tears dripped from Mathilde's eyes. "I only hope that you can keep Charley from following in the dreadful footsteps of his forbears. He carries a terrible legacy in his blood."

Agnes glanced down at Charley, who now wrapped himself around her. "Charley will not be raised by an evil man who would teach him to lie and cheat and steal his way to glory and riches. I pray that he will grow strong and learn a trade and support himself with honest labor, far from battlefields and tournament grounds and gambling houses."

Mathilde nodded. "You're a brave and steady girl, Agnes, and I'm sure Charley will take after you. Has the Countess given you shelter in her castle?"

Agnes nodded. "For now. I don't yet know where we shall go."

Mathilde drew in a shaky breath. "Would you...might you..." She looked down at the ground. "Would you consider returning to Neversend to live with me and my girls? I do consider it your home. I swear never to blame you for—for what happened."

Agnes, sturdy as an oak, with her young daughter in her arms, seemed to consider this for a moment. "Neversend has been my home for as long as I can remember. Although I've suffered there, I've experienced great joy there, and your daughters have been the only close friends I've ever had. I would gladly return if the law allowed me to."

She turned to look at Ela, who drew in a steadying breath. "As Sheriff of Wiltshire I'm in full support of this reunion. I realize that Justice de Braose might not see matters the same as I do, but when he returns for the next assizes, I shall make a strong case for you both. In the meantime, I propose that Agnes return—with her children—to Neversend on a trial basis."

A smile crept across Mathilde's careworn face. Agnes, calm and steady, smiled at Mathilde. "I shall look forward to serving you again, mistress."

"Oh no. You shall never serve me again. You can help me manage Neversend along with Joan and Helene, but not as a servant. You are the mother of my grandchildren and I consider you to be my dear daughter."

Tears sprang to Agnes's eyes. She handed Tilda to Mathilde, who took the infant with such tenderness that Ela felt a tear creep into her own jaded gaze. "I wish you both many happy years building a new life for yourselves as well as the children. May God be with you and guide all your actions."

"I shall tell Tilda all about you, my lady," said Agnes. "So that as she grows she shall know that my life, as well as her own, were saved by a great lady who was once sheriff of all Wiltshire."

THE END

AUTHOR'S NOTE

Tournaments were a controversial entertainment throughout the middle ages. Tournament contests could foment resentment between powerful nobles or even between localities, so prohibitions against tournaments by both kings and popes were a regular occurrence. They were banned from England until the reign of King Stephen in the mid 1100's. Prior to that time, knights would travel to the continent to compete. Early tournaments often featured a *melée*, where armies of knights would battle each other and incur grave injuries. By Ela's time these were largely replaced by the one-on-one contests more familiar to us. Even so, they could turn deadly, and Ela's grandson William—her son William's oldest son—died from injuries sustained in a tournament at Blyth around 1256.

Ela's son William did indeed petition Henry III in an attempt to claim the earldom from his mother. We know from a letter that William wrote to the Pope years later, that the king had turned him down: "my kinsman and liege lord, hath bereft me of the title of earl and of that estate, but this he did judiciously, and not in displeasure." The king's lawyers no doubt reminded him of his obligations to Ela under the expensive agreement she made with him shortly after her husband's death. Ela never did pass the title or estates to William and we can only speculate about her reasons for retaining them until her death. She outlived her son William, who died in 1250 while on a crusade in Egypt. Ela also outlived William's aforementioned son and heir who died from his tournament injuries. When Ela finally died in 1261, the title passed to her great-granddaughter, Margaret Longespée.

If you have questions or comments, please get in touch at jglewis@stoneheartpress.com.

AUTHOR BIOGRAPHY

J. G. Lewis grew up in a Regency-era officer's residence in London, England. She spent her childhood visiting nearby museums and riding ponies in Hyde Park. She came to the U.S. to study semiotics at Brown University and stayed for the sunshine and a career as a museum curator in New York City. Over the years she published quite a few novels, two of which hit the *USA Today* list. She didn't delve into historical fiction until she discovered genealogy and the impressive cast of potential characters in her family history. Once she realized how many fascinating historical figures are all but forgotten, she decided to breathe life into them again by creating stories for them to inhabit. J. G. Lewis currently lives in Florida with her dogs and horses.

For more information visit www.stoneheartpress.com.

Cover image includes: detail from Codex Manesse, ca. 1300, Heidelberg University Library; decorative detail from Beatus of Liébana, Fecundus Codex of 1047, Biblioteca Nacional de España; detail with Longespée coat of arms from Matthew Parris, *Historia Anglorum*, ca. 1250, British Museum.

Made in United States
North Haven, CT
03 July 2023

38504980R00164